Lessons in Falling

An Out of Office Novel
Book 1

Christy Schillig

ISBN: 9798218739430 paperback

Cover designed by Sam Palencia, Ink and Laurel

Edited by Cassandra Dunn

Published by Christy Schillig

 Formatted with Vellum

Dedication

This one's for you, Shultzy, for being the person I look forward to waking up to every day and for being the best example of an educator who cares.

Author's note

Hello, Amazing and Supportive Readers:

I wrote this novel before the pandemic in my fifth or sixth year of teaching, still bright-eyed and bushy-tailed—ready to take on the world of education. After the better part of a lifetime battling my own mental health conditions, I found myself needing to help the students with their battles. Naturally, as so many of you know, finding resources and ways to help never came easily, and the empathy that I work so hard to teach often threatened to swallow me whole. I don't want that feeling for you.

Though this is a work of fiction in every way, there are themes in this novel that are very real and very painful. I want you to take care of yourself when reading—and in all aspects of life. This is a love story—an adult love story, but beneath that core, this novel revolves around the need for support for mental health conditions including but not limited to eating disorders, body dysmorphia, and agoraphobia—particularly in the adolescent years. Within this novel, we also deal with grief, abandonment, loss of a parent (off page), medical situations, on page sexual content, on page alcohol consumption, off page drug consumption, and harsh language.

Please read with care and I hope you enjoy your time in these pages.

Always,
Christy

If you or someone you know is struggling or in crisis, help is available.
Call or text 988 anytime in the US to connect with a trained crisis counselor. This is a confidential service and is available 24/7.

Prologue

Devon

Lesson 1: Mind the cord.

I can separate that night into two equally awful halves, the sum of which makes a rotten messy whole. I could also get away with blaming the entire shitshow on my little sister, Tara, but that would be unfair. Convenient, yes. Partially deserved, absolutely. But ultimately, unfair. The brunt of the blame fell on me. I spread my wings knowing full well I was more penguin than eagle. And sure enough, I landed flat on my face in a puddle of Midori.

But there was a piece of me that needed that sister trip out to Chicago—that wanted to escape the comfortable routine of teach, eat, sleep, repeat back in South Jersey. A small, needy, unrelenting part of me that craved something new and begged to step on that sticky stage and wrap my fingers around that spittle-covered microphone. I needed to break my rules. Throw caution to the windy city. Prove to myself that I was more than lesson plans and take-out with mom.

Or maybe I just did it to shut Tara up.

Either way, it was time for some attention-seeking behavior. That's what we'd call it in our classroom when a child wouldn't stop calling out or blew his nose four times in a class period like an amplified tuba. All excusable when you're in middle school, mapping out your identity slowly and painfully, like an American driving in Britain for the first time. But as an adult—a semi-sober adult? Aw. Hell. No.

None of this knowledge changes the fact that I let Tara write my name on a little scrap of paper beside a splash of tequila and a stick-figure cartoon she drew of me making out with the perpetually annoyed DJ. I couldn't blame the man for that scowl. I'd be perpetually annoyed too if I had to listen to dozens of people murder the same songs every night with their booze-beats on. Karaoke MC was not a profession for the faint of heart.

"Misssss G!" he bellowed.

I looked at Tara, her honey-colored hair still floating in impossibly perfect waves around her face despite the heavy dancing and drinking she'd been doing for the last two hours.

"That's you," she said, sliding a shot of tequila my way. I downed it despite the fact that I'd blasted through my four-shot rule.

"No shit." I stood slowly. Kept my focus straight ahead as the DJ repeated the name only my students used for me. Just before the clapping and cat-calling could drown out my voice, I turned to Tara again and reminded her.

"No videos!"

Her hands went up, showing me that her weapon of choice was not in her grasp. Like her beautifully manicured fingers couldn't pull it off the table by the time I hit the first note.

"I know the rules," she said, rolling her heavily lined eyes.

Of course she knew the rules. She'd been breaking them to drive me crazy since she was five, mixing up my hair-color-organized barbies and leaving toothpaste all over our shared sink. I gave her one final warning look and turned back toward the stage steps, mounting them slowly to avoid a Jennifer-Lawrence-Oscar-fall moment. I kept my eyes on the black cord that ran the length of the stage like it was a live wire, tiptoeing alongside it as it twined up the microphone stand and disappeared into the bottom of the metal cone that I wrapped my sweaty fingers around. A thousand scenarios flashed through my mind. What if I tipped over in my heels? I slid my feet over the wooden planks to remind myself I was in my sensible teaching flats—much to Tara's dismay. What if I forgot the words? My eyes focused on the huge screen beside me. Right. Words on screen. The key mechanics of karaoke. Besides, how could I possibly forget the words to "Black Velvet" after hearing my mother belt it off-key every morning on the way to school?

Familiar music began to drown out the chatter around me as I squinted against the spotlight and let out a deep breath. I sang all the time—much to my students' discomfort. But this was different. These weren't my people out in the audience. These were adults. Full-on, coffee-drinking, bill paying, grown-ass adults and anyone over the age of fourteen made me itch. I found Tara's Cheshire grin in the audience and shook my head. See, Tara. I can let go. I can still have fun.

The title of my song flashed across the screen just as I recognized the beat of what certainly wasn't the opening chords of "Black Velvet." I looked to the DJ, expecting him to see his mistake in my wide helpless eyes. He didn't blink. I shielded my eyes and glared at Tara. Sneaky, sneaky, sis. She had her arms up as she did the opening moves to the routine we'd rehearsed every day for six months in preparation for her 7th grade recital. The neon red exit sign glowed behind her and I calculated the chances of making it out before she reached me. She was small, but scrappy. Years of her pinning me took the wind out of my sails. There was no escape.

I looked down the barrel of the microphone and caught the lyrics, my voice soft and shaking.

This here's a jam—

A few people in the back started to cheer and dance while I gained momentum through the first verse of "Bust a Move"—a classic that predated my existence but was played ad nauseam in our living room in the early aughts. I let my shoulders loosen as my hips moved to the bass. Tara was now right in front of the stage doing her full routine like she was still twelve in a fluorescent leotard. I sang louder as the second verse hit—used my teacher voice.

I crossed my arms in time with Tara as I rapped and did a little kick-step to mirror her own. Adrenaline coated my nerves and I let myself go—a mistake I rarely made. My eyes remained on my little sister and time blurred. We were back in front of her mirror, laughing like morons with our backwards hats and tinted sunglasses.

Next day's function–

I was working the stage, the words coming so confidently that I didn't even need to look up. Two slides left. Four steps right. Who needs a lyric screen?

I was Young MC, bitches.

Everyone was dancing now. I was killing it. I held the microphone out so Tara could sing the "ah ah yeahs" and the people behind her leaned in to sing along. My hands were suddenly free of the burden of the microphone and I took the opportunity to do what the moment called for—the running man.

But the man did not want to be running.

Not that night.

That cursed black cord betrayed me—reached out and coiled around the toe of my left shoe like a hungry python—causing me to teeter back once and then lurch too far forward. I reached out to the microphone stand with the desperate hope that it was cemented to the stage. My fingers closed around the silver pole, my ankle choked by the black tentacle, and I fell into the space in front of the stage. I hit the ground. And somehow, laying in the puddles of spilled mixed drinks and shoe bottom residue, dangling from that cord like a newborn still attached to its mother, I wasn't even close to rock-bottom. Rock-bottom was coming hard and fast, because the universe wanted to prove that humiliation, like the number line, is infinite.

Chapter One

J eff

Lesson 2: Satan has one dimple.

The sound of a woman rapping from behind a curtain in recovery pulls me away from my post-op report. I try to ignore it and purge the details of the procedure I just did into the microphone, but the lyrics are just familiar enough to keep pulling my attention from what I need to do. I speak louder.

"41-year-old male presents to ER for removal of retained foreign body in left foot at—"

"I'm SO SO SO SO SO C-C-COLD," the female rapper yells and I lose my place. I press pause on the dictation device and turn from the desk, looking around me for a free nurse or an intern, but they are all with patients. One more week of this. One more week of residency and then it's off to my fellowship. Goodbye being the orthopedic bitch called in for every trauma. And unfortunately, goodbye Chicago, my home. But it's only a year, and then I'll be right

7

back with my family, finally starting the elusive career that's been dangling out of reach for so long. I let out a breath, place the dictation device down beside the computer, then head toward the voice.

"I'm a popsicle—an ice cube. I'm a Klondike Bar!" She's excited about the latter. "What would you dooooo for a Klondike Bar?" she sings.

I slide back the curtain slowly, so the patient doesn't get scared, but the hooks clamber over each other in a messy, metallic clatter. My effort is wasted because she's got one eye open staring up at the fluorescent bulbs lining the ceiling like she's glimpsed straight into heaven. She doesn't seem to register my presence, but then she speaks.

"One eye works," she says to me, as I crane my face into view above her. "I'm a pirate. No. No. A cyclops." She lowers her voice like she's telling a ghost story around a campfire. "I eat sheep—and men."

Her pupil dilates as I block out the light from above, the black soaking into the amber pool around it. She focuses on me.

"Mmmmmm, I'll eat you. You're tasty," she murmurs. "Nom, Nom, Nom."

I can't help but smile at that. It's been a long-ass two days since I've slept, and this loopy creature is a welcome reprieve from my exhausted irritability. She's shaking again, her body's response to the anesthesia draining from her system. I reach into the cabinet beside the monitors and grab a stack of blankets then spread them across her one by one. She figures out a way to open the other eye and watches me silently as I make my way to the foot of her bed to grab her chart.

"Devon Gallagher. 32. Female. Initial Diagnosis: Ruptured Achilles Tendon," I read to her. Ouch. Six to twelve weeks in a boot. Poor thing.

"Poor Devon. I hope she recovers. That sounds serious," she says. "Boring. But serious."

I flash her a comforting smile. I could be done with my post-operative report by now, halfway out of the hospital for the first time in 48 hours, but there is something about Devon Gallagher's lifted brows as she studies me.

"You're Henry Cavill, aren't you?" she whispers, then presses her lips together, waggles her brows.

I let out a laugh at the way she looks around her, as if this is some big secret she needs to keep. As if the paparazzi will jump out from behind the curtains on either side of her.

"No, I'm Dr. Harrison," I correct.

She smiles and—holy shit. Smile doesn't do that thing justice. Her entire drowsy face lights up. It's like driving onto the Las Vegas strip for the first time.

"Righttttttt. Dr. Harrison," she says, trying to wink. Both of her lids are fluttering like she's having a seizure. "I promise I won't tell," she whispers. She tries to lift her arm beneath the blanket, and it slides limply off the bed.

"You broke my arm!" she yells, forgetting all about the fact that I'm Henry Cavill. She's pissed now, her sweet doe eyes suddenly narrowed at me like I've thrown her puppy into a well. I put my hands up.

"Devon, your arm is not broken. Your muscles are regaining control. It'll take some time," I explain. I'm using my calming voice. The one I perfected during my round in pediatrics.

"My neck works," she says proudly, twisting it back and forth. "Chest. Check. Stomach. Check. Va-gi-na. Check!"

I swallow my chuckle. Thank goodness she won't remember this. But she's not done. She mistakes my wide eyes for confusion and clarifies.

"You know. My peachy. My lady treasures. My box o' love. That last one was carved into a desk at school. Anywhoooo, I'm glad that you didn't break my undercarriage like you broke my arm. I need it— though not as much as I'd like to need it. I haven't needed it since— was Clinton president? No. No. I was just a wee tot then," she says in a terrible Scottish brogue. "Good Ole' Billy and his frisky willy. He'd probably use my vagina for me."

I have to pull the curtain closed between us to hide my laughter.

"Where'd you go? I guess you don't care about my vagina either. 'I'm Henry Cavill. Blah blah. I can have *all* the vagina with my perfect jaw. Blah blah.' Well, I've got news for you, buddy. This one's special. Dusty, yes. But special. Just needs a little feather duster and voila! Good as new."

Holy shit. This is too much. I look around for someone to share this with—anyone at all—but the only nurse in sight is bent over the computer hammering away at the keys.

"I'd probably get more booty if I let Tara and Mer put me on Timber—or if I wasn't always home with Mom. Mom's fault. Ultimate cock-blocker, that woman—"

I find myself nodding in agreement, thinking of my own mother and the way she told my first girlfriend how I'd sit in my room and watch "Saved by the Bell" on repeat. Devon Gallagher keeps on yammering behind the curtain.

"And I coulda gotten laid tonight—I mean I looked smokin'—but someone roofied me and brought me to you, Henry. So, you see, the only real solution is for you to have sex with me. Let's see if I can get this gown off—"

I take a deep breath and slide the curtain back open to stop her from stripping, but Devon just smiles. No sign of intent to undress. Her big, deep eyes are wide and excited.

"Peek-a-boo!" she sings.

I step to the right side of the bed and tuck her dangling arm back below the layers of blankets. She seems to have forgotten about propositioning me.

"I'm going to go now, Devon. You need to try to rest. And when you wake up, you'll feel much better," I tell her. But I don't move to leave. She blinks up at me and grins.

"You have one dimple."

I nod. Her dark hair spills around her like an ink blot on the pillow. I can smell her coconut shampoo.

"Satan has one dimple."

I don't nod.

"Satan. Lord of darkness," she whispers and tilts her head, signaling for me to lean closer. I can see the tiny flecks of gold in her blurry, unfocused left eye. "Could you help me become more like you? Teach me how to let loose a little. And possibly send me a lover? A generous one. I've heard you can be very, very persuasive." Her voice has gone low and raspy and she pushes her full bottom lip into a pout.

"I'll do my best," I whisper back. And I know how insanely unprofessional it is, but I really cannot resist that pleading look she's giving me beneath those absurdly thick lashes. I want to use this woman's uninhibited brain like a gumball machine. Stick a quarter in and see what color comes out next.

Susan appears across the bed and I jump back like she's caught me with my pants down. She doesn't seem to notice as she checks the monitors and then smiles down at Devon. I step back but Devon is still watching me as Susan checks her IV and tells her she needs to rest. Her mouth opens to speak, and I put my finger to my lip and wink. I force myself to turn away and head back to the computer. I need to finish this report. Check in on my patients one last time. Send my first month's rent to the landlord in Philadelphia. Text my Mom and sister back about the farewell party to celebrate the end of this never-ending residency and the beginning of my final one-year stretch as a fellow. I need to sleep. And then sleep again.

An hour later, just before I leave the recovery bay, I pull Devon Gallagher's closed curtain to the side and look at her peaceful, sleeping face. And though I know she will forget all of this, somewhere in the small irrational area of my brain, I hope she remembers me.

Chapter Two

D^{evon}

Lesson 3: The internet is public and permanent.

Eighth graders can be ruthless. If they even detect the slightest weakness, they will circle it like wolves then each take their turn to attack. So, standing in front of my class today with my bad leg bent atop my steerable knee scooter was like leaving a trail of blood and guts across the snowy, predator-filled tundra.

"Ms. G, can I catch a ride to my next class on your handlebars?"

They snicker in unison before the next wolf takes a shot.

"My little brother doesn't need his stroller anymore if you want to try that."

Haha. I smile and shake my head.

"My Grandma has a rascal you can borrow. Just make sure you fill it with gas before you give it back."

That one actually makes me chuckle. My turn. I give them a big bright grin—lots of teeth—and say, "You guys done? Get it allllll out of your system now because it's gonna be a long ten days till summer filled with quizzes and tests and—"

They all groan. Heads go down to desks. Apologies are muttered. Defeat apparent in the slumping of their shoulders. That's right, little wolves. This bleeding bunny still has all the power.

"No, but seriously everyone. Write down your homework—" Another groan. "Oh please. It's one problem. And get your notebooks out. We have to finish up our lesson on scatterplots. There is learning to be done, my people." I clap twice as they start to take action.

June is possibly the worst month of school. They've taken all their standardized tests. The sun is shining outside the windows that can't be opened. The "air conditioner" wheezes weakly above us, blowing nothing but our warm, stale breath around the room. And all that the kids and teachers want to do is get outside and have some much-deserved fun. But the world would fall from orbit before an administrator supports you actually enjoying your school day. Math class is for mathing only.

"Ms. G?"

I turn from the Smartboard at the sound of Madison's soft voice. Her notebook is open and ready to go as always.

"Yes, Maddie?"

There's murmuring and Maddie looks around, her cheeks redden, her foot taps beneath the desk. Her peers around her are shaking their heads. Some are mouthing the word "don't." I sigh. What are these goons up to?

"Ms. G, I think you should know that there's a—"

"Solar eclipse tonight!" Jonathan interrupts from beside her.

I take a deep breath and adjust the Velcro on my huge black boot, ignoring the concerning fact that Jonathan is in eighth grade and thinks the sun comes out at night. There's an aching in my calf that I just can't seem to shake, but I can't complain. It's my own fault for refusing to take anything for the pain. I thought resting for a week in bed would help. It had not.

"No. Jonathan, she has a right to know!" Madison's voice is louder than I've ever heard it. You tell him, girl. I'm impressed. But I'm also very, very nervous.

I pull my shoulders back and look between their faces. This class has been one of the best I've ever had. They're hard workers. Mostly kind. And they love to laugh.

"What's going on?" I ask, narrowing my eyes at Jonathan who puts his hands up in surrender.

"There's a video of you!" Madison blurts out, her face now covered in crimson blotches while the other students shake their heads and cringe.

"A video?" I ask. I'm not catching what she's throwing. "For yearbook?"

Madison lowers her head to her desk and Jonathan speaks up.

"We decided not to tell you because—well—it's not—like—"

"Who has the video?" I ask, still stuck in the fog.

Twenty blank stares look at me with pity.

"Ms. G, *everyone* has the video. It went viral," Jonathan explains, his words slow and even like when I need to introduce a new formula to a student with a math allergy.

Viral. The internet. Right.

Oh. My. God.

I wheel down the row toward where Jonathan is sitting, rolling over folders and notebooks. There are baskets under the desks, but heaven forbid our students ever use them. I put my hand out.

"Show me," I squeak.

Jonathan doesn't move. He looks across the room to someone for help, but nobody dares.

"I can't. We can't have phones. Remember?" His eyes are wide. He runs a hand through his hair.

I know they all have their phones. Tucked in socks. Zipped in pencil cases. Snuggled into bras or waist bands. But no one will risk the dreaded "automatic Saturday detention." I roll my eyes and start to reverse, ignoring the sound of crumpled paper beneath my wheels and the cry of "my toe" that someone fakes as I go. I want to kill Tara. One fucking rule! No videos.

I get to my laptop and type in my name. All that comes up is the school website. The Rutgers University website. The newspaper articles about how I organized a group of teacher volunteers for Chop. No viral video.

"Type in 'Karaoke Fail'," Kamaiah tells me from the front row.

And I do.

And there it is.

I press the play button and watch myself. Two slides left. Four steps right. Then the final verse. I look good. Happy. Like I'm having more fun than a kid on a carousel. And then I'm passing the microphone down to Tara who looks legitimately gorgeous staring up at me like I'm Beyonce and she's my biggest fan. My arms go out. I see the moment I misjudged. The left toe of my flat connects with that stupid black cord. And as I pull my arms in and switch my feet, my mouth forms a round O mirroring my eyes, and the realization on my face as I reach for the microphone stand is nearly too comical to be real as I tumble off the stage, the crowd clearing graciously to assist gravity.

Whoever made the video edited the scene so the moment I disappear beneath the crowd, I reappear in slow motion reverse, rising like a phoenix, my talons clutching the silver pole as I stand back on the stage and fall—over and over again.

Did effing Spielburg produce this video?

You can see every flicker of emotion that crosses over my face: the joy of performing, the confusion, the fear, and finally the flinching resignation. I hit play again and someone gets the lights so I can watch it as it's meant to be watched.

"Look, Ms. G. 5.3 million views!"

I look up from my laptop screen and toward the voice, confused. It's Aiden, with his toothy smile pointing at the Smartboard. I look slowly to where he's pointing and realize my laptop is projecting onto the screen for the whole class to watch. Not that it matters. There's no way they haven't seen it already. This is what comes from stepping outside my box and breaking my rules. I'm going to kill Tara. Why did I let her talk me into this mess?

Then my eyes lift over their little heads and find Mr. Donato, the head principal, staring at me like I've lost my damned mind. Even his mustache is angry. I snap the laptop shut. The Smartboard goes black and the students groan. The light flicks on. Then a few of the kids follow my gaze, craning their necks to look over their shoulders. I hear some giggles. A few gasps. One muffled curse.

"Ms. Gallagher, could I have a moment alone with you in my office?" Mr. Donato turns and doesn't wait for my answer. Our badass guidance counselor, Elizabeth, steps into the room and her eyes are filled with apology when I roll by her. The students are silent, watching me like I'm being led to the gallows. I force a smile and wink to let them know it's all going to be alright and I hear Lizzie's too chipper voice as I shut the door behind me.

"So, how 'bout those scatterplots?"

Sister, Sister

Devon: I'm going to kill you.

Tara: I guess that means you saw it. I swear
to you. I DID NOT TAKE THAT VIDEO.

Devon: I'm still going to kill you.

Tara: Come on. It's not that bad.

You look really HOT. And you still got it.
Until—you don't.

Devon: I'm glad you think it's funny. My
boss didn't.

Tara: Who, the asshat with the Captain
Hook stache? That man wouldn't know
funny if it sat on his face.

Devon: Tara, he wants me to take sick leave
for the rest of the school year "to rest and
recover."

Tara: I'm sorry, Dev. But maybe it'll be good
to get some time off? I've gotta go.
Michael's coming into the conference room.

Devon: Ten years of teaching, T. Not once
have I missed the last day of school.

How am I going to say goodbye to my kids?

Tara: Could you write them postcards? Or
send something into school?

Good news is they can always watch the
video when they miss you.

Devon: You are so dead.

Tara: BTW there might be a GIF out there,
too. Just type in karaoke.

Or failure.

Or so embarrassing.

Devon: Oh. My. God!

Chapter Three

Devon

Lesson 4: The last day of school isn't as fun when watching from your mom's Toyota.

I've borrowed my mother's car to make sure the school resource officer, Dante, doesn't recognize me and come over for a chat through the car window. I'm ducked down, the brim of my Phillie-Phanatic-embossed baseball cap parallel to the top of the steering wheel, my eyes level with the pitifully low number on my mother's odometer. The last thing I need right now is for the staff and students to see me parked out in the lot like some creep.

I see the related arts teachers come out of the school first. Mr. Wisneski with the '80s style boombox on the shoulder of his Hawaiian-print shirt. Ms. Simpson clasps along to the tinny music blaring from the speakers while Mr. J, our music teacher, uses his fingers to conduct. I hear the chorus of "School's Out for Summer" and the familiar tug of bittersweet anticipation courses through my chest. I should be out there. Smiling and fist bumping and hugging my students to send them off to high school with the feeling that there is a family here behind them, wishing them well.

My boot feels heavy against the floor of my mom's old Toyota. The car is hot, my sock inside the boot sticking to my ankle with sweat, but I don't dare to turn on the ignition and possibly draw attention to myself. I imagine the students catching sight of me and rushing the car with their phones, a pubescent paparazzi, dodging school buses like Regina George did not. I duck down lower.

I refocus on my building, tamp down the rising melancholy, and watch as the first homeroom of sixth graders skip, speed walk, and sprint out of the building hooting and hollering like maniacs. They are still so small. The babies of the middle school and I imagine them in two years, legs long and spindly, cheeks less round and cherub-like, sitting at the desks of my classroom. This first class has broken the flood gates. Now hundreds of children are rushing out the doors, a phone in almost every hand as they take selfies, Snap each other and film Tiktoks to the boombox beat.

The teachers are herding them onto the buses, their faces a mix of amusement and exasperation. They still need to get inside and clean their rooms, go through the tedious checkout process that awaits them. But not me. I'm on paid sick leave and obviously making the best of it as I adjust my shorts to avoid furthering my swamp ass.

Pathetic.

I catch sight of Mr. Donato's mustache as he ushers a group of seventh grade boys onto bus 29. Seeing him still makes the anger course through my veins and pour into a fireball in the center of my chest. I take the mature route and flip him off, keeping my finger beneath the steering wheel just in case I accidentally photobomb one of the 8,000 selfies being shot at the moment. Obviously, that would be my luck.

Headline: Young Teacher/Karaoke Failure Caught Flipping-off Students in Instagram Photo.

I've given a decade to this school—ten years of putting my students at the forefront of my mind and actions—and here I am holed up in a 2012 Corolla wearing my "oh the places you'll go" shirt like I'm a crazy Stan. I reach for someone to blame—but my scapegoat sister stopped bleating when she swore she hadn't broken the social media rule.

What about Donato? Surely I can dole out some blame in his general direction. Never once has the man had my back. It's not like I released the video—or ran an illegal karaoke ring in the school auditorium. But still here I am with my tail between my sweaty legs.

And it's not the first time he's made me—or other educators—feel this way. Countless times I've asked for help or support and he's told me to stay in my lane—that I'm stepping out of line. That the mental health of my students is not my concern. And countless times I've limboed beneath his red tape to figure out a way to help. How low can you go? Really, effin' low if a kid is in crisis. Subterranean even.

My focus is recaptured when my students start filing out of the building. No skipping or running for these goons. No way. They are far too mature for such shenanigans. They saunter. I find myself smiling, my eyes tearing up like they do whenever I hear the graduation song or see a student in their cap and gown. Many of them are hugging the teachers—I can almost hear their heartfelt thanks and feel the discomfort of the approach to embrace. Hands and arms down around hips? The diagonal tilt? The one arm side hug? It's all part of the awkward adolescent package. The package that I signed up for. Those are my goddamned hugs. And I need them right now.

I try to remind myself that I'll see them around town. At Target, where they all line up for pink drinks and look at me like I'm well outside my rights to be spotted on their turf, then reconsider and want to take photos like I'm some rare spotted tiger. And some of them I'll see often, the few who have shared lunch with me each day and opened up about their pain and their issues. Those few always stay in touch. Like Syd has and always will.

I wait until the very last student disappears onto their big yellow bus and I rest my forehead against the steering wheel. The farewell beeping starts as one bus after the next files out of the parking lot like that arcade game, Centipede, the drivers' honking drowning out the opening of "We Don't Need No Education." The students are nearly hanging out of the windows, some waving, some videotaping the teachers who are all sending them off with their hands in the air, yelling a chorus of wishes of good luck and see you next year.

And then it's quiet.

The teachers turn and head back inside and I turn the key in the ignition, adjust my boot so it's away from the pedals, and drive home to my mom with the less than comforting thought that there is always next year.

Chapter Four

J eff

Lesson 5: It's a small world—and it is rapidly getting smaller.

It's not even mid-August and Philadelphia is already a sweltering mix of body heat and food truck odors. In the two-block walk from the orthopedic building toward my new (new to me but very, very old) Washington Square apartment, my back has produced enough sweat to soak through my scrubs and make me want to dive into any of the fifteen hipster bars I've passed for the sweet relief of a cold beer and some air conditioning. Chicago isn't much better, but at least you can find some relief when a breeze rolls off of Lake Michigan.

My phone vibrates in my pocket and I lift it out expecting to see a call from Kevin, the trauma surgeon that I'm meeting for drinks. I tried to get my own co-fellow in the spinal cord injury program, Dustin, to tag along, but he did not seem interested in anything other than consulting on the bone resection he was performing later. It would be a long twelve months of fellowship if I didn't "branch out," to quote my mother. It seems silly to make friends when my expiration date here is closer than a bag of frozen peas. But I don't want to wallow in my homesickness, either. I slow my stride and check the screen. Speak of the devil.

"Hey, Ma."

"Honey! I was worried. The nurses told me you were in surgery, but I wasn't sure they knew who you were," she explains. Somehow, she makes the dumbest shit seem perfectly reasonable.

"Right. Well, I was in surgery. Everything good at home?" I ask. I can hear Sam in the background, her little voice singing something about stinky feet and Uncle Jeff. No matter how many times I explain what an orthopedic surgeon is, Sammy's convinced I touch feet for a living.

My mom puts her hand over the mouthpiece and tells my 8-year-old niece she should drink some water to dilute her high. Before I have a chance to ask what the hell is going on, she comes back to me.

"Sorry, hun. I caught Sam gnawing on the sugar cubes we give the horses and she's out of her mind—bouncing off the walls. Everyone is good."

My mom tells Sammy not to tie the dogs together and I wait until she can refocus. "I just wanted to make sure you're all settled in. There's a care package on its way!"

Jesus. "Ma, you really didn't need to—"

"Oh shush. Everyone needs a little t.l.c.," she tells me.

This may be true, but a Donna Harrison care package has little to do with what most people would consider t.l.c.

"It's only been a few weeks," I remind her. And if she keeps up at this rate, I'll have at least 40 strange packages to deal with by the end of this fellowship.

"And I miss you already, J.J."

I can hear the tears in her eyes. The familiar pang of homesickness rips at my obliques. Eleven more months. That's it. Then I can start my career close to home. Help my sister with my niece. Make sure the therapeutic riding center my mother runs has everything it needs.

"I miss you too, Ma. But I gotta go. I'm meeting some people from work—"

She's clapping, possibly jumping up and down.

"You made friends!" she chirps.

A man in a suit looks at me as he passes, his brows pulled together in amusement. I realized after graduating from medical school that I'd never be older than six in her mind.

"Alright, Ma. Gotta go! See you on our Zoom call on Sunday," I promise, picking up my pace when I see the sign for The Rusty Hammer.

"I love you, Jeffry James," she tells me. I smile because I've heard it so many times that it is engraved on my frontal lobe.

"Love you, too, Ma. Tell Sammy and Sis the same."

"Will do." I hear her yelling to Sammy before she even ends the call, making sure to give her my love the second after I ask her to. The woman is nothing if not reliable. But she's proven that every moment of my life.

I duck into The Rusty Hammer and search the long, crowded bar for the familiar blues of scrubs and find Kevin's carefree grin just as he sees me and waves both hands over his head. He's sitting beside a dark-haired woman in scrubs who is eyeing me over the rim of a highball glass like she's a crocodile and I'm an unlucky wildebeest crossing her river.

Kevin pulls the stool he's tilted against the bar off the wood ledge and knocks on the metal seat. I sit and Kevin slides a pint glass in front of me.

"Jeff, this is Meredith," he says as I hold out my hand to her. "Mer, Jeff."

She slides her hand into mine and tilts her head, her eyes narrowed, studying me. Seconds tick by, long and slow. But this woman keeps looking right into me. I break eye contact first and look down at the tattoo inside her wrist—a sketch-like rendering of a pair of lungs surrounded by watercolor streaks.

"Kevin, we can't hang out with this guy" she says, still staring at me.

"Come on, Mer. Leave him alone—"

"You know the deal. No one better-looking than me." She smiles and I hear the theme song from Jaws. I slide my hand out of hers as she continues, "I already made an exception for Devon."

"Nice to meet you. I thought you'd be a guy from the way Kev described you," I say, lifting the beer to my lips. "But now I feel like a sexist shit."

"Did he say I was tall, dark, and handsome?" She tilts her head.

"No. He said your balls were way bigger than his," I tell her and she grins wider.

"They so are! But I know Kev didn't say that. Kev would never say balls. He would have used the word testicles. He's refined. Private school boy. Studied at St. Timothy's Academy of Deuchedom or some shit." She jabs an elbow into Kevin's ribs and he shakes his head.

"Are you funny, Jeff?" She doesn't let me answer. "I think he might be funny, Kev." Meredith is still looking at me with narrowed eyes. "You sure you don't want to uninvite him? You know Devon's a sucker for funny."

Kevin ignores her. Keeps his pretty blue eyes right on me.

"Meredith's a CT surgeon, so lucky you. You'll be seeing her around the hospital." He pats my back. "Now she won't just have me to emasculate."

"You need to be a man to be emasculated," Meredith shoots back, leaning across the bar to get a refill. The young bartender hurries over and she reaches up to squeeze his man bun. He doesn't even flinch. "Jeremy, can I get another Brown Derby, please? And something light for Devon."

Bartender Jeremy nods but doesn't move. He's hypnotized. Catatonic.

Kevin's phone pings on the bar and Jeremy's trance is broken. He scurries off to get the drinks and Kevin lifts the screen to eye level, reads the message, and stands.

"Dev's here," he says, lifting his drink toward the door. I swivel in my chair for an introduction and freeze as I take in the oddly familiar brunette standing behind my stool.

Those wide bright eyes—glowing now with alertness. That gorgeous smile—more cautious than it was that night but still so arresting that I nearly tip over my stool as I stand and face her. I find myself hoping for some reciprocal recognition as she puts her hand out to me and ignores Meredith's low whistle. One side of her mouth lifts further and I take her hand and nod like an idiot as she says,

"Devon Gallagher. Nice to meet you."

Chapter Five

D^{evon}

Lesson 6: It can always get worse.

The new guy is staring at me like I have three breasts. He's still holding my hand in his firm grip and I lift a brow while I count the uncomfortable seconds. I must look like an ex or something because his green eyes are wide and surprised. I know it's not because I look good. I'm a sweaty mess from cleaning and setting up my classroom all morning and I can still smell the Expo cleaner spray on my hands despite the way I scrubbed them. The kids call it funky cheese spray. And they aren't wrong.

...8-9-10. This is getting weird, though I can't say that staring at this guy is hard work. His chin is—

"This is Jeff," Kevin says. And the new guy finally snaps out of it and lets go of my hand. I hear Mer clear her throat and I pivot my body so she's not behind me. I know better than to let Meredith stand behind me. Always keep danger right out in front.

We grab a table toward the back of the bar and Meredith and Kevin flank me while Jeff lags behind. I turn to find him staring back at the door like he might bolt, but then his broad shoulders deflate, and he rounds the table to take the chair across from me.

"How was school?" Kevin asks me.

"Empty. Thank the lord," I say, realizing too late how that might sound to the new guy. "I had a rough year," I tell Jeff with a small smile.

He lifts his hands. "No need to explain. My sister's a teacher," Jeff says.

I like him already. Teacher relatives are automatic brownie points in my book. But he's still watching me with that look—faintly surprised and fully amused. There must be something in my teeth. I tighten my lips.

"Kevin, he has a sister," Mer says, swirling her bourbon. "Maybe you could break your epic dry spell. It's such a waste that your last name is Johnson and you never use your—"

"Meredith, try not to scare Jeff away," I say, swatting her thigh.

"Too late," Jeff says under his breath. Willing to engage in a pissing contest with Mer? I give him another brownie point.

"Speaking of dry spells," Kevin starts, turning to Jeff, "tell the ladies that story you told me about that woman—from your residency."

Jeff chokes on his beer. Sprays a little of it onto his scrubs. He shifts in his seat and looks everywhere but at me.

"I'm gonna grab some napkins," Jeff says, retreating toward the bar.

Meredith immediately leans in, her voice low, but not low enough.

"Umm, is it just me or did Dr. Centerfold hold onto your handshake a little longer than socially acceptable?"

Kevin makes a sound and looks away.

"I'm just saying." Mer lifts her brows. "Maybe someone's hot for teacher."

"Or maybe someone watches too much porn," I respond. "Besides. He's a doctor."

"Right. Your rules. Do you have a rule that says 'I must die alone surrounded by felines'?" Mer asks.

Oooof. Can't say that one doesn't hit too close to home. I have a recurring nightmare about sinking in kitty litter like it's quicksand. It's the number one reason why I don't get a cat. I take a big sip of my beer to cover my shiver and spill a little in the process. I already have a smear of red on my jeans from where a leaking pen attacked me while cleaning out a student's forgotten pencil case. I take another long swig, trying to forget how sad it was clearing out my room with none of my colleagues or kids around. The school is so depressing when it's empty—like a stuffed animal left behind on a playground. And though I didn't want to face my colleagues yet, I miss the energy of being in session. And the laughter.

Jeff comes back to the table with a shot and another beer instead of napkins.

He's barely in his seat before Kevin tries again.

"Jeff, tell the girls that story," Kevin says, leaning toward me. "You'll love this." He nudges my arm. "Devon loves funny medical antics."

I so do. It's probably not something to be proud of, but I can't get enough of the dumb shit that happens in the hospital. There's something about the way the doctors take the most chaotic, ridiculous situations and create order and precision—my brain really likes that. It's the same way I feel when I plug a coordinate point into a linear equation and it comes out equivalent.

I wait for Jeff to entertain me, but the color has drained from his face. He shakes his head.

"No. I really shouldn't. I don't want to break patient confidentiality," Jeff says, looking toward the exit again.

Kevin chuckles. "I think it's a little late for that, man."

Jeff lets out a long breath and looks up to the ceiling before giving me a sad look.

"It's ok. Really. You don't need to tell us," I say. The guy looks miserable. "Kev, leave him alone. It must be a guy thing," I say with my nose wrinkled in disgust.

"I promise, Jeff, you can't offend Devon. And obviously, you can't offend Meredith. They'll love it," Kevin insists.

"Do your best. I dare you," Mer tells him. Her eyes glitter with the challenge.

But Jeff doesn't notice. He's still staring at me, two lines deeply creased between his dark brows, making a perfect number eleven above the bridge of his nose.

"Ok fine. I'll tell it," Kevin says when the silence stretches on too long. Jeff opens his mouth to say something, but Kevin rambles on. "So, Jeff is trying to dictate a post-op report in recovery last month when a woman starts rapping that song you love, Dev. What's it called?"

"Bust a Move," Jeff says softly.

I nod. I like this woman already. We like the same music. And though that song is cursed and I have sworn it off for life, I imagine my dance with Tara and smile until the image of me falling off of the stage wipes it away.

"Right," Kevin continues. "The woman starts yelling about how cold she is and the nurses are all busy so Jeff has to be her savior. When he goes to help her, she decides that he's Henry Cavill and starts to talk about her vagina—a lot."

Weird. I'd had like seven sex dreams about Henry Cavill's chin in the last month. That's probably the average Cavill fantasy rate for most Americans. Oddly enough, I'd also had a few steamy dreams starring Satan. I blame that on bingeing *Lucifer*.

"She proceeds to tell him that she hasn't gotten laid in eons—paints a clear picture about how dusty her lady bits are—"

Meredith is chuckling and shaking her head. Poor patient. I can totally relate to dusty bits. Finding good help is impossible these days.

"After propositioning him to end her drought, she decides that Jeff is actually Satan and enlists his help to get herself laid."

For some reason, heat rushes to my face and my gaze lands on Jeff. His face is contorted like someone's pulling off his fingernails, but Kevin doesn't notice.

"Jeff, what did she call her vagina, again? Her love cushion?"

Jeff shakes his head, his eyes locked on mine, his shoulders slumped. The impossible starts to click in place. That song. Cavill. Satan. I'm fixating on the formula for the probability of mutually exclusive events—it's approaching zero when Jeff sighs.

In a voice so soft it begs for forgiveness, he says, "Her box o'love."

Oh God, no. No. No. No. NO!

Kevin and Meredith are laughing, completely unaware of my horror, and I stand to push back from the table. The metal chair screeches against the cement floor. I mumble something about the bathroom, and I stumble toward the front of the restaurant, my eyes blurry and burning as I haul my boot through the oblivious bar patrons. I'm overreacting. It's just a coincidence. There is no way that I am that woman. I was halfway across the country. This is impossible.

But even as I push into the bathroom stall, breathless and dizzy, the image of "box o'love" scratched deep on the desk in the front row of class flashes on my lids and I know without a doubt. The rapping, Cavill-loving, Satan-worshipping, dusty vagina is mine.

Chapter Six

J eff

Lesson 7: What or who happens in residency should stay in residency.

On instinct, I follow her as she stumbles toward the front of the bar. Meredith watches Devon limp across the space as if the display is nothing out of the ordinary and Kevin stands, justly confused. I say something lame about having a sister as an excuse to try to help. Surprisingly, Kevin buys it and sits back down. And though my sister has prepared me for a lot of shit in life, I'd say running into a random patient who shared humiliating, drug-induced info is definitely not on that list. I stand against the wall across from the bathroom and wait. I should give her time. Let her process the impossible.

I don't do any of that. I knock and push the door open.

"Devon. It's Jeff. Can I talk to—"

"No!" she yells. I hear her breathing hard. "No, thank you," she says more softly.

I step into the space between the sinks and shut the door behind me. One yellow flat and her black, robotic boot are visible beneath the stall, the flat tapping against the black and white tile.

"I'm really sorry. This is—I had no idea—"

"That you were spilling my subconscious onto the table for a few laughs," she finishes.

I scrub at my face. "I had no idea I'd ever see you again and—"

The door of the stall swings open and she steps out, her eyes narrowed on my chest.

"So, you thought, let me use this poor, defenseless patient as the punchline of my joke so I can join the male doctor fraternity at Jefferson. How refreshing. Just what the world needs. Another privileged white guy, throwing other people's humiliation around to boost himself up. I'm shocked you didn't tape the whole damn thing and add another viral video to my repertoire."

Oh shit. She is pissed. I have no idea what she's talking about with the video thing, but her finger is in my face and her chest is rising and falling so heavily beneath her "You Matter" t-shirt that my eyes wander for a fraction of a second and she laughs, a humorless, empty chuckle.

"My face is up here, Doctor. Didn't they teach you that in med school?" She shakes her head and murmurs something to herself about misogyny and I'm staring at her like she's backhanded me.

I'm an idiot for telling Kevin that story, but I wanted so badly to share it with someone—to say it aloud so I could relive the way she stared up at me with those melted caramel eyes—to hear her giggle echo in my moronic, thick skull as I recited the details of the night I'd played over and over again in my head.

"I'm so sorry," I tell her again. She's washing her hands. Scrubbing them really hard, her fingers attacking her wrists, the water steaming, as hot as her rage.

"For what? Humiliating me or staring at my tits?" She tilts her head and watches me.

"Both. Though really it was more of a glance."

A young blonde pushes through the door and looks between us before hurrying into a stall. Devon grabs for a paper towel behind me and has to crane her neck a bit to keep eye contact. She's got her lips in a tight line as she smacks and twists the paper towel between her palms.

"Can't you find another friend group to tag along with?" she asks me, tossing the balled-up towel into the trash.

I could. I could try harder with Dustin or just spend more time in the common room between procedures. I could call Ray, a pediatric neurologist I befriended during residency who landed across town at UPenn. I could even walk around Washington Square and make small talk with my neighbors. Or I could just do what I'm here to do for the next part of a year, put my head down and perfect my skills, and forget about trying to fill my few hours outside the hospital with anything but sleep. But I shake my head. None of that sounds like fun to me now.

"Sorry, Dev. I think we might just have to handle this like adults," I say with a shrug.

"Don't call me Dev. I hate adults," she bites back, then pushes a piece of hair that has come loose during her rant behind her ear and lets out an overstated sigh. "Fine. I'll ignore you. You'll pretend like you've never seen me before in your life. And no one has to know. I was drugged up. None of it was true anyway. I happen to have zero dust—down there. Freshly-swiffered or whatever."

I bite down hard on my cheek to keep from laughing. Her eyes find mine, and she widens them, waiting for me to agree. I nod. "Right. All lies. And I've never seen you before. Or heard you refer to your vagina as your lady treasures or whatever."

She puffs up again, her finger back in my face. "This is not a joke. I'm going to trust you despite the fact that I have no reason to, besides your sister being a teacher. But I don't have to like you."

The toilet flushes behind her and the blonde woman reappears, keeping her eyes on the sink. She risks a side glance over at Devon in the mirror and then turns, opens her mouth to speak, but Devon stops her by putting a hand up.

"Yes, I'm the girl from the video. And yes, it was all real," Devon blurts out, her cheeks still streaked with red.

The blonde pulls her brows together and shakes her head.

"I just wanted to tell you that you have a piece—" she points to Devon's ass, "of toilet paper stuck to your—"

Devon reaches for it like a dog chasing her tail and misses. I grab it for her and toss it into the trash as the innocent bystander hurries out of the space without drying her hands.

Devon pulls in a long breath and looks back up at me. Then at the door.

"I can see why I thought you were Satan," she says quietly.

I try not to smile but fail. Which obviously pisses her off more. She tosses me one last teacher glare and then marches—no, limps aggressively—out of the bathroom.

I prop both hands onto the edge of the cool porcelain sink and look up at the industrial A/C vent that snakes through the space and then back at my reflection in the mirror—slightly bemused and more than a little flustered. I'm a goddamned surgeon. I'm trained to handle life-altering situations with calm and poise. But that—that was like standing in the center of one of those hurricane wind machines—equal parts terrifying and exciting. And I've got a pocket full of crisp dollar bills out and ready to do it again.

She told me off. I was solidly and thoroughly put in my place—maybe for the first time ever by someone other than my bossy little sister and my mom. I mean, she's just thrown every ounce of her pissed-off, five-foot-four indignance in my face along with that aggressive finger and told me the-fuck-off. So why the hell can't I wipe this stupid smile off my face?

Chapter Seven

Devon

Lesson 8: Chickens are always a good idea.

I drop the arm full of groceries onto the oversized island in my mother's kitchen and catch sight of her through the window above the sink. She's sprinkling feed across the lawn, her lips moving as the chickens frantically swarm around her feet, pecking so fast that you'd think she'd never fed them before—when in reality any single chicken from her flock could feed a neighborhood.

I imagine the ridiculous conversation she's having with her feathered fatties as her mouth opens and closes. *Bernice, save some corn for Athena, you chunker. Cheeks! Be kind to Betsy!* Her chickens are her only chance to socialize besides her overweight golden retriever, Brutus, who is currently waddling around the yard happily sniffing chicken butts.

The chickens had been Tara's idea—a way to get mom outside more often—and at the time I'd thought it was crazy. But now, watching her smile as she sprinkles the kernels, I have to admit that Tara's hairbrained scheme might have worked. Though I'd never tell her that.

I'm nearly done putting away the groceries when the back door slides open and my mom comes inside, her long chestnut hair pulled back so the fine lines around her eyes are visible in the light that fills the space. She sees me and smiles wide, as if I didn't just see her yesterday. Brutus sees me and wags his tail twice, then plops heavily onto the tile floor beside the air conditioning vent. Life is hard, Brutus.

"Hey, hun. No hospital today?" she asks, making her way around the island to wash her hands. They are still covered in the chalky residue from the chicken feed. She gives me a little hip bump as she scrubs, and my boot defies inertia. I nearly topple over. The damn boot is like an anchor.

"I'm going to head over with Syd this afternoon," I say and my mom nods. She knows Sydney well. My former student has pretty much been a part of this family since she graced my classroom four years prior. Her ongoing battle with anorexia lit a fire under my ass that grew so hot it still burns holes in my underwear, but I have yet to find a way to harness the flames other than taking course after course about adolescent mental health and visiting the twelfth floor of CHOP each week with Syd.

"You didn't need to come all the way home, hun. I had some food left in the fridge," my mom says.

"You have eggs, Mom. And you eat them twice a day. Besides, I needed to get out of the city. Kev and Mer wanted to get brunch and there's this guy that Kev—"

"A guy!" She actually drops the bag of apples she's putting away.

"Slow your roll. He's a dick. And a doctor. Doctor Dick."

Her shoulders instantly deflate. I consider telling her the entire messy tale that's been swelling inside like a water balloon on the end of a fire hose—delineating the embarrassing Friday bathroom scene from two weeks ago and all of the so-far-successful attempts to avoid said embarrass-er in between. I'd leave out the fact that the dick in question is insanely hot. Obviously. That detail is irrelevant. But when I open my mouth to speak my stomach gurgles once and lets out a long, dramatic groan. My mother shakes her head and releases an exasperated breath.

"So busy taking care of me that you forgot breakfast?" she asks.

I don't answer. I don't need to.

My mother sighs and gestures to a chair as she stares at my boot. "Sit. You're not supposed to be on that thing all day."

I do as I'm told despite the fact that I hadn't moved off of Meredith's couch for hours the day before. Mer's couch is my soulmate. And maybe I'd part with my soulmate to go for a little stroll, prevent the atrophy in my bad leg, but it is too damn hot in the city, the modern glass buildings downtown reflecting the heat between them like the walls of a microwave and the brick facades of the townhomes that run through South Philly baking to a deep shade of brown like clay left in an oven too long. Couple this excruciating heatwave with my discomfort with being on my own in the city, and you have a Devon-sized ass indent on the cushion of Meredith's leather couch.

Tara can't understand what my "issue"—her word not mine—is with the city. We share the same blood, the same adventurous early childhood. We've faced the same pain. But where she thrives in NYC and craves the energy of the crowds and the thrill of the new, I prefer the safety and comfort of the known. Like my mother. Just not as bad. *Yet,* Tara would add when I defensively insist that I am nowhere near as bad as mom.

I watch my mom's capable hands as she piles the fresh cut lettuce from her garden onto the rolls I bought. An image of her from our years before the accident flashes on my lids, like a dream you want to remember but can't flesh out. My mother seemed unstoppable then. We traveled constantly, following Dad to conferences across the world, people-watching in cafés along the Seine and crunching soft snow beneath our skis in the Tetons. Did those things really happen? It's impossible to align that fearless and strong woman of the past with this slightly soft, homebody version before me. Or to imagine a little me in her wake.

"How's your sister?" she asks, eyeing me as she spreads the Dijon.

Still a pain in the ass, I want to answer. But *still kicking ass* is a more accurate response. Tara's worked her way up from intern to lead designer in one of the fast-growing brands in fashion. She might be a thorn in my side sometimes, but she's all rose to the rest of the world.

"She's fine. Leaves for Milan tomorrow," I remind her.

She wrinkles her nose at the mention of Milan as if the city is a piece of balled up toilet paper stuck on her shoe. She doesn't necessarily like the idea of Tara's travels—or her life choices in general—even if she planted the seed of wanderlust that has grown like a weed inside my sister. But Mom never comes out and directly says anything. Just a passive-aggressive comment here and a pointed facial expression there. It's one reason why Tara rarely visits.

"So, you two have made up then?" my mother asks, already knowing that Tara and I have never fought for longer than a day and that was when she cut up my favorite blanket to make a sundress that was actually cute as hell. I couldn't tell Tara that, either.

"Yeah. We're fine. I can't really blame her for Chicago," I explain, and my mom lifts her brows as if to say, why the hell not? She approaches the table with our lunch, and I wait until she sits to ask the same question that I ask every day.

"Want to make reservations for tonight? Get out for a little bit?" I know the answer. But if I don't at least ask, I feel like some sort of dirty accomplice.

She shakes her head, her frown lines deepening as she swallows an oversized bite. "And waste all these good groceries you just brought?" She takes another bite of her sandwich and chews slowly, studying me as I pick at the cheese on my own. "You sleeping here tonight?"

I nod, knowing I should just stay at Mer's. I mean, her apartment is only three miles away from the Children's Hospital of Pennsylvania. But the guys are going over tonight to watch the new Tarantino movie. And while I love Quentin as much if not more than the next dark and twisted soul, I know that "the guys" now means Kevin *and* Jeff, and risking another night with Doctor Dick is low on my to-do list.

"I'll make us some homemade pizzas," my mother says. And I have to admit homemade pizzas sound a lot better than sitting cross legged on the couch thinking about whether or not the annoying guy two cushions away is wondering if I'm still sexually unsatisfied. I feel heat rush to my face.

"Perfect," I say around a piece of tomato.

"Girls night in." My mom grins.

Again.

I smile right back, trying not to imagine the disappointed look and the sharp kick on the shin by an overpriced heel that Tara would be giving me if she were here. Just one more thing not to tell her. Besides, Tara isn't here.

She's out there—living her life.

Chapter Eight

J^{eff}

Lesson 9: Wherever you go, there she might be.

Finding parking at the Children's Hospital garage should be a requirement for canonization. After twenty minutes of circling and false hopes, I finally manage to squeeze into a vacancy between two minivans covered in a variety of "Proud parent of..." magnets and bumper stickers. Even the zombie-stick-figure-family window sticker in the back of the Honda Odyssey I'm passing doesn't get the dopey-grin reaction out of me that it normally would. I'm anxious about being in a children's hospital, exhausted after an absurdly long lumbar fusion that faced several complications, and once again, I'm sweating like I ran a marathon.

I find the garage elevator that smells of warm piss and rust, step inside, and press the button that will get me to the tunnel that leads to CHOP's lobby. I should have rescheduled, should have explained to Ray that the routine procedure hadn't gone as planned and that we should meet up for drinks next week instead, but I've already been forced to change dates on him twice since I arrived, and Ray deserves better. Shit, he deserves a medal of honor for the things he witnesses in the pediatric ward.

I lean against the handrail and shut my eyes as my stomach lurches upward. I'll stay for a beer, eat something greasy and comforting, and then put a real date on the calendar—a day where we can meet someplace less depressing than this. A day when we both have off, so we aren't scrambling to get a meal while Ray's beeper threatens to go off at any minute for some emergency.

The elevator dings and I open my eyes to find my new favorite wide-eyed brunette staring at me with signature annoyance.

"Jesus. H. Christ," she growls, crossing her arms as her teenage companion steps over the crack onto the elevator.

"What are the odds?" I ask, taking her in. She's been avoiding me since that afternoon at the bar, always making some lame excuse to leave the moment I arrive, and I can't say I wouldn't do the same, but my stomach does another flip and I can't blame the elevator because we aren't moving.

"Really good when the universe hates you," Devon deadpans. The doors start to close, but she doesn't uncross her arms and I'm impressed by her commitment. There are few people in this world who would choose to stand on the third floor of a sweltering, stinky parking garage rather than step into an elevator with me. The thought makes me grin wider as I put my arm out to stop the doors just in time.

"Do you want to stand out there and wait for a magic escalator to appear or—"

She lets out a long breath and her hands fall by her sides, then she steps onto the elevator sideways, dragging her boot across the dingy carpet, so she can watch me the entire time.

Someone clears their throat and I release the door and turn. The girl she's with is smiling so big it makes my jaw hurt and she's looking between us—back and forth—her neck twisting, her pierced brow lifted toward the gray-blue streaks in her hair.

"Sydney, this is Jeff Harrison. Kevin's doctor friend and overall pain-in-the-ass," Devon explains from the farthest corner of the space.

Sydney puts out her hand and I take it. She can't be a day over seventeen and I'm about to ask how they know each other when the young girl beats me to it.

"Ms. G is my life coach," she says, twisting at her eyebrow ring with her free hand in a way that makes my own brow bone ache.

I look at Devon who is shaking her head emphatically.

"I am no one's life coach," she promises. "Syd is a former student. We volunteer in the ED ward together."

"Eating disorders," Sydney clarifies, and I nod, all too familiar with the abbreviation for what my sister struggled through for most of her post-pubescent years.

"It's very nice to meet you, Sydney." I release her hand though she doesn't seem to want to let go. Her fingers linger on my wrist. "You've chosen an excellent life coach," I tell her.

Devon shuts her eyes as if the mere sight of me is causing her pain and I chuckle. The elevator lurches to a halt and the doors ping open. I sweep an arm out to let them off, accepting Devon's warning look with a smile. Her message is loud and clear. *Remember your promise.* How could I forget?

Though it's obvious Devon is hauling ass, pulling her boot along beside her as fast as her little leg can manage, I match her stride easily and walk between them.

"Do you work here, Dr. Harrison?" Syd asks.

"No," Devon answers. "He's just here to torture me."

"I'm here to meet an old friend," I tell the girl and she nods.

The lobby opens up before us, a wide marble expanse enclosed in sheets of glass to let the natural light flood the space—an architect's doomed attempt to combat the unavoidable melancholy of a hospital for sick kids. The sound of coughing and crying fills the cavernous space, bouncing off the tall panes of blueish glass. I'm suddenly back in my third year as a med student. The eight weeks I spent rounding in pediatrics pulled my heart so thin it could have crumpled like tissue paper. I consider turning back around.

I open my eyes to find Devon looking back at me while Syd chats with the nurse behind the desk.

Her head tilts a little and her face softens. I quickly speak to cover whatever it is she's found in my expression: "I'm coming over to Meredith's tonight in case there's some imaginary dog you need to walk or a very pressing manicure you need to have."

She hesitates, narrows her eyes at me. Syd appears with a visitor sticker and holds it out to Devon.

"I'm not around tonight," she says quietly, and I'm shaken by the change in her voice.

I nod and scramble for something to tease her with. Of course, she's not going to be around. She's never around. I wonder if my increasing presence in Kevin's life is hurting her social life more than she's letting on and something like guilt nibbles at my gut.

"If you want, I don't have to—"

"I like to be home. At my mom's," she cuts me off. "Believe me, Jeff. It's not all about you."

There she is. I lift up my hands.

"Right. Just trying to be nice," I tell her.

She rolls her eyes and turns away, pulling Syd alongside her as she limps past the check-in desk.

"See you around, Dr. Harrison," Syd hollers over her shoulder and I give her a wave, watching as the teen nudges Devon with her elbow.

"He's so hawtttttt," Sydney says, bouncing alongside her and Devon shakes her head and tries to shush her without success. As they round the corner, Devon glances back and I meet her gaze and flash her one last smile before she disappears. I lower myself into a leather chair and shoot Ray a text to let him know I'm here. And despite the sad sights and sounds I've avoided for many years, I think maybe visiting Ray at his hospital wasn't such a bad idea after all.

Chapter Nine

Devon

Lesson 10: Breakdowns can lead to breakdowns.

We are halfway between the hospital and the Ben Franklin Bridge when my mom's trusty-rusty old Corolla lets out a rattling belch followed by a dragon puff of smoke from beneath her hood. I reach across Syd's lap like my arm will protect her from the billowing black smoke that wreaks of oil and carcinogens while I pull the car into the empty parking spots along the side of Vine Street. Why did I decide to drive this ancient P.O.S. anyway?

"Remind me why we drove this dinosaur again?" Syd asks as I poke frantically at the release button to unbuckle her seat belt and push her out of the car. Syd swats my hand away. "Jesus, Ms. G. I'm seventeen. I think I can unbuckle myself. And the car is *not* on fire. Relax."

She releases the seatbelt with ease and gives me a look like I'm an overbearing mother wiping something off her face. I lift my hands in surrender.

"I'm sorry. Instinct," I explain, checking my side mirror for traffic and then sliding out of the car into the fug. My booted foot is immediately puddled in sweat. Drivers are beeping as they pass, like their horns are going to help expedite the death of the car and clear the clouds of noxious fumes from the expressway. I can feel Syd's eyes on me as we look on helplessly from the curb.

"Let's put your granny panties in the window and abandon it," she says.

I give her a look and discreetly pull up my jeans to make sure my underwear isn't showing. I was having such a good day. I mean, I ran into Satan in the elevator up from hell, but besides that. The kids at the hospital were responsive and grateful for the free tutoring. Syd received early acceptance to Rutgers—my alma mater. Cue proud tear. And the falafel-truck guy on the corner in front of UPenn gave me a freebie. Now I have to break it to my mom that I broke her antique-on-wheels while trying to give it the exercise it deserves and I'll be missing our girls-night-in date.

"I'll call a tow truck. You call your mom," I tell Syd.

She slips her phone from her bra and I shake my head. How is that comfortable? I dig through my teacher bag and find mine an hour later. Before I even have a chance to Google, Syd is done with her call.

"She can't come in. She's got a shift until nine and no one can cover," she explains, toying with her eyebrow ring. She does that when she gets nervous.

"It's fine. We can get an Uber—or hang at Meredi—"

"Yes!" Syd exclaims. She's met Meredith twice and has not shut up about her since. Kindred spirits, those two. I imagine them both in leather pants starting bar fights or slaying vampires or some shit. "Do you think that hottie from the elevator is there yet?"

Damn it. I forgot Jeff is going over.

"Easy there, stalker. I think that Meredith might actually be at the hosp–"

"Oh no you don't! You think I can't smell your bullshit? Please!"

The look she's giving me is so condescending that I've forgotten how to form words.

Syd lifts her phone and shows me Meredith's contact. Yikes. Who gave her Mer's number? I can't even imagine the conversations these two are probably having behind my back.

Syd: *Dr. Meredith, have you ever taken mushrooms?*

Meredith: *Of course, Syd. Who hasn't?*

"Yeah, I'm gonna need you to delete her from your contacts. ASAP. Let's just get an Uber home," I try.

Syd rolls her eyes and presses the call button then walks a little bit up the block so I can't hear her private conversation with my best friend. I miss eighth grade Syd. The one who hung on my every word like I was Athena, Goddess of Knowledge. I want a take-back, but it's too late. Now with Meredith on board, I'm stuck in this mess. I take in a deep breath to calm myself and choke on the fumes.

I'm just hanging up with the tow company when Syd reappears by my side looking like a kid on an Easter egg hunt. Her smile does little to soothe my nerves as I look at the traffic blurring past the hunk of metal before me.

"She's coming to get us," she tells me with a little bounce.

I lift a brow. Appraise her with new found respect. I was sure we'd have to walk. Drag my boot across fifteen humid city blocks then face Dr. Dick lookin' like a swampy beast.

"She gave up her parking spot?"

I'm legit in shock. Meredith's Audi has not left her coveted spot off of Passyunk since before the pandemic. She must really love the kid. Not that I can blame her. There's just something about Sydney. She went to war against herself and her body and she came out on the other side with this warrior's spirit that makes everyone stronger around her. I pat her on the back.

"Well done, Young Padawan," I tell her.

"What the fuck's a Panda Wand?" She wrinkles her nose in disgust.

Ugh. Generation Z.

"Language! Come on, Syd." I ruffle her hair and she smacks at my hand. I point to the Starbucks on the corner and say, "I'll buy you a pink drink and explain the inner workings of the Star Wars universe."

"Oh gawd. Please don't," she mutters as we head toward the crosswalk.

Ignore her, I do.

Chapter Ten

Jeff

Lesson 11: Whatever happens on tequila isn't real-a.

"I brought some burritos just in case you guys were–"

I pause at the top of Meredith's staircase and look around like I'm in the wrong apartment. Painted floors. Check. Navy bookcases. Check. And the phallic watercolor over my right shoulder certifies that I'm in Meredith's bachelorette dungeon.

Devon leans back against the leather couch cushion and crosses her arms over her chest.

"You brought us burritos? Isn't that nice! Devon? Isn't Jeff so nice for bringing us burritos?" Meredith asks from the kitchen. I hadn't noticed her there.

Devon doesn't answer.

"Actually, I only brought two—"

"Perfect because it's just me and Devon. Kev got called in for a gunshot wound and Syd just got picked up!"

Meredith's voice is way too chipper for discussing a gunshot wound, but I force my eyes away from Devon's face and drop the paper bag of food on the round table that we used to play cards on Thursday. I turn to find Mer grinning at me. Two weeks hanging out with her after work and lunching together at the hospital and her smile still brings my arm hair to attention. She opens the fridge with a flourish.

"Pick your poison," she tells me.

"I'll have whatever you two are drinking," I say, and Mer's smile turns to something even more devilish. I glance over my shoulder at Devon, but she's busy pretending to study the remote.

"Dev, you cool if I share el Blanco?" Mer asks.

"Si," Devon says and it's the unexpected sibilance of her response that makes me realize what I've just walked into.

"Are you two drunk?" I ask with a chuckle.

"Lightweight is," Mer answers, looking over my shoulder at Devon as she pours me a glass of tequila.

Devon forgets that she dislikes me for a moment and smiles.

"I am mildly buzzed," she says. I can't help but smile back.

"You're in my spot," I tell her. She looks around at the couch and then back at me with wide eyes like I've just stuck my finger into the tiger's cage at feeding time. And I might be that stupid, baiting her when she's obviously tipsy. But it's really hard to resist.

"Let's be clear, Doctor Dick—"

Doctor Dick? When the hell did I get that nickname? I bite back a chuckle.

"This couch and my ass have a longstanding relationship." She rubs the leather like she's petting a dog. "And no one—not even some smarmy surgeon from the Midwest—is going to wheedle his way in between my butt and this cushion."

I take a sip of the tequila and try to look offended.

"I have no intention of butt wheedling. And smarmy?" I whisper into the bottom of the glass. "I was aiming for charming."

She shakes her head slowly and says, "You missed."

"Are you two done with the foreplay? I'd like to eat my burrito without wanting to vomit," Meredith chimes in as she slides into a chair at the table in the corner.

Devon says yes and I say no. Meredith rolls her eyes.

"What's the deal with you two anyway?" Mer takes a giant bite of the burrito and closes her eyes.

I look to Devon to respond but she is glaring at me. I can practically hear her voice saying, *Don't you dare, Dr. Dick.* So I shrug and drop into the chair beside Meredith, who's looking between us while making out with her burrito. She swallows and takes a sip of tequila.

"Alright. If you two aren't gonna fess up, I'm gonna have to start throwing out guesses. Devon, did Jeff sleep with your mom?"

I laugh and Devon pulls her boot off the coffee table and makes her way over to join us.

"Not yet," she answers seriously.

"Alright, then he looks like that guy who seduced you that night at Woody's then had his friend steal your purse while you made out in the bathroom," Mer says lifting her chin.

Devon looks at me. "Holy hell. He does look like that jerk! Man, could he kiss, though. He did this thing with his tongue..."

She tilts her head as her voice trails off and she smiles up at the ceiling. I rub a hand over my face and wait for the next attack.

"I give up. I know you have a thing against doctors, but this is something else, Dev. You've been avoiding him like he's an airborne STD—"

"Would it still be sexually transmitted if it's in the air?" I ponder aloud, but they ignore me. I might as well keep sipping my tequila and watch the show. But I'm too curious. "What's her issue with doctors?"

Devon is giving Meredith the same warning look that she gave me just moments ago. Mer looks down at the ruins of her meal and pushes a few beans to the side of the wrapping.

"Nothing," she says. "Devon just has some—you know—rules."

"Doesn't everyone?" Devon asks.

I shake my head and she looks to Meredith for support. Her expression says fat chance.

"Come on. You might not talk about them, but you have rules. Like no having sex on the first date—"

Meredith laughs. Loudly.

"Fine. Then, no relationships with a friend's ex."

I nod. That's fair.

"Tell me more about these rules," I say leaning toward her. I'm curious in a way that should trigger an alarm. But apparently my warning system is broken.

Devon shakes her head and presses her lips together.

"It's not like they are written down somewhere. It's just—like—loose guidelines I follow for myself, for work and stuff. Like grade all tests the day they're taken. Keep a master notebook in case a kid misses a day. Etcetera and so on," she explains while she studies my face for a reaction. I don't give her one.

"I'm not talking about your teacher rules. I'm talking about life rules. And they most certainly are written down," Meredith corrects. Devon's forehead crinkles as she watches Mer stand up and walk to the kitchen.

"No they aren't. That would be overkill. It's not like I'm Moses walking around with his tablet thing."

There is some rummaging behind me in the kitchen and I turn.

"Rule number 1. No dating doctors," Meredith reads. She's holding up what looks like a used cocktail napkin.

Devon puts both hands on the table. "What is that!?"

Meredith smiles. "It's from that night that Tara took us to the drag bar in NYC and you got pulled up on stage after smoking that—"

"Ok. Ok. I remember," Devon says, wincing. "Well, I remember the drag bar, but I don't remember you playing secretary."

Meredith plops back into her seat, napkin dangling from her fingers. Devon goes to snatch it and Mer lifts it out of reach then lets it flutter into her hand.

"Oh my gosh. These are so embarrassing!" Devon laughs.

Mer nods.

"But it can't get much worse, right?" she asks and I realize the question is directed at me.

"I don't think you have anything to be embarrassed about," I tell her. She tilts her head and studies my face. Her hair spills over her shoulder. She looks back at the napkin and starts to read.

"Rule number two. No smoking unidentified substances."

That one makes sense. I nod as she continues.

"Rule number three. No sex on the beach."

Before I can ask why not, Meredith looks my way and puts a hand between her and Devon like a shield then whispers, "She got sand in her yoohoo once."

"Rule number four. No poppin' squats."

"Public urination ticket," Mer explains.

I'm way out of my league with these two.

"Rule number five. No tequila after midnight." Devon shakes her head.

"She turns into a gremlin."

I chuckle.

"Rule number six. No social media." She looks up at me. "I'm a teacher! A goddamned professional!"

I resist the urge to make a comment about her viral video. Instead, I nod hard so she stops staring at me. I have yet to let her know that I've done some light stalking and found her karaoke exploits. 65 million views and at least a million of them were me. I couldn't get enough of her running man.

"Rule number seven. No dating doc—wait how many times is that on here?" Devon looks over the napkin at Meredith.

"As many times as your stoned ass rambled it. Four maybe, five times."

Devon blows out a puff of air that sends the napkin onto the floor. We both lean to pick it up at the same time and nearly bonk heads.

"Sorry," I whisper, so close I can see the way my breath moves a stray wave hanging near her temple. I expect her to make a smartass comment, but she's staring at my mouth, her bottom lip pulled between her teeth in a way that makes me take in a sharp breath.

The sound of a throat clearing pulls Devon from the trance and she lets her lip pop back into place.

Shit.

"I'm gonna go have a cigarette," Mer says.

"She doesn't smoke," Devon tells me as Meredith heads toward the bedrooms. "Lung surgeon and all that."

I nod, trying to take my eyes off of her mouth.

"If I'd known your plans had changed, I could have skipped tonight and given you some time with your friends," I tell her softly. Olive branch extended.

She shakes her head. "It's fine. This isn't a custody battle. We can coexist. Besides, you woulda missed all the fun." She points to the napkin that still lies on the floor between us.

"It is fun. You are fun."

She narrows her eyes at me, suspicion radiating off of her in waves, but I hold my ground. I refuse to look away. I'm gonna push my luck.

"You know," I start, "I noticed that your rule specifically said no *dating* doctors."

Keep pushing. No whammy. No whammy.

"Yeah. Let's not have this conversation. I'm feeling too good for a limp down memory lane—"

"No. I'm not asking why. I'm sure you'll tell me your reasoning when you're ready," I say and she swirls her glass and looks down at the tequila cyclone she's created. There's something in the line of her mouth that tells me she might never be ready to tell me. I forge ahead,

"It's more the wording I'm interested in. Specifically the verb part of the rule."

"Mmmhmmm. What's your point?"

She lifts her glass to her lips and I wait until she has a mouthful of tequila.

"Well, you never said anything about any of the other verbs you might do with a doctor."

"Like sledding? Or playing tennis?"

I lift a brow.

"Considering my condition," she points to the boot, "I think those verbs are out."

"Those weren't the verbs I had in mind," I say.

She narrows her eyes at me and takes a sip of her tequila, then swallows slowly before asking, "Are you propositioning me?"

"It's only fair. Since you started it."

"I was on—I don't even know what I was on!" Her voice hits a pitch I've never heard before.

"Is that a no then? Should I change the wording on the official document?" I reach for the napkin and she bites her lip. She's fighting a smile and this somehow makes me feel something. Pride, maybe?

"No need to amend the document," she says softly. Her eyes widen. She wraps a piece of hair around her finger and goes to cross her legs, but can't lift her boot off the floor. She gives up with a frustrated growl and crosses her good leg over the bad. I realize my hand is frozen in midair.

"I'll allow sex with doctors," she tells me, her voice low. I swallow hard. "Just not with you."

"Ooof."

She nods excitedly. "Burn, right?"

Victory shines in the neat line of white teeth gleaming my way.

"That's a shame because I brought that feather duster."

Her smile slips into an annoyed frown.

"Meredith!" she yells loudly, keeping her glare trained on me.

Meredith appears, winded, and looks around the room for the emergency.

"What the hell, Dev? Why'd you yell like that?" she asks.

"I just wanted to make sure you were still here to help me hide the body."

Meredith looks my way and gives me an exasperated shake of her head. As she makes her way to refill her tequila I hear her murmuring something about getting it out of our systems and inevitability. But none of it sticks. It all just goes in one ear and bounces off my occupied brain. Because I'm too busy thinking of more ways to rile up the smirking smartass at the table beside me.

Chapter Eleven

D^{evon}

*Lesson 12: Never answer the door when a Salvatore brother is on-
screen.*

My last weekend before school traditionally requires an action-
packed weekend of absolute stillness and peace. And there is only
one place in the world right now where I can achieve such a state.
Meredith and Kevin are at work. Tara's still off gallivanting in Europe
like she's a royal. My mom is hogging our house—surprise, surprise.
And I am at my leisure in Mer's empty apartment.

It's just me, my soul couch, and the Salvatore brothers, living life
to its fullest when there's a knock on the downstairs door. I ignore it,
a) because I'm not wearing pants beneath the Drexel Med hoodie
that reaches down to my knees, b) because Damon has his shirt off on
the screen and I forget for a second that someone is knocking, and c)

because going down the steps in my stupid boot requires serious work so I'm not getting up unless I absolutely have to. There's another loud pounding and I realize that we are now in the "absolutely have to" territory.

I pause *Vampire Diaries* and hustle (waddle like a penguin) down the never-ending steps leading to the front entrance that empties onto Passyunk Avenue just as the third loud pound sounds on the triple latched door.

"Alright, alright! I'm coming!" I yell, reaching for the intercom button. "Yes?" This better be good considering topless Damon.

"It's Jeff."

I look up at the water stain in the corner of the staircase ceiling and shut my eyes. It's been a full week since the chance run-in at CHOP and the tequila sodden shitshow that followed, and it has become increasingly difficult to avoid this man and believe me I've given it my full A-plus effort. The upcoming school year should provide a convenient excuse. I knew there was a reason I worked.

I press the intercom button again. "What do you need?"

There's a long pause and I imagine Jeff's dark hair glistening with sweat as the steam from the manhole on the sidewalk engulfs him in swampy clouds. Serves him right.

"Devon! Can you just open the fucking—"

I unlatch the final lock with a smile. Something about Jeff cursing gives me unnatural joy.

The joy vanishes when the door swings open and a wave of suffocating heat sweeps over me and up the staircase. Jeff steps in and closes the door behind him, shaking his head as he looks me over. He's barely sweating in his fitted jeans and vintage tee.

"Watch your language," I tell him, turning and heading back upstairs which requires me to step and heave—step and heave—like I'm Jacob Marley pulling a ball and chain behind me. My mom would smack me in the back of my head for being such an unwelcoming hostess, but I just want to get back to Damon's pecs, hoping he will wipe the image of Jeff's broad chest in his soft gray t-shirt from my annoying thoughts.

"Says the woman who drops the f-bomb like it's a hot potato," Jeff says from behind me.

"I only curse in the summer. I have to get it all out of my system. Why are you here anyway?"

I hold the back of the sweatshirt under my ass to make sure he cannot see any of my—

"I'm not looking at your box o'love. And I'm here because I was invited."

He has found a way to work box o'love into every conversation we've had since our sober introduction. Unfortunately, his determination and creativity impresses me. But he doesn't need to know that. I press my lips together and ignore him as I lower myself onto the couch. I fold my good leg under me and lift my boot onto the coffee table then hit play, watching Jeff's long stride in my periphery as he moves into the kitchen and opens the fridge. I'm used to this with Kevin—the way he makes himself at home at Meredith's and at my mom's—but with Jeff it feels funny. Like we're playing house. He makes his way back out of the kitchen with two bottles and hands one to me.

"Thanks," I murmur, keeping my eyes glued to the screen as I take the beer.

He plops down on the cushion beside me. There's a cushion open at the other end. Who sits in the middle when the end is open? Someone who knows exactly how far I want to be from him. That's who.

"Ya know, I never understood why Elena goes for Damon. Stefan is obviously the better brother," Jeff says.

I hit pause again and turn my neck slowly—exorcist style—use the full force of my teacher glare.

"If I have to do this with you, there's some things you need to know." He's smiling and I want to poke something sharp into that stupid dimple on his right cheek. "Number one, I like my personal space so move over." He murmurs something about the rules and scoots over like an inch, keeping his ass firmly planted on the middle cushion as he waits for me to go on. "Number two, Labor Day weekend is a sacred teacher pastime brought over by the Vikings in the early days of yore."

He lifts his brows.

"Yup. So don't go fudging it up for me."

"It's still summer so you might as well just say f—"

I hold up my hand to signal he has not been called on.

"And number three, don't say dumb shit about the Salvatore brothers. Stefan is boring."

He tilts his mouth upward. I've named this expression "smugly amused" and it appears to be one of his go-to moves when he's near me. "Boring?"

"Yeah, boring. And self-righteous. Sound familiar? No one wants to fantasize about a guy who is morally superior. It's like having a sex dream about a priest—although *Fleabag* season two was pretty dang hot. The Dalai Lama! It's like having a sex dream about the Dalai Lama," I explain. I sound like Tara defending one of her trashy boyfriends to Mom. But Jeff just considers what I'm saying and scratches at the stubble along his chin.

"Are you growing a beard?" I ask him. He's usually clean shaven. Rugged Jeff is throwing me off kilter.

"Maybe," he says, like it's some big secret. "How many more weeks of this?" he asks, knocking on the hard plastic of my boot.

"The foot fetish guy said one more—but if someone had done a better job it would be off by now."

He sighs. "I've told you at least six times that I wasn't your surgeon so stop looking at me like that." He turns his legs toward me and pats the worn denim on his thighs. "Let me take a look, while I'm here."

Nopey, nope, no.

I shake my head. "No way am I letting you mess me up further than you already have."

"I can't believe they let you teach our youth," he murmurs, then reaches out and unstraps my boot.

"They beg me to teach the youth," I correct.

I try to smack his hands away, but they move so fast. He's like a Velcro strap ninja.

"Stop it. My foot smells and I haven't shaved." I'm still smacking away, mostly hitting myself.

He laughs. "Just hold still and let me look. Goodness, you're a child."

He's winning and I'm out of breath. I sit back and hold my hands up, surrendering as he peels off the black plastic and reads my sock out loud.

"I'm a delicate fucking flower." He looks up at me.

"I am." Obviously.

He makes a sound of disbelief. "Have you been doing your strengthening exercises?" he asks, shifting my ankle into his lap. His long fingers are careful. Precise. I can't help but imagine them working their way up—

He clears his throat. "Devon?"

Too much Damon in one day. I know better than this. It's like the time I had to take an emergency trip to the vibrator store after that episode with Buffy and Spike that–

"Devon!"

"What?"

His smile is lopsided. I'm still out of breath and I tell myself it was the ninja hand game and not his fingers on my bare skin. He speaks slowly, like I do in class when I'm explaining bivariate data. "Are you doing your physical therapy?"

Not really. But I'm not going to tell Dr. Superior that. "Yes, Jeff. Can I have my foot back now, you creep?"

He's rolling my sock down in this slow methodical way that is making me dizzy. I stiffen.

"Can you relax your calf?" he asks, as he pulls the sock away.

"It is relaxed. My muscles are just that firm. You know. From all those exercises—Oh god."

His palm cups the bare skin at my heel and my leg jerks at the sensation, and I kick him square in the jaw. Hard. My hand flies to my mouth.

He keeps one hand on my bad foot and pushes his chin back and forth with the other, testing the joints, staring at me like I'm more trouble than I'm worth.

I'm trying not to laugh at the fact that I just punted him in the face, but I'm grinning so hard. "I told you not to do it! But noooo, the patient has no rights. Dr. Jeff knows best."

"Dr. Jeff? What happened to Dr. Dick?"

He lets out a breath and his eyes meet mine and I'm staring, trying to place that color green in my memory. It reminds me of the swimming hole in Vermont that my mom took us to on one of our many adventures from before. He seems to sense that I've gone somewhere in my mind and snaps in front of my face.

"You alright?" he asks. "Did you hurt yourself?"

I just kicked him and he's asking me if I'm alright? His jaw is made of steel. Or that shit wolverine is made of. Aluminum. Aluminumum. Aluminimiuminum.

"Adamantium," he corrects.

Shit, I was saying that out loud?

"I'm fine. Just very ticklish," I lie.

He nods and I look away.

"Hey, Dev. Jeff is coming ov—" Meredith comes to a halt at the top of the stairs, a case of beer in one hand and a pizza balanced on the other. Kevin bumps into her back and she nearly drops dinner. I hadn't even heard them come in. My heart slams against my rib cage. Mer looks at my foot in Jeff's lap and smiles at us. "I hope you shaved those cave woman legs before you let him examine that," she says.

I laugh a little too loudly and pull my foot away from my attacker.

"She didn't," Jeff says, and I want to smack them both as I try to put my sock back on far less gracefully than it was taken off.

Kevin cranes his neck around the pizza box to see what's going on and his lips turn down a little at the sight of me de-booted. When I tilt my head at him he pulls them back up into the warm smile I'm used to.

"Hey, Dev. I feel like it's been ages," he tells me, squeezing past Jeff awkwardly as I whisper, "Should I give him the ass or the crotch?"

The answer is ass. Jeff leans back to avoid it. I giggle as Kev embraces me and earn a glare from Jeff.

Kevin releases me and follows Mer into the kitchen, leaving me and Jeff awkwardly sizing each other up. He tries to help with the boot, and I shoot him the you've-done-enough look I reserve for my eighth graders when they say something cruel. He backs off with a chuckle and lays the boot on the table, then joins my friends—ugh—*our friends* in the kitchen. I guess I'm in the acceptance stage of this unfortunate situation.

I focus on calming my breathing. I should have just stayed in Jersey this weekend—where it was safe. My mom loves *Vampire Diaries*. She doesn't cheer for Stefan. She doesn't sit too close or purposely try to piss me off and make me feel weird—well unless she makes a sexual comment about Damon—but that's a different weird. I focus on the straps of my boot and promise myself to ignore the knocking next time I'm alone.

Chapter Twelve

J eff

Lesson 13: You are in too deep when you think snoring is cute.

I can hear Devon snoring every time I walk down the hall to use the bathroom. The door to Meredith's guest bedroom is hanging open a crack and bear grunts reach me in the hallway. I consider going in, flipping her onto her side so she sleeps more soundly, but I know how absurd the thought is even if the image of Devon waking up and attacking me with those slow swatting hands makes me laugh to myself as I pause by the door.

I can't stop thinking about the way she felt in my hands. The way she reacted to my touch. How her skin hummed against my fingertips or the way her whole body tightened when I took off her ridiculous sock.

"Dude, what are you doing?" Meredith doesn't even bother lowering her voice.

I reach out and shut the bedroom door softly and stare at the brush strokes in the white paint for a moment before I turn to face Mer in the tight space.

"Trying to be quiet so I don't wake Devon," I explain. Mer lifts a brow like she wants to push the topic, but then her trademark grin spreads wide. And I shudder.

"You look more like you are deciding whether to use zip ties or duct tape on your victim." Meredith reopens the door that I've just shut and the bone rattling sound gets louder.

"Duct tape. No brainer."

Meredith studies me until I have to retreat back to the table. So maybe I need to reel it in. Spend some time talking or thinking about something other than Devon. Or maybe not.

"Devon's got a pair of lungs on her," I tell Kevin as I slide into my seat and pick up my cards.

He nods. "Snores like my grandfather. But denies it. Claims it's impossible because she had her adenoids out." He smiles around the rim of his water bottle and leans back. No beer for Kevin. He's on call. Again. The life of a trauma surgeon.

"How long have you two known each other?" I ask, pushing my bet into the center.

"Who? Dev and I? A long time. We were lab partners freshman year at Rutgers."

"And then friends ever since?"

He nods. "We dated for a while in college, but she dumped me before I started at Drexel Med."

I feel his eyes on me and I study my cards hard. Just making conversation. Nothing to see here. I'm definitely not battling some weird thing in my gut that burns when I think of the fact that he's seen Devon naked.

Mer slides back into her chair and I squash the silly burn before she senses it with her supernatural powers. "What did I miss?"

"Jeff digging into Devon's past," Kevin tells her with a laugh. He waggles his brows at me and I shake my head.

"I was just making—"

"Ha. Don't bother, Jeffy." She looks me over like she found me head first in the cookie jar. "It's sad that you think I don't see you. I see you."

Kevin chuckles and she swivels on him.

"Oh please, Main Line. Like you're any better. At least, Jeff's torch hasn't seen the better side of a decade. Luckily, your mutual daddy issues doused that shit."

Kevin's neck turns an uncomfortable shade of pink and he whispers some choice words Mer's way before throwing his cards face down into the center.

"I fold," he says, standing and looking down at Meredith. "I'm gonna go easy on you tonight because I know your time of the month is coming. But next week, you're done."

Meredith looks up at him like she's hurt. "When our cycles synced, Kev, you promised you wouldn't use it against me."

He lets out a long breath and turns to me.

"You need another beer?" he asks.

I nod. I feel like a complete shithead. How had I missed that Kev is into Devon? Of course he's into her. I mean, who wouldn't be, but I should have seen it. I was too busy looking at her to see him looking at her, too.

"I'm sorry, man. I had no idea you had a thing for her," I say.

Why am I apologizing? Nothing is even going on between the two of us. She's made that clear. Shit, I sound even more like a prick.

Kevin shakes his head. "Meredith likes to invent shit. Devon and I are ancient history. She's like a sister to me."

"That's what Jamie Lanister said, too," Meredith murmurs and I lose a little of my beer down my chin.

Kevin's pager beeps so loudly that my hand jerks and knocks over my stack of chips.

"Shit. I've gotta go in," Kev whispers as he looks down at the small screen. He's out of his seat grabbing his bag before we even have a chance to ask if he needs anything.

"Good luck," Mer yells after him as his footsteps pound on the stairs. The door shuts with a slam and I reluctantly meet Meredith's gaze.

"Is it me or has he been on call every weekend this month?"

She nods and shrugs her shoulders.

"He chose trauma. And since I know you're dying to know, that is part of the reason why he and Devon broke up," she says, pushing her huge messy pile of chips forward. "I'm all in."

I keep my eyes on my cards and pretend not to be interested in what she's telling me. I'm not that good of an actor.

"She ended things because he wanted to be a trauma surgeon?" I push my chips in and meet Meredith's gaze. "I call."

"I said part of the reason. But yeah. That's too close to what her father was. And after the shit she's been through—I can't say I blame her. Doctors are a no go. Sorry, Jeffy." She narrows her eyes at me. "Alright show me yours and I'll show you mine," she says, lifting a brow.

I want to ask for more, but something stops me. I've already trespassed on so many of Devon's secrets that I can't bring myself to dig deeper. I want her to tell me these things—when she's sober and alert. But if what Meredith is saying is true, what the hell am I doing letting myself obsess over all these details?

I spread my triple sixes on the table and Meredith doesn't blink. Thank goodness Devon is asleep. She'd have a field day with Satan references. There's a loud snort from the back room and I can't help but smile.

Then Meredith lays down a full house and my smile disappears.

"This isn't even fun anymore," she murmurs as she pulls the chips back towards her.

"Yeah it must be hard. Winning all of our money every time we play."

"Listen, I'm gonna go to bed, but you're welcome to stay,"

Meredith says, pushing back from the table. "Do you want to follow me back and watch me sleep, too, you fucking weirdo?"

I stare up at her.

"Good night, Meredith."

"Sweet dreams, buddy."

I sit at the table for a minute, nursing my beer, processing everything I've just learned. It's not like Devon hasn't been forthcoming. Shit, she's given me more information about herself than I've gotten from any woman I've ever dated. Albeit unwillingly for the most part. Still. Here I am trying to dig under her fence when she's hung a huge red sign for me in blinking neon lights. No trespassing. Off limits. Dead end.

And the truth of the matter is, everything in Philadelphia is a dead end for me. I've got eight more months here. Then it's back to Chicago. Where I'm needed by my family—by my sister, by my niece, by my mother and the business. Their fence has a sign, too, but it says "Welcome Home." I should be focused on my career. I should stop looking forward to the chance of seeing Devon like a virgin on prom night. I should get my shit together.

Should.

Sister, Sister

Tara: I'm stateside and I've got news. You up for a visit this weekend?

Devon: News!? Like you finally decided to move home?

Tara: Don't be ridiculous. I'm taking you to dinner and then we're going dancing.

Devon: I just got my boot off!

Tara: Exactly. Perfect timing.

Devon: And it's the first week of school. You know how tired I get the first week.

Tara: Yeah. Must be tough to work four days after having a full summer off. I'll leave work early and head down on Friday. Meet you at Del Frisco's at six. Bring the crew.

Devon: Are you going to invite Mom?

Tara: That seems like a waste of breath. But I will.

Devon: Give her a visit at least. Before you come into Philly.

Tara: I always do.

Devon: Except for last time.

And the time before that.

And the time before that.

Tara: Bite me, perfect daughter.

Chapter Thirteen

Devon

Lesson 14: They are worth the fight.

The adrenaline has drained from my body and I'm running off the fumes of three-hour old instant espresso wafting from my Don't-Make-Me-Use-My-Teacher-Voice mug on my desk. I always feel terrible for my E period class, last of the day, drinkers of the dregs of my instructional juice. But this group is really getting the backwash.

My leg is aching. Every throb makes me think of Jeff's deft fingers on my calf on Friday. That particular memory has caused me to solve three integer problems wrong and forget most of the names I work so hard to learn on the first day. And to make matters worse the spinning wheel of death on my ActivBoard has been circling for nearly three minutes and there's really only so many times you can push a kid to tell you about their summer before you realize that their summer was probably really effin' boring and they are embarrassed to share.

"Anyone else do anything fun this summer while we wait for our technology to cooperate?"

Crickets.

This group is quiet. I only got four smiles at my specialty tee that I had made the day after I signed my contract with the district. My first-day-of-school shirt. *Welcome to The Best Year of Your Life.* It makes me smile even when I read it upside down. I'll consider this class my challenge for the year and breaking their adolescent armor my herculean quest. I will make them love me, gosh damn it.

The ActivBoard gives a visual hiccup and the next math problem flashes up on the screen.

"There it is! Go. Go. Go."

The students stop staring at my forehead and turn to each other, throwing answers across the room despite my repeated attempts to shush them while they search for the red solo cup with the answer written inside. I love watching the groups try to pick up the cup with their doohickey—a rubber band with four strings tied to it, one string for each group member.

"Don't overstretch it, Hulk Hands!" I tell a boy who's already broken two rubber bands by pulling the string too hard. He nods, eyes intent on the task. His team almost has their doohickey around the cup.

"No touching the cup, Billy. Only the string. Goooood!" I love the way their little noses crinkle in consternation while they focus.

"Nice job, Jill and team! Get it to the table." It's shocking that I wasn't a cheerleader. I'd have made a damn good one. Wasted on the soccer field if you ask me. Jill's group has the solo cup secured in the doohickey and they are hovering around the table in the back of the room, working together, pulling the strings so that it stands upright without falling. The rim of the cup makes a satisfying plop sound as it drops from the rubber band's clutches, then wobbles once and settles. The team members cheer and jump up and down.

"Keep going everyone. I need to check if they're correct," I yell over the groans of defeat. I glance at the integer problem on the board and then slip through the chaos to check the inside of Jill's Team's cup.

"Negative ten is correct! We have a winner!" I clap and the bell rings over the sound of trash talking and whining.

"Alright everyone, notebooks tomorrow! Let the math begin!" I holler as they rush out of my room to check their phones. Bunch of addicts.

I limp toward my desk to check my phone, hoping there's a response from Dr. Dick and crew about my invite for Friday night. It's not that I care if Jeff comes. In fact, I really hope he doesn't. Tara is like a vulture with fresh roadkill when I bring around new men. She'll pick him apart and probably embarrass the hell out of me—not that there's anything left to be embarrassed about around Jeff. But still, I'm just curious to see how he responds, this being our first text convo and all.

My arm is elbow deep in my oversized teacher bag when I notice one student lingering in the back corner of the room, stacking up the cups and collecting the doohickeys for me. My chest does that hot air balloon thing that it does every time I witness an act of kindness. Her hair is cut short, the edges razor cut in different layers, and she's dressed in sweatpants and a sweatshirt that's two sizes too big. When she looks up from the table, I'm shocked to see familiar blue eyes sunken into a face that's changed too much since I saw it last year.

"Jessica!" I try to sound more excited than surprised. I've worked with this girl in math club for two years and I barely recognize her. And it's not the haircut.

"I'm so excited you're in my class this year." I keep my face as neutral as possible though my insides are gasping and clenching. Even after all of the master's classes in child psychology, it was Syd who taught me that any reaction to physical appearance can be detrimental.

"Me, too, Ms. G," she says with a small smile. She reaches out to hand me the cups. Her sweatshirt slides back from her wrist and I note the sharp edge of the joint bone jutting out. My heart cracks like thin ice.

"Did you have a nice summer?"

She hesitates, then nods. Even that effort seems to exhaust her.

"It's gonna be a good year, Jess. See." I point to my shirt and she blesses me with a breathy laugh.

"See you tomorrow, Ms. G."

"Looking forward to it," I tell her.

I watch her grab her books and head out the door into the hall. There's a loud pop and I wonder if it's my heart busting through my sternum then I realize I've squeezed the solo cup too tight and cracked the plastic. I lower the stack of cups to the table and let out a long, coffee-scented breath.

I'm trained for this now. I've been through it with Syd—with countless others after her. I've got a masters in adolescent psychology and several certifications in mental health advocacy. But none of those pieces of paper can stop the walls of my over-stretched heart from snapping like the rubber bands that Hulk Hands broke during the game today. Watching these kids battle—watching them suffer—it has been the most difficult part of my life. And that's saying something.

I look to my wall of inspiration and focus on the bold letters of the poster Syd gave me.

You are worth the fight.

Now if only I could get these kids to believe it.

Chapter Fourteen

J eff

Lesson 15: Murphy's law is strongest when you are at your weakest.

I have forty-five minutes to get out of the hospital and across center city to Del Frisco's. During rush hour. There are still two patients I need to follow up with, a bundle of paperwork to be filled out, and I need to touch base with Dustin who is taking my on-call shift tonight so I can be at this dinner. I should've just declined the invitation. But when her name showed up on my phone for the first time, my thumbs took on a mind of their own. All of the cold hard logic I forced down my own throat last weekend didn't stop me from reacting like Charlie with the golden ticket when her text danced across my screen.

I'm rushing to get changed, pulling on a suit jacket I haven't worn since graduation, hoping that I'm not the tool who shows up over-dressed, when Jonathan, a new nurse on the ICU floor bursts into the on-call room. His face is red and his dark hair is sticking out all over the place like he's been grabbing at it.

"Dr. Harrison, I'm sorry. I know you need to go—"

"Take a breath, Jonathan. What's going on?" I ask. Poor guy just started last week and already looks like he's going to have a coronary.

"It's Mr. Peterson. Something's not right. No movement from waist down."

Shit. Dustin performed a discectomy on Peterson this morning. The hardware must have slipped.

"Jonathan, get the OR prepped and page Dustin—"

"OR three is ready. And that's the thing. Dustin's not here. I paged him and then Cherisse told me he left over an hour ago. Dr. Greer left at noon, as well."

Fuck. My attending is out of town and Dustin left me hanging. Alright, maybe he forgot. I reach for my phone to let Devon know what's going on and the screen won't light up. It's dead. I rustle through my gym bag searching for a charger, shrugging out of the suit jacket as I dig. Then the memory hits and I look up at the bright hospital lights overhead.

I left my charger by the treadmill at the gym.

"I'm scrubbing in. Get Peterson into the room and on the board. Have someone contact his family," I say, reaching for my scrubs.

I need to get in touch with Kev or Mer. I slide my phone back into my pocket and hurry out toward the nurse's bay.

"Cherisse, love of my life," I start.

"Mmmhmmmm? Now what do you want?" she says barely looking up from her computer screen. I know better than to pull the emergency card right now. Cherisse and the nurses deal with a hundred emergencies a day and barely bat a lash.

"Could you charge my phone for me and help me get in touch with someone?" I give her my most irresistible half smile.

"You look like you had a stroke. Don't smile like that. Does this look like the geek squad back here? I don't have time for your tech issues, Dr. Harrison—"

"I'll bring breakfast trays from Talula's every weekend in September," I say.

She puts her hand out for my phone.

"Please call Dr. Kevin Johnson in trauma and let him know I got held up with a patient. Thank you, Cherisse. You are a lifesaver."

"Extra cheese danishes on those trays, Doctor," she murmurs, spinning away from me in her chair.

"Of course," I tell her over my shoulder as I rush toward the elevator. Every footstep against the tile echoes my internal cursing and worries. Where the fuck is Dustin? And I hope to hell we aren't too late for Mr. Peterson.

The elevator doors open in front of me and I step inside. The sharp smell of bleach does nothing to hide what this elevator has seen.

I hold my breath and focus on the long night ahead.

Chapter Fifteen

Devon

Lesson 16: Pack a Snickers.

I'm getting hangry. Like turn-green, flip the table kind of hangry. We are waiting on Jeff's arrival to order entrees and I've polished off a bread basket filled with dainty biscuits to no avail. Luckily, the soft lighting of the restaurant and the flow of chatter and laughter has me distracted from the enormous pit in my gut that I can't blame entirely on my hanger as I steal a glance at Jeff's empty seat. Unluckily, my sister and my soon-to-be-ex-friends won't stop recounting my top ten greatest hits.

"Can we please not tell this story again?" I ask my ice water. But no one seems to hear me.

"Where were we again? Montgomery Park?" Tara asks.

"No. Behind Thomas Mansion," Meredith corrects. "Remember Devon tried to get in?"

Is it possible to hate your friends and sister? I look to where Jeff should be seated again and try to tell myself it's a good thing he's not here yet for this nonsense.

"How much snow did we get that night, T?" Kev asks. He turns his perfect white smile on me and I glare at him. We'd been dating for a while at the time, well past the point of awkward butterflies and desire to be perfect. But nowhere near comfortable enough to deal with the "Shitty Sled Incident," as Tara and Meredith have fondly entitled it.

"Enough that I had off from high school for three days. And enough to have to dig a hole when Dev's stomach started to hurt," Tara laughs. Her curls bounce softly off her shoulders and I imagine sawing one off with my messy butter knife.

I shake my head and glare instead.

"I had to sled the rest of the night with one sock," I say softly, and Kevin pats my hand across the table.

"I offered you my sock," he says, pressing his lips together, eyes glittering.

"My hero. Too drunk to drive me to a restroom, but just drunk enough to de-sock for the lady," I say and he inclines his head and pretends to tip his imaginary cap. I can still hear the sound of his laughter that night when I complained that my toes would fall off from frostbite.

"Not to change the subject or anything, but I believe we are here for a reason," I remind them. Everyone looks at Tara.

Tara's smile is otherworldly. I've seen it bring grown men to their knees when she gives it her all. And right now, she's giving it her all. Kevin is leaning toward her, his upper body tilting across the table so hard, he might fall face first into the empty breadbasket. Where the hell is the breadman?

"I've met someone!" Tara tells us in a breath.

Meredith groans while I say congratulations. Monogamy is not Mer's cup of chai.

"So does this mean I have to stop sexting you?" Kevin asks.

"Of course not," Tara replies seriously.

The door at the entrance pushes open and I crane my neck to see if it's—

"You ok, Dev?" Tara asks, turning her neck and looking toward the door.

I nod too hard and pinch my neck.

"Of course. I'm excited for you!"

And I am. Don't get me wrong, I want my sis to meet the one, but Tara meets a lot of someones. She's stunning. Magnetic. Someones are lining up around the block for my baby sister. Have been since we were in high school. So, while I'm happy for her, I'm not moved to make a toast or do a cartwheel.

"I can't wait to come up to NYC and meet him. I'm so hap—"

She lifts her hand to stop me and her stack of bangles slides down her wrist toward her elbow.

"And I'm moving to Milan to live with him," she finishes. And I need someone to shut my mouth, to shake me back to consciousness, to give me chest compressions. But my useless doctor friends don't do a damn thing to help.

"You're what?" I sputter, suddenly wishing I'd ditched Kevin and Mer to meet her here alone.

She meets my eyes and I see the unspoken challenge. *Try to stop me.* I've seen that look before so many times—when she was eight at the top of the waterfall in Lauterbrunnen, when she'd found that sky diving pamphlet beneath her wiper in high school, or when she'd stepped foot in that run-down flat in the meatpacking district in NYC fresh out of design school. There was no stopping Tara once she had that look.

"I know this seems sudden," she begins.

"A heart attack is sudden. This is—"

"But, I actually met Marcello on my last trip to Milan—he owns the hotel I've been staying at—and we've been talking over the last several months and, Dev, I'm in love with him."

Holy shit, the look she wears as she says this. How am I supposed to compete with that? No amount of reasoning or logic will wipe away the dopey, eye-sparkling grin that she's got plastered across her face. I fan myself with the menu, but it doesn't help.

"Are you guys hot?" Meredith and Kevin are looking down at their laps like they are performing surgery down there. "Why didn't you tell me—before—when you met him?" I ask and she presses her lips together and waits for me to reflect.

Alright, so I'm not the person you'd call when you want to hear "go for it." I get it, I'm reserved. Cautious. She of the rules and what ifs. But I'm still a little hurt that she's hidden something that's earth-shattering enough to make her pick-up and move across the world and leave the city she loves—and me—in the dust. Though at this point I'm used to the dust. Don't even need my inhaler anymore.

I go through the motions—take a sip of cab—put down the glass. Pretend to listen as Kevin asks her a question. But I can't hear much beneath the ringing in my ears as I total up the distance between Italy and my mom's house, all four thousand of the miles bouncing around my skull like a bowling ball between bumpers. New York had been far enough. Hopping on the train was a task reserved more for Tara than it had been for me, with her ability to travel light and on a moment's notice, without the anxiety that clawed at my ribcage and the thoughts that stormed my brain every time I had to leave my comfort zone. But there is no trip home from Milan on a whim. This trip requires planning. This trip requires a jet. Breathe in for four. Hold. Breathe in—wait.

A dark-haired man pushes through the door and my heart jumps then falls when I realize it's a stranger. Where the hell is Dr. Dick?

"Your job?" I ask finally, sneaking another glance at the door. I check my phone screen again to see if he's texted. My throat feels swollen. Jeff is usually annoyingly early.

"Will be in Milan. Michael's already set me up there."

God damn it, Michael. Why do you have to be such a good boss? Why can't you be more like Principal Ass-stache?

"That's great," Kevin says beside me. His eyes meet mine and I nod. It is great. Great. Great. Great. "Devon, are you alright?"

My chest is constricting, squeezing my heart like a sponge, and I let out a breath to give my insides more room. I just need to breathe. But the oxygen—where the fuck is all the oxygen? Meredith's hand finds my shoulder and I turn slowly so I don't get any dizzier than I already am.

"Dev, I think you need some air. Come on, let's get you outside—"

Her fingers twine through mine and I'm being towed around the tables of happy, oblivious diners by Mer, like a little girl dragging her doll behind her. Tara stands to follow and Mer points back to the seat. She obeys.

When we push through the glass doors, the humid night air does nothing to ease my chest.

"What's going on? I can't remember last time this happened," Meredith demands, looking me over.

I put my hands on my knees and stare down at my bootless calf. It's like half the size of the other calf. I hate that Jeff was right. I should have done my exercises. I hate it more that he isn't here right now and that my heart is bursting out of my chest with the need to know he's ok. I hate most that if I just stuck to my gut, avoiding him at all costs, I wouldn't be hyperventilating on Broad Street ruining my little sister's life news. Even if that news has another family member leaving me.

"She's moving to Italy," I murmur to the curb beneath my feet, pulling in sharp breaths between words. I lift my watery gaze up to Mer's. "Has Jeff." Breath. "Texted you?" Breath.

Her face changes. Realization hits. She reaches for her phone in her back pocket, checks her messages, and shakes her head. Then she presses a button and holds the screen up to her ear.

"I'll call the hospital," she says to me, rubbing my back with one hand while I focus on my breathing. She's so stunningly calm. Part of her training, I'm sure. No freaking out when your scalpel is hovering over someone's aorta. She watches me out of the corner of her eye as she speaks, "Shelly, it's Meredith Brown. Can you page Dr. Harrison for me and have him call me immediately? Yup. Ok. Perfect. Thank you."

She turns to me. Looks me over again and shakes her head with a small smile.

"I'm sure he's fine. He will call us, Dev." She pats my head like I'm a tiny child.

Meredith is calm but not so great with the warm and fuzzy.

"I knew you were freaking out about T, but," she pauses, wrinkling up her nose. "I didn't know you were thinking of—you know—your—"

I put my hand up so she stops. No need to go there. Why would she realize something like that? It's not like talking about it will fix a damn thing, and it barely ever affects me like this. Anymore, at least. But tonight was different somehow, with Tara at the table and Jeff's empty seat. Then the heart wrenching news that my sister is moving across the world. It triggered something. Somehow it took me straight back to that night, sitting at the table with my *dad's* empty seat.

"It's no big deal. This is Tara's night. Let's get back inside," I say softly, now that I can breathe again.

Meredith nods, but her lips turn down and she looks me over, diagnosing like I'm a patient.

"Fine, but just give me a signal if you need to get out again. Touch your nose or rub your nippl—"

"Alright. Alright. Let's go."

The moment we push through the doors, Tara's almond shaped eyes lock onto mine, worried and confused. She has the same amber flecks as me and right now they are catching the light from the low-hanging lanterns dangling over our table. I sit down slowly and work up the strength to do the right thing despite the dagger twisting in my chest. It was hard enough to watch her go two hours north. This will be hell.

"To love in Milan," I offer, my voice as shaky as my hand lifting the wine glass.

"You'll really love him, Devon," Tara tells me, and I look up from the knot in my napkin and nod as we clink our glasses together and sip (chug) our drinks.

"Of course, I will!" I sound unconvinced. Unconvincing. Unconvincable.

But Tara just turns back to Meredith as she asks whether Marcello has any brothers. *Marcello?* Really? How long can a man named Marcello last? I signal the waiter for a refill and chastise myself for being so petty. I'm sure Marcello is a perfectly lovely man and I want my sister to be happy—to find love. Someone that will choose her and not some job. Someone that will show up and fill the empty seat.

When the waiter makes his way back to the table with the bottle of red, I try to discreetly let him know to keep it coming. The wine is too smooth and Tara's news is too much and Jeff's seat is still glaringly unoccupied. And even through the warm haze that has suddenly settled around me, I can already see that this night is going to be shittier than the great sledding explosion of 2014.

Chapter Sixteen

J eff

Lesson 17: Better late than never—sometimes.

When I finally arrive at the bar, it's close to midnight. I'm wrecked—physically and mentally from the hyperfocused state I was in all night trying to make sure the patient could walk again. But when I talked to Meredith after getting her page three hours after she sent it, she'd hinted that something wasn't right with Devon. So, I hauled ass over to the Public House in Fishtown, despite the fact that I can barely keep my eyes open.

It takes me a minute to spot Kevin in his crisp, baby-blue button-down, leaning against the bar looking out over the dance floor. The strobe lights and pounding music are doing nothing for my headache. When he turns and sees my approach, I think I see his lips turn down, but the lights flash off and then back on, and his normal warm smile is plastered on his face.

"Hey, man. Rough night?" he raises his voice over the music, signaling to the bartender to get me what he's drinking.

"Rough doesn't cover it. Did you get Cherisse's voicemail?" I yell back.

Kevin hesitates. Then pulls his brows together and slips his phone from his pocket and checks the screen.

"Shit, Jeff. I didn't even see it." He doesn't meet my gaze.

The bartender arrives with my beer and I tell Kevin not to worry about it. No harm, no foul, right? But the gnawing in my gut tells me that there's harm—and the harm might be what Meredith was hinting at with Devon.

Before I can open my mouth to tell Kevin what happened, a woman covered in sweat pushes through the crowd toward where I stand at the bar. Normally, sweat makes people look like drenched rats, but on this woman it works. Her makeup glistens like she's been professionally sprayed for a photo shoot. She's gorgeous—and very familiar—and when she smiles up and high fives Kevin, I know immediately who she is. She's an exact replica of her sister—except where Devon has chosen to keep her hair dark, her freckles uncovered, her eyes natural and bright—Tara has lightened her hair and made her eyes into something dark and sexy.

Tara squeezes in between Kev and me and asks the bartender for a glass of water while I locate Devon and Meredith on the dance floor. They are playing some sort of tag, spinning away from all the men who approach, trying to avoid their grinding crotches like a game of frogger.

"You must be Jeff," Tara yells up at me.

I nod and hold out my hand to her while she sips her water through the straw.

"My sister is pissssed at you!" she says, taking my hand, biting the straw, and lifting her brows.

"What else is new?" I say back, but my stomach dips a little.

I look back at Devon. She doesn't look pissed. She looks like she's having the time of her life, pushing some guy in a silk shirt back to the group of guys he came from, while shimmying her ass to the beat. But the man isn't getting the hint and I see her spin too fast to avoid him and wince. Her hand goes to her calf and I take a step toward them, ready to help her off the floor, but a manicured hand grabs my arm and stops me.

I follow the fingers and arm up to find Tara eyeing me over the rim of her water glass.

"You going to rescue the damsel in distress? That'll just piss her off more," she tells me.

"I'm just worried about her. I'm an orthopedic surgeon and she had a really bad Achilles rupture. She really shouldn't be dancing just after she got her boot off. It's my job to make sure she's ok." This makes perfect sense. "Also, I kind-of fucked up when I first met her, and I need to—I don't know—show her I'm not a dick."

"So, you're gonna prove that to her by staring at her like a creepy stalker or rushing in and mansplaining her recovery?"

One side of my mouth pulls upward. Tara doesn't mince words. But neither does Devon, so I'm not surprised.

"She told me by the way—about your 'fuck-up'." She uses air-quotes and tucks a blonde curl behind her ear. There are cuffs and piercings hugging the side of her lobe all the way up to her cartilage. "I think she's more embarrassed than anything. Devon doesn't talk about her sex life much. She's annoyingly private. And she's super cautious. So feeling something—well she has a way of morphing the entire spectrum of emotions into anger."

I nod. I respect that she's not one to kiss and tell. And the anger thing makes sense to me. Not everyone had a professional to teach them about emotional regulation. "Yeah, well sometimes it's easier to just rage and yell. Rather than be vulnerable."

She looks me over, narrows her eyes like she's appraising an antique at an auction.

"I really wouldn't go out there, though. She's drunk and I can't be held responsible for what she does to you."

I laugh and wait for her to break a smile, but she just lifts a brow and waits.

"Thanks for the warning. I'll take my chances," I tell her with a grin and she lets me go.

I push through the crowd and stop short when I see Devon with her back to some guy, swaying with her arms up over her head. A tiny flash of skin is exposed over the waistline of her jeans and I swallow hard. Meredith is giving her the thumbs up like she approves of this creep behind her. The man puts his fingers on the little sliver of skin and I'm suddenly no longer tired. I head toward her and the guy sees me coming before Devon does. I give him a look and point between Devon and myself and he puts his hands up in surrender. Devon is still swaying with her eyes closed, so I slip into the stranger's place and put my hands on her hips. She moves her ass against me and I can't see straight—and I can't blame the strobing lights.

Meredith is spinning and when her eyes finally meet mine over Devon's head, she pushes her lips together then bolts from the dance floor. Devon goes to turn and I tighten my grip, lower my head over her shoulder.

"I'm sorry I was late," I say into the space below her ear, breathing in her scent.

She freezes in my grip. I release her and she turns slowly and looks up at me.

Her amber eyes are wide. Her dark curls wild around her face. She's so fucking beautiful. And, man, is she pissed.

"I thought you were dead," she yells, her eyes narrowed on my mouth. Her fists are clenched by her side and a trickle of sweat slips from her neck, down her clavicle beneath the v at the top of her black silk top. "You couldn't fucking call? What are you some kind of celebrity—so important that you can't pick up the phone and let me know you're alive?"

A woman bumps into her back and Devon lunges forward toward me, wincing a little as I steady her.

"I'm sorr—"

"Don't bother! It's my stupid fault for thinking it could—for giving a shit." She shakes her head and turns to walk away from me. I put my hand on her arm to stop her and she looks over her shoulder at me. Her eyes are glistening—and it's not sweat. The shock of seeing the pain in her eyes stuns me silent. I let her go and watch her limp away.

What just happened here?

The answer to that question disappears into the women's restroom. And this time, though my palms are still burning where they held her hips, I know better than to follow her.

Chapter Seventeen

D^{evon}

Lesson 18: If you call him, he will come.

Tara is sprawled out beside me, her honey-gold loose curls still perfectly intact against the silk pillowcase she brought with her. My mouth is dried shut and my eyeballs are being pushed out from the inside. I curse Tara for breaking the tequila after midnight rule. Then curse her again for looking like she's at a goddamn wellness spa instead of the other side of a sweaty, drunken night.

Good news is I didn't rupture anything last night—well maybe what's left of my dignity when I lost my shit in front of Jeff. A minor meltdown, really. Nothing to write home about. I'm sure he didn't even notice.

I flex my foot and wince. My calf feels like a knot the size of a cantaloupe has formed inside it. I swing my feet out of bed and use my toes to search for the foam roller Meredith bought me. She'd bought me a massager, too, that worked wonders on my neck until Tara informed me it was actually a vibrator.

"Did Meredith go home with butt-chin?" Tara asks my back.

"Yup." I don't risk nodding for fear of an immediate concussion.

"Nice, he totally looked like Spartacus..."

"I am Spartacus," we both say in a deep voice. Mom has a thing for the Douglas men.

My foot finds the bag handle and I slide off of the bed and land on the floor with a thump. It makes my brain rattle, but I focus on digging my fingers into the unfolded clothes to find what I need. I pull it out and lay it on the floor, shifting my weight so I can attack my calf bump. I bite hard on my lip, and still a groan comes out through the side of my mouth.

"Are you alright down there?" Tara's pretty face appears over the edge of the mattress, her eye makeup smudged just enough to look like she's done it on purpose.

"I'm fine. Arrrrrrrgh." Knead the dough. Roll the dough. "Can you go mess up your face?"

She pulls her nose up. "You look like you need help. Do you want me to call Meredith to come home?"

"Nooooooo." Shit, this hurts. Maybe I should stretch. I kick the roller to the side and reach for my toes and the pain sears through the back of my leg. I'm squinting so hard there's a throb in my temples.

"What about Kevin?" Tara says as she rolls out of sight.

"You can't call either of them. Meredith likes to have morning sex and Kev is out on the Schuylkill rowing merrily along." And I don't want to say the words that are forming in a cloud in my head, but the pain in my calf can't just be from mixing Cab with tequila so I let out a cleansing breath that reeks of alcohol, and tell her in a strained voice, "Call Jeff."

She looks at me, searching my face for some signal that I remember last night.

"I know. I know. But he's an orthopedic surgeon and he's used to my humiliation. Just call."

She grabs my phone from the charger on my nightstand and puts in my code that hasn't changed in 15 years. She's squinting at the screen, scrolling with her thumb.

"Dr. Dick," I murmur, and she just shakes her head and smiles as she presses the screen then lifts my phone to her ear.

I pull my leg in and bend it over my good one then let my fingers press and push into the ball above my heel. It feels like I'm sticking my fingers into an open wound.

"Jeff, it's Tara—yeah we are ok—sort of. No. We slept at Meredith's. It's Devon's heel—she's in pain and I'm not sure—ok." She's nodding, staring at me, her lips turned down. "Right. Ok. Thanks, Jeff." She presses her thumb to the red circle and drops my phone on the crumpled sheets.

"He's on his way," she tells me, and I find myself surprised by the fact that I'm not surprised. I knew that he would come. Despite my mini-breakdown while breaking it down.

Tara gets down beside me. "He wants me to elevate your ankle and put ice on it. Do you need help getting back in bed?"

I shake my head and pull myself up on the nightstand putting my weight on my good foot then plop back into bed. The effort makes my head spin, but I've lost track of what's messing me up. Tequila or the pain? Or Jeff.

Tara disappears to play nurse and I'm left with my fuzzy memories of last night. Jeff must think I'm a lunatic—crying like that on the dance floor. It's almost been twenty years since my dad died. But somehow, sometimes, it feels like I'm still sitting at that table holding Tara's little hand, watching my mother talk to the police beside the hostess stand at his favorite restaurant. A pain in my chest takes the attention away from my calf. I rub at my face then catch sight of myself in the mirror hanging over the closet door. Yikes.

"Tara?" I yell.

I hear her footsteps hurrying back.

"Can you buy me makeup that looks like that—" I point to her face, "—the day after?"

"Jesus, Devon. I thought you were in pain," she hisses then disappears from the doorway.

"I am in pain. I saw my reflection. It was very, *very* painful," I tell her. I'm gonna buy a silk pillowcase. That'll do it. I slide my finger over the shiny pink covering of her pillow while I watch myself in the mirror, imagining that I'm soaking up the magic and my face will suddenly be less puffy and hungover.

Tara reappears with a bag of frozen peas and a bottle of water. She tosses me the water and grabs the magic pillow from my hand. She lifts my ankle and slides the pillow and the peas beneath my heel, then lowers my foot like it might break into a thousand pieces.

"Drink that," she inclines her head toward the bottle, and I twist off the cap and obey. "Before he gets here, we need to talk."

"I know. But brush my teeth for me while you talk."

She rolls her eyes but scurries off to the bathroom and comes back with my toothbrush and a dixie cup. I press my teeth together and pull my lips back like a horse and she thrusts the items at me. I guess I'm brushing my teeth myself.

"Alright, tell me what's going on," she says.

Here we go. This is the first time Tara and I have been alone and sober since she broke her news. Did she see my heartbreak? Was I that transparent? She knows me well enough to understand that I would never want her to leave, but she's studying me right now like I'm one of her sketches and I need adjustments.

"What's going on with you and Jeff?" she asks.

The toothpaste goes down the wrong pipe and I sputter. Drool leaks out over my lip and drops onto my t-shirt. I wipe my mouth with the back of my hand and stare at her.

She lifts her brows and waits.

"Nothing!" My voice is too loud. Too squeaky. I spit out some toothpaste and try again. "Nothing is going on. He's just a friend.

Some doctor who made me into the punchline of a cosmic unfortunate coincidence."

"You know that *I know* that isn't true. I saw the panic attack when he didn't show up at the restaurant. And, unfortunately, I also saw the scene from dirty dancing at the club."

Annoying, nosy-ass, know-it-all.

"You saw me reacting to the fact that my only sister is being swept away by Marcello the Italian pirate. That's all you saw," I lie.

There's a knock on the door and Tara is still staring at me like she can see right through my dry, bloodshot eyes into my shriveled, slow-motion brain. She pushes her lips together and gives my leg a patronizing pat then stands to answer the door.

"You have toothpaste on your chin," she says over her shoulder.

I let out a breath the second she leaves the room and I feel my heart fluttering in my chest. I look down to tell it to knock off its shit and realize I'm braless. My favorite shorts have tiny holes trailing up my inner thigh. I'm a god-damned mess—and not even a hot one. But there's no reason to care. It's just me and my annoyingly perfect little sister. And Jeff. Who just keeps getting to witness me at my best.

He appears in the opening to Meredith's guest bedroom, a dark circle of sweat makes his tee shirt cling to his chest, like he's been working out hard. Or running across town in this awful heat to assist a crazy woman. His eyes are so filled with concern that I'm suffocated with that deep gut-wrenching empathy I feel when my students cry and need comforting.

I give him a little wave and he shakes his head and steps into the room.

Chapter Eighteen

J eff

Lesson 19: House calls are never a good idea.

Devon is sitting up against the headboard with her foot propped up on a pillow and an ice-pack of peas beneath her ankle, and I'm immediately reminded of the first time I saw her. Her dark hair spilling across the white linens of the bed in the recovery ward in Chicago, her glassy eyes smiling at a hundred funny thoughts that skittered through her loopy brain.

Instead of a blue hospital gown she's wearing a t-shirt that says, "Underestimate me. It'll be fun." And a pair of shorts that might as well be underwear. I take a deep breath and step inside as she waves and scrunches up her nose in apology.

"I knew you were in pain last night," I tell her, sitting on the end of the bed very gently.

"Must be nice to know everything. Can we blame this on Meredith?" she asks.

"As long as I don't get blamed. We could blame the dozens of creepy men chasing after you. You had to do a lot of fancy footwork to keep them at arm's length." I reach for her painted blue toes and stop. "You're not gonna dropkick me again are you?"

One side of her mouth curls upward. "No promises."

I wrap my hand around her foot and scoot closer so I can get under her knee with my other hand. She lets out a small gasp and I meet her eyes to check for pain, but she is looking down at her lap, no sign of pain on her face. I lift her foot and can see the ball in her calf immediately.

"Jesus, Devon. Did you stretch at all last night?"

Her eyes meet mine and she looks annoyed. "Yeah, Jeff. Didn't you notice me doing the lotus pose on the dance floor?"

"Alright, alright." I slide my fingers down over the bump onto her heel. Everything seems to be intact as far as I can feel. "I want you to come in and get an MRI just to make sure you didn't tear it again."

She groans. "Can't you just tell?"

"I can't see through your skin, Devon. This bump is definitely a muscle knot." I run my finger over the tennis ball in her calf down to her heel, "and the tendon isn't completely ruptured, I can feel that." I push gently again into her heel and feel for a tear. "But you have a fair amount of swelling and I can't be sure you don't have a tiny tear and if you do, you need to rest—get back in the boot and stay off your feet."

"Surgery again?" she asks, her tone exhausted. "The kids are ruthless when I have to use that scooter thing."

"No, a tiny tear wouldn't require that," I say, placing her foot back down on the peas. "You can teach in a boot."

"Not the way I teach," she murmurs.

She looks so sad that I pat her shin and she looks up at me.

"Ok. We can blame this on me," I tell her.

She smiles, but it's only a shadow of what she's capable of.

"You want me to try to get this knot out?" I push my thumb into her calf muscle, and she jumps a little. I grin at her narrowed eyes. "It's gonna hurt like a bitch."

"Are you some kind of sadist?" she asks seriously. "Like Steve Martin in *Little Shop of Horrors?*"

I laugh. That movie gave me nightmares for years when I was little. But I watched it over and over again none-the-less.

"Maybe. Either way you gotta work that knot out," I tell her, and she sighs and tilts her head back against the headboard.

"Alright. Do your worst." Her eyes are closed tight and she's biting her lip. I have to look away.

"It'll be easier if you roll over onto your stomach."

She opens one eye and looks me over.

"Is this so you don't have to see my face when you hurt me, you sicko?"

"No. It's so you can scream into the pillow."

Her eyes widen and the amber around her pupils seems to melt. The words hang there between us. I'm suddenly aware that my hand is still on her leg and that I'm sitting on her bed and her chest is rising and falling beneath that ridiculous tee. She's not wearing a bra. She rolls over just as my eyes find her hard nipples.

I let out a slow breath that does nothing to help the situation beginning in my pants.

"Alright, you ready?" I ask her as I get into position.

"No," she murmurs into the pillow.

"I'm just going to stretch you first," I explain as I slowly rotate her ankle and pull out her toes.

She grunts a little and then giggles when my fingers accidentally brush along the balls of her feet.

"Careful. You might get kicked again," she warns.

I push my thumbs into the lump on her calf and make a small circle. She tenses, her hands grip the sheets and the sight of her fingers wrapped around the linen makes my throat go dry and forces me to look away.

"You ok?" I ask as I work the tissue in slow circles.

She turns her head so I can see the side of her face.

"I'm fine. Get the damn thing out and stop fucking around," she tells me, and I chuckle and push a little harder, causing her to turn her head back into the pillow and let out a low groan.

"Ummm. Am I interrupting something?"

I jump a little, but Devon doesn't flinch. Tara is standing in the doorway holding two mugs of coffee, her mouth stretched into a wide smile.

"Shut up, Tara. He's getting the watermelon out of my calf." Devon rolls over and sees what her sister is holding and lights up. "Oh, Angel of Mercy. Coffee." She claps. Actually claps.

I take a mug out of Tara's hand and thank her then watch as she holds the second cup just out of Devon's reach.

"You want this?" Tara asks.

Devon's eyes turn to slits.

"Promise you'll come to Milan in the early spring," Tara demands, pulling the coffee back slowly as Devon's fingers reach forward.

"That's not even remotely fair. And isn't it cold? Couldn't you pick a nice Hawaiian?"

"Then I'll drink it." Tara takes a sip.

"You know I can make my own damned coffee," Devon says.

"I used the last of the grinds and I doubt you can walk on that." Tara gestures to her bad leg.

Devon shoots me a look and then stares at my mug as I lift it to my lips. I let out a long mmmmmmm.

"Dick," she murmurs. "Fine, T. I promise to come to Milan in the spring if you promise to visit Mom twice a month until you leave."

Tara scoffs. It's like watching a chess death-match. I can't help but wonder why the hell Devon wouldn't want to go to Milan. Or why Tara needs to make a promise to see their mother. I'd kill to see my own mother right now.

"That's a bit much," Tara begins, but Devon gives her a look that could have started global warming and Tara shrugs. "Fine. I promise."

Devon lunges for the coffee and I'm shocked it doesn't spill everywhere. She puts her lips to the cup like it's the holy grail. They both turn to me at the same time as if they've just remembered I'm still there.

"Can you get her in for an MRI today?" Tara asks.

Devon smacks her. "Eavesdropping again?"

"It's not eavesdropping when the two of you talk so loud because you forget I'm here," Tara says. She has a point. I'd forgotten about her.

"I can take her over to the hospital and get the imaging done whenever she's ready," I say.

Devon shakes her head as she blows the steam from the dark surface of her mug.

"I've got to meet Syd at the Children's Hospital today at two. And it's your day off, Jeff. You've already done enough," she says, and I meet her eyes. It always catches me off guard when she shows her softer side. I clam-up, like I did last night on the dance floor.

I focus on my mug, take another sip of coffee and pull my shoulders up and let them fall like it's no big deal. And really, it's not. The truth is, after everything that happened last night, the way she looked at me—the sadness there, I couldn't stop thinking about her. I left the bar to give her space and recover, but she didn't leave my mind. And when the phone lit up this morning with her name, it was the first time I felt at ease since my hands were on her last night.

"I can take you to CHOP after the imaging. My car's in the Jefferson lot. It's the least I can do after missing dinner last night." I shrug.

Devon winces at the mention of last night then meets my gaze over the rim of her mug and I see her wheels turning. I'd pay my first year's salary to see into that head.

"Ok," she says, blowing again on the coffee.

"Ok," I echo. Her lips are so—

Tara clears her throat and I slosh a little of my coffee onto my wrist.

"Yup. Still here," she tells me with a smile. "I'll drive you two over to Jefferson on my way out. Dev, get dressed."

I stand and head out of the room. Just before I pull the door shut, I see Tara put her hands on her hips and stare at her sister with lifted brows. Devon studies her coffee like she's about to swan dive into it, then I'm staring at the white painted wood of Meredith's guest room door thinking *What the hell am I doing?* for the second time this month.

Chapter Nineteen

D evon

Lesson 20: You are not alone.

The parking garage of the Children's Hospital looms over us, the entrance crammed with cars all waiting in line for the ticket to pop out of the machine.

"Can you please just tell me what the radiologist said?" Jeff asks again, as he pulls up another car length.

"You don't need to park. Just drop me at the main entrance," I tap my finger on the window pointing to the lobby, "—unless you're meeting your friend again."

"Seriously, Devon. Stop changing the topic." He takes his foot off the brake and we coast forward again. Serious Jeff is so annoyingly pushy.

"I told you what he said. He said you really fucked up my ankle. Left some sort of sponge inside my body that's causing that big bump on my calf—"

"Do you take anything seriously?" he asks, cutting off my shenanigans.

"Yes." Not really. Well, maybe sometimes algebra. Even though I do like that funny cartoon that asks the kid to find x and he just circles the x. Drugs. Drugs are serious. I make sure I don't joke about drugs because I once overdosed on marijuana in high school. Though that's a pretty funny story, too. Shit, what do I take seriously?

"I take mental health seriously," I say.

Jeff reaches out the window and grabs the ticket then shoves it in the pocket in his shorts. He seems to be processing my statement about mental health as he pulls the car into a spot near the elevator. I still can't get over the fact that he's driving this tiny little hybrid. I'm so used to Kevin's gas-guzzling Tahoe.

"Well, that's good—about the mental health thing. But can you take your own health seriously for a second? Did the radiologist mention a tear?" he asks.

I put both hands on the console between us and stare right into his eyes. I make sure my face is deadly serious.

"In the sponge you left behind?"

He tilts his head back against his headrest and lets out the world's longest puff of air.

"You. Are. Impossible," he says, staring at his car roof for divine intervention.

"Impossibly awesome," I murmur as I push open the door, step out and then lower my head back in. "Thanks for today. *Seriously,* Jeff. I appreciate all of it."

And I do. I would have been waiting for hours at any other imaging center to get the MRI, but Jeff got me right in and introduced me to Cherisse, who is obviously my soulmate because she told me she blackmailed Jeff for cheese danishes. Then I had a radiologist read me the results only moments later. Please. Like that ever happens in real life. All of it was because of Jeff. I smile and push the car door shut.

I'm surprised when I hear the driver's side door shut and footsteps behind me. I turn and he's beside me, matching my stride.

"Dr. Devita made you a disc of the imaging," I tell him, pulling out the CD from my purse and handing it to him. He snatches it from me like I might pull it back.

"Easy boy. Are you meeting your friend again?" I ask as he presses the button for the elevator.

He clears his throat a little and looks at his apple watch.

"I was thinking of coming up—with you—if that's ok?"

Is it ok with me?

"Why wouldn't it be ok?" I shrug. I mean I'll get an excited earful from Syd about it for sure. And the girls might swoon at his feet, but who am I to deprive them of the simple joys in life?

He follows me to the elevator and presses the arrow, then holds the door open for me. I lean against the glass and watch him select the floor for the tunnel. My gears are grinding now, and I can't get them to stop. I understood Jeff's run across town to check on my ankle. He just isn't the type of guy to ignore anyone's call for help, especially if it's in his area of medicine. And escorting me to Jefferson? Yeah, I get that, too. He works there and could pull the strings. But this? Few people want to spend their day off from the hospital in a hospital.

"Jeff?"

"Hmm?"

"I don't want this to come out wrong or anything, but why are you coming with me?" And like most things that come out of my mouth it sounds too direct. Sugar-free and sharp.

"I'll tell you that if you tell me what happened last night," he says softly, his eyes on the side of my face.

Shit. Never mind. He's not getting any more of my crazy until he shows me a little of his. If it exists.

"I'm not sure what you're talking about. Too much tequila." It's not a total lie. I risk a glance his way and find him studying me.

He nods once, a small smirk playing on his lips. "Alright, then. I guess we'll both be left in the dark."

The doors open and he gestures with one arm for me to lead the way. I narrow my eyes at him as I pass. This just makes him smile wider.

Syd is standing against the glass windows on the right side of the light-filled waiting room. She looks up and sees me approaching and her smile fills me with warmth. But then she sees Jeff beside me, and I understand the true meaning of the phrase second fiddle. If I thought what I got was a smile, there's no word in the dictionary for what her face does when she sees him.

She tugs my arm forward and leans into me, attempting a whisper, "You brought Dr. Hotass! The girls and Sean are gonna freak."

I turn to Jeff hoping he didn't hear, and he lifts his brows at me and asks, "Did you come up with Dr. Hotass? I like it a lot better than Dr. Dick."

"No. Your ass isn't hot to me," I tell him, taking the visitor tag Syd's holding out to me and slapping it on his chest with more force than necessary. He barely blinks. I turn to the receptionist desk and sign him in beneath our names while he asks Syd how she's doing.

On our way down the hall, Syd squeezes between Jeff and me and loops her elbows around ours.

"Alright, Jeff. Here's the dirt. Kayla is a veteran. She's been in and out since I was here two years ago. I love the girl, but you can't believe a thing she says. Sean's new to treatment. This is his first stint and he still doesn't understand why he's here in the first place. Denial isn't just a river in South America—"

"Africa," I correct.

"Yeah. That's what I said." Syd throws me a look. "Anyway. Abby shares a room with him. She hasn't spoken a word to anyone since she was admitted three weeks ago. The nurses have no choice but to NG tube her because she's silently refusing." Syd takes a breath when the elevator arrives.

"The NG tube feeds them through their nose," I tell him, and he looks at me like no shit Sherlock. It's easy to forget he's a doctor when he's wearing a Space Jam t-shirt and a pair of Chicago Bulls basketball shorts.

"I told Kayla I'd help her with her pre-calc so you two can chill in Sean and Abby's room or see if the nurses need anything," I say, knowing Syd prefers to spend her time with Sean. He responds well to her. All of the patients respond well to Syd. She's a force.

"Stick with me, kid," Syd tells Jeff with a nudge. And he gives her a smile that would have knocked me out at 17. But she's still standing.

The elevator door opens to a space that takes my breath away every time I step into it. Natural light pours over the floor and walls like syrup. There are deep plush couches and barnwood tables and white shelves lined with books of every color like a beaded friendship bracelet stretched across the interior walls. It's quiet and warm—a safe-place I imagine whenever I need a break from my fast paced, out-of-control life. I breathe in the clean scent of lemons and wave to three nurses at the bay.

"Hey, Devon. Syd." Gina steps out from behind the counter. "And who is this?" Her eyebrows disappear into her dark curly hair as she wraps her arms around Sydney and eyes Jeff over her head. I hear Syd attempt a whisper into Gina's ear. "Dr. Hotass." The girl needs serious help in the volume control department.

"I'm Jeff."

He steps forward and extends a hand that Gina takes with one arm still around Syd's shoulders. Gina saw Syd through the worst of her battle against anorexia and the bond that they formed during that struggle is nigh unbreakable. It's the silver lining that Syd never lost sight of.

"Ah, you're the new guy. The Jefferson surgeon..." Gina trails off and looks at me.

"Jesus, Gina. Don't tell him we talk about him. He's already approaching maximum ego," I say and then hurry the hell out of there before she says something to further embarrass me. Jeff grins and I pretend not to see it as I slip into Kayla's room and plop down in the first chair I see.

"Rough night last night?" Kayla's voice is raspy from the damage she's done to her throat.

I nod and meet her eyes, the red lines still so pronounced that there's barely any white around her iris. I can remember when Syd looked like this. When her elbows and knees jutted out from her skin beneath the sheets and I could see bones through the gown that the human eye was never meant to see. Syd's cheeks were sunken, but Kayla's are slightly puffy, her body's inflammatory response to the damaged salivary glands.

"I danced myself back to the hospital," I tell her, pulling my nose up into a regretful wince.

"At least you went out with a bang," she says. "I'd kill for some dancing."

It's a simple enough statement, but I hear what she isn't saying. Syd has trained me to see and hear the voice of the eating disorder in even the simplest of phrases. Does Kayla really want to dance or is it the need to burn calories screaming at her right now?

"Pre-calculus is just as fun as dancing." I grin and Kayla literally sinks down into her fluffy white pillow, her angular chin slipping out of view last.

"Can we not?" she murmurs.

"Yes, we can!" I say in my cheerleader voice and she cranes her neck back up and has the decency to look embarrassed for me.

"My book is in the study room." She starts to stand and I lift my hand to stop her. If she goes to get it, she'll be gone forever, avoiding the introduction to the radian circle like it was sent from hell to collect her soul.

"I got it," I tell her, and she narrows one eye at me in a look that says, *Touché, you pain in my ass.*

I head back out into the common area and watch the city move through the long expanse of glass. Cars crawl around the corners of the busy square in front of the hospital while pedestrians hurry up and down the flanks of 34th street. Always so busy. I'm exhausted just looking at it. I turn my gaze upward to the skyscrapers grappling for purchase in the soft blue sky. The spire of the Comcast Building pokes out above them all, claiming its victory beneath a soft streak of white clouds. It's a beautiful view—if you're into that sort of thing.

I slow down a little as I pass Abby and Sean's room, curiosity overruling my good sense as it always does. I hear Syd's squeaky laughter and Sean's deep chuckle. Jeff's voice is next.

"The worst part of all of it is that it is all so deeply unfunny, ya know. But we have to laugh. To get through it."

"So, what happened to your sister?" Syd asks. I picture her leaning toward him, eyes wide, her fingers spinning her eyebrow ring like they do when you've got her rapt attention. And Jeff certainly has her rapt attention.

"She battled it until she was nineteen and went for six months to inpatient treatment near here actually—at Renfrew. She beat it there. I mean she still battles. But now she's winning." There's a heavy pause, then Jeff says, "She's got a daughter now. And she's happy. Genuinely. There is an entire life to be lived—after."

"Only if you win," someone whispers and I crane my neck, trying to peek around the door frame.

It's Abby. And this is the first time I've heard the girl speak.

"Not everyone wins," she says and the pain in those words makes my chest so heavy I have to lean back against the wall.

"No. You're right, Abby. And it's not as easy as I just made it sound," he whispers. "But you're here and you're fighting and that's the first step."

"True," Syd admits.

"And I'll tell you the same thing I told my sister every time she refused a meal and had to have that tube shoved up her nostril." Jeff pauses and I can feel every ounce of pain drift off of him into the hallway as he remembers. "You are not alone."

"Amen," Sean says.

I close my eyes and echo that *Amen* in my head. Jeff has personal experience with this. No wonder he was willing to come. Pieces of the Jeff shaped puzzle are starting to click into place in my head. And as I open my eyes and push off the wall, still reeling from the emotion beneath his words, I can't help but admit that I no longer want to avoid him at all costs.

I want to know more.

Chapter Twenty

J eff

Lesson 21: Bad news will find you at your worst.

It's the first week of October and I'm already approaching my burnout point. It hasn't happened since I moved to Philadelphia, but this week has really pushed me past my surgical threshold. I've been moonlighting as many shifts as possible to save some money. And every time I opened up a patient, whether it be a routine hip replacement or a run-of-the-mill ACL tear, some sort of complication was waiting beneath my scalpel. While I love the challenge, my eyes feel like they're bleeding and my hands are cramping and sore.

I need to sleep. For a day or two. I know I brought this on myself, not resting on Saturdays like I usually do, but I don't have a single regret. Spending time with those kids makes me remember why I wanted to be a doctor in the first place. It makes me remember why I'm here and who I'm doing this for.

Of course, spending time with Devon is a damn good fringe benefit. There's something about being with her that takes the edge off, like the feeling you get as you stare out at the sea with the water running over your feet. Devon has that effect on me. She makes things softer—easier to process.

My phone vibrates in my pocket just as I sink into the cushions of the Ektorp I bought last month from the huge Ikea off Delaware Ave. My chest feels empty—stripped of all energy and emotion and I pray to anyone who will listen that my patients are ok and that it's not the hospital calling again with some new unexpected emergency. I'd have to dig deep. Too deep.

The picture of my mom with Sam on her horse in front of her appears and I accept the Facetime call.

"Oh, J.J. You look exhausted!" She's yelling and I turn the volume on my phone down. I know better than to explain to her that she can speak in her normal voice. I also know better than to explain to her that she needs to back off the camera. Her forehead takes up half of my screen.

"Yeah, Ma. It's been a rough week."

"Did you get my last care package?" she asks excitedly.

I wish the answer to that was no.

"Yes. Thank you so much—"

"Did you read the article I attached to the box of condoms?"

It was more like a crate of condoms. And the article she's referencing had to do with the rise of STDs in New York City. And it was dated six years prior.

"Yes. I got the article about New York City from 2019. You know I'm in Philadelphia, right?" I ask. I shut my eyes and wait.

She sighs as if I'm a moron. "J.J. that's two hours north of you. These things can travel—"

"Ok, Mom. You're right. Thanks for the condoms. Is Sam there?"

My mom doesn't bother to cover the mouthpiece when she yells for my niece and the small beginning of a fatigue migraine crescendos to a full-on pounding skull-splitter. Nothing like a mother's voice to bring on the cortisol. But then there is a rustling and my mother's forehead disappears and the heart shaped face of my sister's perfect offspring comes into view.

"Sammy, are you taking care of Gran?" I ask her and she shakes her head and gives me a look, then smiles off screen at my mother. The wallpaper behind her starts to slide out of view and I see her swaying ponytail as she passes the hutch filled with the white and blue china my grandmother left to my mom. The girl is on a mission, her tongue poking into the side of her cheek. She looks down at me, her eyes wide telling me to wait and then I hear the screen door squeak open and her footsteps on the front porch, the background is all blue sky, like my niece is floating in the clouds.

"Uncle J, she's acting kinda weird. Her and Mom keep fighting about something called a morgue edge. I dunno," she tells me, checking over her shoulder.

"A morgue edge?" I repeat. My exhausted brain is trying to process what Sam's trying to tell me and I can see by the way she's chewing on her rosy bottom lip that she's upset about whatever the hell it is. Then it clicks.

"The mortgage," I say more to myself than to her. I push up from the couch and stand, suddenly feeling nervous.

"Yeah. That's what I said." She rolls her deep green eyes at me.

"Sammy, love, can you put Mommy on?"

She nods and lets out an annoyed breath then holds me at her waist so that I'm watching the underside of her chin as she makes her way back into the house, passing light fixtures and door frames that tell me her route. When the onion-light fan appears on screen above her, Sammy looks back down and I make sure to give her my most comforting smile. If I wasn't worried, I'd feel a little angry at my sister for letting the poor kid hear their arguments. Though knowing Sammy, she'd have figured out a way to hear them no matter how hard they tried to hide it. She's a stealthy little thing. There's not much you can keep from her.

"Love you, Uncle J," Sammy tells me with a grin. "Enjoy the feet."

I chuckle. "Will do. Love you, kid."

My sister appears and I lift a brow. "Take me away from little ears," I instruct, then continue pacing back and forth until I hear a door shut and see my sister look back at the camera.

"What the hell is going on with the mortgage, Jen?"

My sister lets out a breath.

"We weren't going to tell you. You worry too much. Sammy is so much like you—"

"Jen."

"Ok. Just don't get all crazy. The riding center needs equipment so Mom had a choice to make," she explains. "Invest in the business or pay the mortgage."

"How much does she owe?" I pull in a deep breath to prepare for the blow.

"Twenty thousand." My sister pulls her nose up and flinches as I curse.

"Shit, Jen. Why didn't you tell me?"

"Just calm down. I've got this under control. I called the mortgage company and they've got us on a payment plan and foreclosure—"

"Foreclosure! Can you make the payments?"

She looks over her shoulder. But I can still see the tears.

"I gotta go, J.J. I'll call you later."

The screen goes black.

What the hell is going on over there? I know my mom's therapeutic riding center has never done much more than break even, but that was never a problem before. Twenty thousand dollars? A year from now, I'd be able to cover that in a few months with my salary. But right now, with the rent to this apartment and the paltry fellowship stipend and the student loans finally calling in the enormous pile of debt I accumulated from eight years of education, there's no way in hell I can cover that.

I stare at the dark screen of my phone hoping that Jen's picture pops up and she tells me that this is some sort of joke. How is she managing this? The stress must be eating her alive. God, I hope *she's* eating. I can't think like that—can't let my mind spiral back into the past to the time before Sammy. It was a miracle her body could even conceive after what it went through.

I sink back into the couch, grab a pillow and squeeze it to my chest. If I sleep, just for a little, maybe this will go away. Maybe it'll seem more manageable on the far side of a nap. I lay myself down and catch my reflection on the unlit iPhone screen. I look like I've been dragged through the deepest circle of hell. I shut my eyes, but I know damn well that sleep won't come.

Chapter Twenty-One

Devon

Lesson 22: "No" is a complete sentence.

Most teachers get really worked up about Back to School Night. But there is something so powerful about the partnering of parents and educators. And though adults are certainly not within the same sphere of comfort as their offspring, I do love the moment that the parents walk in and look around the room with that awkward sense of déjà vu, and I get to guess what child they belong to. It's a game I've played every year for ten years. A game that has sadly diminished in challenge as the denominator of my score has lessened over time and post-pandemic attendance has dwindled to hover around thirty percent. So far tonight, I've gotten thirty-two out of forty correct matches, and I narrow my eyes and focus on the line of the man's jaw in the back of the room as he wanders around the last row looking like a lost dog.

"Davie?" I say to him over the heads of the other seated parents who I've filled in about my game.

A woman who must know Davie's dad hollers, "Yes!" and I put my hand out to introduce myself.

"I'm Devon Gallagher," I tell him.

"Grant Dean," he replies with a smile, making his way over to the desk beside the woman who confirmed his identity. Davie Dean is a great kid. Polite. Kind. She has her father's smile.

"Alright, so now you get to feel why we all need to go to chiropractors by the time we hit thirty," I say as I make my way back up to the front of the class and survey the way the parents fidget in the uncomfortable desks.

"Obviously, I have a spiel. And since this is the last period of the day, in this case night, if at any time during my spiel you want to go off script just let me know," I tell them.

A hand flies up in the back.

"Yes? Johnny's mom?"

"My son has a crush on you," she says with a huge grin.

Ugh. Poor Johnny. No wonder he's so quiet. Obviously, humiliation is a household item.

"Ok. Maybe not *that* off script," I tell them and there are a few laughs around the room.

I start my speech, using my slides on the Smartboard to talk through the challenges of the eighth-grade curriculum. It's eight fifteen at night and the last thing these people want to hear about is the Pythagorean Theorem (though it's literally the coolest lesson in 8th grade), so I move it along fast then focus it back on the kids and how they can get help. A few of the parents jot this information down, and I assure them that it's all posted on Google Classroom. They just keep jotting, maybe so they don't need to look around the room at their peers or make eye contact with me. Sometimes I do wonder if certain people ever escape the adolescent stage of development and its chronic inflated awareness of others' judgy thoughts.

"Do you guys have any questions?" I ask, mildly distracted by my phone buzzing on my desk chair. I wonder if it's Jeff. We've been texting and I've decided he's textworthy. Lucky him.

"Why are those posters in a math class?" someone asks from the right side of the room. I try to refocus, wiping Jeff from my mind.

"Those?" I look at the superhero posters I got at Five and Below. "That's the Marvel universe! X-men in the front, Thor, Hulk, the rest of the Avengers. There is so much math in Ironman that—"

"No, no—the others," the woman says. I'd guessed her child wrong and now I've forgotten who she belongs to. This is obviously Jeff's fault because he's occupying important real estate inside my brain. Like a squatter not letting anything else in.

"My mental health posters? Those let the students know that I'm an ally," I explain. I can feel myself come alive as I smile at the woman. This discussion is so important to me and I'm very excited to be asked since, honestly, no one ever does. Every opportunity to educate is significant.

"An ally to what?" she asks. Her eyes are narrowed, and I keep my smile easy even as I'm starting to suspect she already knows the answer to this question.

"To all of my students really, but particularly those posters speak to the kids battling something we can't see," I tell her evenly.

She makes a face. I hold the smile steady, like ten men holding up a steel beam. Breathe in. Breathe out. Wax on. Wax off.

"As I'm sure you are all aware, part of our district's mission statement reads, 'We cultivate resourceful, resilient citizens by teaching social-emotional and academic skills in a nurturing learning environment.' That's what I uphold in this class. That's what those posters support," I tell them, avoiding eye contact with the mother to the right who is burning a hole through my forehead with her glare.

The bell rings and I wish them all a good night and a great school year, then make my rounds to the few parents who have older children that I've taught in previous years. They fill me in on their kids' accomplishments and struggles, and by the time the final adult meanders out into the hall, my phone reads 9:15. Well past my school night bedtime. I check my missed text messages and there's nothing from Jeff. My disappointment is pathetic.

"Devon, can I speak to you for a moment?"

I look up from my phone to see my principal, Mr. Donato, standing uncomfortably in my doorway in his suit and tie—the picture of Back to School Night pomp and circumstance. I slide my phone into my purse.

"Of course," I tell him, and he steps inside of the classroom.

He surveys my walls like he's in a museum taking in paintings instead of integer rules and inspirational quotes. I clear my throat.

"Since it's getting late," I prompt.

He refocuses on me, but his eyes don't meet mine. His gaze hovers around my hairline, which always makes me want to stand on my tippy toes.

"Right. Of course. I'm sure you're tired, so I'll just make this quick. I'd like to request that you take down some of the posters around your door," he says, shifting his weight from one foot to the other.

It is suddenly very hot in the room.

"I'm sorry? Could you say that again?" I manage. The whiteboard behind him looks like there's a red haze over it.

"Informally, of course, as a friend. I believe that it would be in your best interest to take the crisis poster there—and maybe the mindfulness—definitely that one," he points to my UCLA Mental Health Support poster, "—off of your wall. We can put them in the guidance office, where they're better suited."

I hear unfamiliar laughter and realize with a start that it's coming from me. I am a person who respects authority. Respects rules and expectations. When I was told that mental health was not my area of expertise, I went back and got my masters. When he asked me to take leave to recover from surgery, I took the leave to recover. But this.

Fuck. No.

"No," I say.

Mr. Donato flinches a little, like I've bitch slapped him. And I wish I could. I ride out the wave of righteous anger.

"I won't take those posters down. And I certainly don't care about my best interest, Mr. Donato. I only act in their best interest." I point to the twenty-six empty seats in front of me. Tomorrow they will be filled with the trusting faces of my students, Jessie hiding amongst them, still shrinking in plain sight despite the protocol I'd followed to get her help. She is badly in need of every ally the school—no—the world can offer. No way in hell am I making this place less safe.

Mr. Donato flattens his mouth and looks me over. I lift my brows.

"Anything else?" I ask.

"Do you know who that mother was?" he says stiffly.

I shake my head and refrain from telling him how many shits I have to give about that mother's ignorant opinion.

He lets out a long breath.

"That's Mrs. Stoner. The school board president."

Of course. Stoner. *Jessica Stoner.* That woman was Jessie's mother. No wonder Jessie hasn't gotten the help she needs.

I look down at my feet and blow the anger at my toes. Out of the corner of my eye, I see Mr. Donato take his leave. When he's gone, I stare at my posters until my eyes blur and the words have no meaning.

Dr. Dick

Dr. Dick: Kev and Mer are coming over for
cards tonight.

Devon: How'd you get my number?

Dr. Dick: From the three hundred texts that
you've sent me. Do you want to come? We
need a fourth.

Devon: Yeah, Kev mentioned it. I'm super
busy.

Dr. Dick: With what? You get done school at
2:15 and we are your only friends.

Devon: I've gotta put out my outfit for
Monday. And wash my hair and plan my
jokes. And FYI, I'm drowning in friends.
Elena, Bonnie, Caroline. Joseph, Madison,
and Sal.

Dr. Dick: Did you just name the characters
from Vampire Diaries and three of your
students?

Your jokes are better unplanned.

Devon: Aww. You think I'm funny.

Dr. Dick: Oh please. You know you're funny.

Devon: Alright. Alright. I'll come to poker night.

Dr. Dick: Too easy.

Chapter Twenty-Two

J eff

Lesson 23: Care packages from Donna should not be opened around others.

I'm just finishing up my fifteenth voicemail to my sister when the doorbell interrupts my plea/demand that she call me back. I toss my phone onto the kitchen counter and make my way to the intercom beside the window, pulling the white lace curtains to the side to see Meredith, Devon, and Kevin standing on the brick sidewalk that lines Washington Square. The lace between my thumb and pointer finger, along with every other item in this fully furnished apartment, would not be my first choice, but eight months was too short a time to give a shit about interior design. I watch Kevin shift the pizzas he's carrying to his other hand as Devon catches sight of me staring down and lifts her hand in a what-the-fuck-let-us-up gesture. I buzz them up.

"Pizza, beer, and strippers," Meredith calls from the foyer at the bottom of the steps as I hold the apartment door open.

"Bring them up," I tell her.

Devon carefully makes her way up the steps. She must still be in pain. Hopefully, she'll let me check out her ankle tonight. She's dressed in full sweat clothes, her hair in a top knot still wet from the shower and somehow, she looks gorgeous.

"Did you put out Monday's outfit?" I ask her.

She reaches the top of my steps, a little out of breath, and I don't step aside.

"I put out the whole week. Failing to prepare is preparing to fail," she explains while brushing past me, lifting her chin. She makes her way into the kitchen and starts putting the beer into my fridge like she's done it a thousand times, even though it's my first time having any of them here.

"Hey." Kevin puts the pizzas on the coffee table and looks around the apartment. "No wonder why you didn't want to host. This place looks like my grandmother's grandmother lived here."

"What? You don't like lace?" I ask, picking up a doily from the end table and tossing it at him like a frisbee.

"Only for the thongs he wears," Meredith says from behind me. I turn to find her trademark grin stretching the tan skin around her eyes. She's holding a box that I know must be another care package from my mother. Apparently, financial troubles aren't as important as sending me well-intentioned-but-insane gifts. My phone rings from the counter, and with the exceptional timing she's always been known for, my mother's face appears on the screen. But before I can get to it, Devon accepts the call on speaker.

"Hey, Mom—"

"J.J., did you get the package? I have my tracker up and it says delivered." She sounds excited about this one which doesn't bode well for me.

Meredith is still smiling as she brings the package to the counter and puts it down next to the phone.

"Yeah, it just arrived along with some friends." I start to tear the tape off the box, but the loud ripping sound doesn't drown out my mother's excitement.

"I'm so glad you made friends. Is the handsome, blonde rich guy there? Calvin?"

"Jesus, Ma. You are on speaker and Kevin is blushing."

"Don't worry, Ms. Harrison. You aren't the first mom to notice my good looks," he tells her, and Devon nods her confirmation.

"Who else is there, J.J.? That pretty little thing you've been volunteering with?"

Oh lord. Really, Mom? I can feel Devon's eyes on my face as I keep my laser focus on lifting the flaps of the box. There's an insane amount of packing peanuts inside. I'm elbow deep in them by the time I can think of how to answer my mother's embarrassing question, but Devon beats me to it.

"I'm guessing that's me—Devon. How are you, Ms. Harrison?" None of the snark and sass is in her tone that I'm accustomed to receiving. I imagine this is the polite voice she uses with her students' parents.

"Oh yes! Devon. I've heard a lot about you, honey. You're a schoolteacher like my Jenny!"

Devon smiles like she always does when she talks about her students. "I am. How's Jenny's year going?"

"Oh wonderful, honey. She loves her class this year."

"Mom, what is this?" I cut in. I've found a box labeled Almond Moo in the swooshing abyss of foam.

"It's an Almond Moo, honey!" She says honey like it could be substituted with dipshit.

What the eff is an Almond Moo? I hand it across the counter to Devon and she lifts the lid and takes out the pitcher-like object.

"I've seen these before on a telecommercial!" Devon tells her in an excited voice.

"What does it do?" Kevin asks from over my shoulder.

I want to tell them all to stop asking questions—to stop humoring this absurdly kind but misguided woman, but my mother is answering him before I can open my mouth to speak.

"It milks your nuts, dear."

Meredith's jaw drops to her navel. Kevin presses his lips together to hide his smile. And even Devon lets out a small burst of a giggle. But it's Meredith I keep my eye on, her dark pupils are gleaming as her mind pokes and prods at every avenue she could take.

"I'm sorry, Ms. Harrison. Could you repeat that?" she asks, a slow smirk spreading as she stares right at me.

"I said it milks—your—nuts." My mother articulates every consonant in a way that makes Meredith's eyes widen with joy.

"Ma, don't—"

"So, Ms. Harrison," Mer cuts in, "if Kevin borrows the Almond Moo, will it milk his nuts, too?"

"Don't answer that, Ma."

"Is that, Meredith? The scary one?" she asks. "Of course, it will, dear. Just make sure Calvin cleans it after J.J. uses it just in case. You don't want to mix nut milk. It'll ruin the flavor."

Meredith nods as if this isn't the first time she's heard this bit of advice. I pick up the phone and press the speaker button before she can ask my mother for any more pearls of wisdom on milking nuts.

"Thanks for the gift, Mom. Can I call you tomorrow?" I ask, shaking my head as I walk away from my friends' belly laughs.

"Of course, honey. Tell your girl to have a great school year."

She's not my girl. I look at Devon who is looking at the bottom of my brand-new nut milker.

"I'll tell her you said that. Can you have Jen call me?"

"Of course! Enjoy your nut milk, hun." I cringe. "Talk to you tomorrow."

"Love you."

"Love you more."

I toss the phone on the couch and point my finger at Meredith who puts her hands in the air as I step forward.

She looks at me with the serious face I imagine she uses to give bad news to patients. "Let's get this party started and milk some nuts."

Chapter Twenty-Three

D^{evon}

Lesson 24: When you can't cope, run.

I love the sound poker chips make when you let them spill from your fingers into a pile. Almost as much as I love the fact that my pile is bigger than that of the two men surrounding me. Meredith is the only one with a bigger pile, but I think she secretly flies to Vegas twice a year to play in tournaments. I cast a glance at Jeff beside me. He smiles wide and I lay down my cards face-up and sit back slowly, enjoying the way his smile slides downward into a frustrated frown of begrudging acceptance.

"D.J. Stephanie. Michelle. Uncle Jesse and Joey. Full house. Again, lady and gents," I purr, not waiting to see if anyone can match it as I pull the chips from the center of the bird-covered tablecloth into my area, stacking them neatly but loudly. The tablecloth looks like it was plucked straight from an estate sale in Savannah, just like the embroidered throw pillows and the birdcages in the built-in bookshelves. It's embarrassing to admit that I've imagined Jeff's apartment several times and I couldn't have been more off. No bachelor's leather couch or iron bar cart stocked with whiskey and man drinks. Jeff is living amongst antique lace and floral patterns and every time I catch sight of him against the backdrop of daisy-spotted wallpaper I giggle at the juxtaposition.

Two groans and a murmur of approval reach me over the satisfying clicking of my chips and I look up to find Kevin grabbing his pager off his waist.

"Hospital again?" I ask.

He nods, looking vaguely apologetic. "I'll see you guys tomorrow. At Devon's?" he asks, looking down at me with tired eyes. I nod.

"Mom's making chicken parm," I tell him.

"Did one of the chunky chickens die?" Meredith murmurs.

"You're sick," I tell her.

She smiles.

"Good luck in there, Kev," Jeff says.

"Thanks, man. Good luck losing to the women," Kev says, grabbing his messenger bag.

When Kev disappears down the steps, Jeff stands to get another round of beers and I idly check my phone, clicking on my sister's Instagram account to peruse the beautiful people and their beautiful things. Just because I don't have my own social media following doesn't mean I can't use it to stalk. Tara has perfected the art of selfie—her hair impeccably coifed—her makeup rivaling the paintings I've seen in the galleries dotting South street. Her pictures of her new beau, Marcello, are just as gorgeous. He's dark where she's light, his thick black hair swept to one side while his brown eyes stare into my American soul, convincing me to buy Italian. No wonder she's moving to Milan. The man is fine. And no filter could make an ass that tight.

I scroll up further and marvel at the masterpiece that is my kin. She's even got the lighting down, the way the moonlight streams through the window behind her and falls over her face, reflecting off the gorgeous cushion cut diamond lifted elegantly off her ring finger. Wait. What?

I click on the picture from today and count again. Thumb. Pointer. Middle. Ring. I'm not great with directions, but that's her left effing hand. My sister is rocking a two-carat rock on the finger of betrothal.

My phone rings and her duckface appear on my screen.

"Ummm. T. Why are you taking pictures with J. Lo's third engagement ring on?"

"Isn't it gorgeous? Devon! I'm getting married." She lets out a little squeal.

"Whattttt?" I'm pacing around the poker table and I don't even remember standing up from my chair. Jeff pushes in all the seats around the table so I don't trip, and watches me with wide, questioning eyes from against the wall, my beer dangling toward me from his outstretched hand. I'm gonna drink that beer real good.

"Yup. Marcello, flew over and surprised me today." She's breathless and I'm trying to match her enthusiasm. But I don't even know this man. He's sweeping my sister away to a foreign country and now he's going to steal the name Gallagher and make her a something that ends with an o. I don't even know his goddamned last name!

"We're going to make dinner at my apartment next Friday for you and the crew—to celebrate," she tells me. She's so happy. So excited. Her tone a pitch higher than I've ever heard. "Mom can't—won't come, obviously. So I hope you can—"

"Of course. Of course, I'll be there," I assure her. And I mean it. I might not know this Italian hottie, might even resent him a bit for his audacity and tight tush, but there's no way in hell I'd miss my little sister's engagement dinner. "Congratulations, T. I'm really happy that your happy."

"I know it's fast. I know you hate fast," she says.

I do hate fast. Fast is scary. Fast is stupid.

"When you know, you know, right?" Ugh. I hate clichés more than I hate fast, I take a long swig of the beer and let the cold bubbles fill my throat and stop me from saying anymore sappy, overused phrases.

"Exactly! I've gotta go though, Dev. They're about to pop the Champ—" There's a loud pop and a cheer. "Facetime in the morning ok? Love you, Devon."

"Love you more."

The call is ended and I'm staring at Jeff who's got his hands sunk deeply in his jean pockets, the full weight of his concern bearing down on me and making me feel guilty for the fact that the announcement of my only sister's engagement requires concern. I try to smile, but I can tell he doesn't buy it because his lips press together and the muscles in his neck tenses. Who has muscles like that in their neck?

"What are you congratulating Tara for?" he asks while I take another long sip of my beer.

"Her engagement," I reply, and he actually winces.

Meredith lets out a low whistle. "Shit. Should I get the tequila? We've got an hour 'til midnight."

"I'm gonna get some air," I say and pull open the sliding door that leads out onto Jeff's tiny balcony.

"That was fast," Jeff says to himself as I pass.

Thank goodness someone gets it. I step out onto the iron grates that hang precariously from the back-brick façade of Jeff's apartment building. The building, much like the knickknacks filling up his interior, is colonial and historic. Jeff steps out behind me and the metal creaks under our weight.

If he's scared that we'll topple the twenty feet onto the green dumpsters below, he doesn't show it. His hand lands on my shoulder and the warmth of it makes me want to lean back against him. I rationalize that desire with the heaviness I'm feeling from the idea of missing my sister. I'm just starved for comfort.

"It was one thing when she was moving there—I mean Tara has moved before—Tara likes adventure. And change—"

"The exact opposite of you," he murmurs, and I feel a small pang of defensiveness. But it fades with recognition. He's right. I hate change. The mere thought of moving sends me into fetal position. Teaching and tenure have tethered me here in South Jersey, like a safety line holding down a hot air balloon. Made my world safe. And there's my mom, of course.

"Yes. But an engagement? I mean, come on. After what we—my mother went through—how could she even consider taking that step so soon? She doesn't know him. He could crush her." My voice cracks. I'm talking to the sky. But Jeff's hand is still on my shoulder, his fingers squeezing me in a way that reminds me I'm not out here alone. I turn myself a little, lift my eyes to his and my breath gets stuck in my throat from the way he's watching me, the way his eyes are soft and serious in the light that finds us from the apartment windows across the back alley. His gaze falls to my mouth and I have to steady myself on the iron railing beside us.

"I get it," he says, his voice low and soft. And I know he does. That he gets me—feels for me. I rock onto the balls of my feet, closing a little of the space between us and I've forgotten what it was we were talking about. My fingers itch to touch his chest—to trace the tight line of his neck and the dark stubble on his chin and—

"Boooooty calll!" Meredith yells from inside and I jump back, knocking one of the potted mums off of its perch.

It seems to fall too fast—like whatever forces at work on the balcony are working in tandem with gravity. I watch it crash onto the dumpster below, pieces of terra cotta clattering over the black lid and onto the cement.

"I'm so sorry," I whisper. But I'm not sure if I'm apologizing for the flowers or for whatever the hell just happened.

I still can't seem to move. Every nerve in my body is standing at alert—live wires severed and set loose in a storm. I look back up at Jeff and shake my head—answering a question that he hasn't even asked.

His eyes are still liquid—like the absinthe I tried in high school. He runs a hand through his hair and opens his mouth to speak, but I turn away. I step back into his apartment, out of the rippling magnetic field. I focus all of my energy on Meredith doing her booty call dance while she holds up her ringing phone for me to see the picture of the hot guy calling her.

"Is that butt-chin?" I ask, hoping she doesn't see how flushed I am. Meredith sees all. The Eye of Sauron. She lifts a brow at me.

"Yup. You ok? You look a bit piqued."

"I'm fine," I lie. Between Tara's news and Jeff's Jeffness I'm anything but fine. "Looks like we can share an Uber," I tell her and head straight for the stairs.

Jeff's voice finds me just before I hit the steps.

"Devon, your money—"

I wave him away without meeting his gaze. "It was just for fun. Thanks for having us."

And I'm down the steps and out into Washington Square faster than I moved before my surgery.

Chapter Twenty-Four

J eff

Lesson 25: Always bring cupcakes.

As I pull the hybrid into the long oak-lined driveway, the sun peeking through the orange leaves overhead illuminating the black shuttered windows of Devon's mother's house, my entire chest has turned inside out. The raw ache of homesickness has me feeling so heavy that when we stop in front of the two-car driveway, I sit there in the driver's seat staring at the mums lining the pathway. Meredith and Kevin get out and close me inside the car to process.

I love this time of year at home. Brisk days, outdoor fires with Sammy roasting mallows, trail rides beneath the changing leaves.

I was hesitant to come—not because of this hollowed out pain in my heart—but because I never got the official invitation from Devon. Her mother insisted that Meredith bring me along, so I'd agreed, looking forward to a home-cooked meal and a peek into Devon's past. But now I realize I should have followed my instincts, stayed behind in the city and rested. Avoided the magnet that is Devon and the reminder that my real life is halfway across the country.

Kevin and Meredith disappear inside the house and Devon steps out onto the covered front porch. Giant pumpkins and gourds are scattered on a haybale beside her feet and she sidesteps them as she approaches the car. Her hair is pulled back to the side, her dark, loose curls cascading down one shoulder, her arms crossed over her chest as she lifts a brow at me and bends to look into the window.

I lower the glass between us and hold her gaze.

"You thinking of coming in?" she asks.

"Nah. I told them I'd drive them for half the price of an Uber."

She smiles and a soft breeze whips a piece of her hair loose from her ponytail. The red leaves of a Japanese Maple rustle behind her. She shivers.

"Let's go, weirdo. I'm cold. And since you managed to weasel your way into an invite from the hostess, you better be ready for an inquisition," she says, patting the roof of the car twice.

I put the glass back up and smile up at her before cutting the engine and reaching for the pink bakery box I brought. The box is out of my hands before I'm even fully out of the car.

"You brought Maggie's! Oh sweet joy. I'm gonna lick all of these," she says, rocking onto her toes while she peeks under the lid of the box.

"They are for your mother," I lie. I know how much she loves these cupcakes, so I took the trip across town to get them. Just so I could see her bounce around like a kid. It was worth it.

"Right," Devon murmurs as she leads me into the house. "I'll take them to her." She stops, glances over her shoulder at me, then bounds up the steps with the box, leaving me staring after her like she's lost her mind.

"You must be Jeff!"

Devon's mother is an exact replica of her eldest daughter. I step forward and offer my hand.

"I am. And I hate to show up empty handed, but your daughter just took off with our dessert to hide them god-knows-where," I tell her.

She laughs, Devon's laugh, and I'm smiling like an idiot at the sound.

"Oh look at that dimple! I'm Kathy Gallagher. It's so lovely to finally meet you." She wipes her hands on the towel over her shoulder then takes my hand in both of hers. Gives me a wink and pulls me in closer. "My daughter talks a lot about you."

Does she now? I shake my head.

"I bet. We had a rocky start," I explain.

But she waves that off.

"Everything with my daughter is rocky. She's all sharp edges on the outside, and gooey kindness on the—"

"Mommmmmm," Devon's head appears over the staircase banister behind us. "Please do not add to my reasons to avoid this man. I just started to tolerate him when he showed up with cupcakes."

Kathy winks at me again and takes my arm, leading me through the hall lined with family photos in a variety of locales and school pictures of Tara and Devon. I try to control my smile when I see a framed 13-year-old Devon with bangs sprayed high and Halloween color rubber bands around her braces.

"Like you looked any better at 13," I hear her murmur from behind me. I toss her a grin over my shoulder.

"I'm sure my mom would be happy to send you a picture if you asked," I tell her as we step into the kitchen. Meredith is filling wine glasses at the corner of the expansive butcher block counter and Kevin is setting the table. The entire back of the kitchen is a wall of glass, the woods behind standing guard over the patch of green where the infamous chickens are waddling around the yard like they own the place. I haven't felt this at home since I left Chicago in June.

Something wet and cold hits my palm and I look down to find the fattest, golden dog I've ever seen nudging his nose into my hand.

"Et tu, Brutus?" Devon says rolling her eyes. "First my friends, now my mom and her dog. What's next, Jeff?"

"Your virginity," Meredith says across the kitchen. Devon's mom laughs. Kevin clears his throat.

"Oh honey, that ship sailed a long, long—"

"Mom!"

This is going to be a good night. A very good night.

Devon must sense my delight because she narrows her eyes at me as she steps around the counter.

"How can I help, Mrs. Gallagher?" I ask while she drops chicken into the sizzling oil in the frying pan. The smell of fresh garlic and olive oil sweeps around the space.

"Call me Kathy, and you can help by drinking some of this wine Meredith and Kevin bring too much of every time they come."

I nod. That I can do. I take the glass Meredith is holding out in my direction and pull up a stool beside Kevin at the counter to watch Devon and her mother as they move around the kitchen, cooking together like they've worked with a professional choreographer. They are so in sync that when Devon looks up from chopping to meet my gaze, her mother removes the knife from between her fingers and bumps her hip against her daughter's to get her to move.

"Go introduce Jeff to the chickens," she says. "They're starting to come up on the deck anyway."

Devon takes a deep breath and a large sip of her wine.

"Come on, Jeff. Let's meet the chickens. Wouldn't want to offend them with our *fowl* manners." She giggles at herself and inclines her head for me to follow.

I stand, ignore Meredith's waggling brows, and follow Devon out the sliding doors onto the dark wood of the back deck. I close the door behind me and turn to find Devon slipping on a pair of gloves that look like they were made for falconry.

"Are those made of chainmail?" I tease.

"Go ahead and joke. Bernice—that fat bully over there—" she points to a chicken that defies the laws of nature, "she's been known to take the fingers of the trusting."

I laugh and hold out my hands.

"Shouldn't I get the gloves? I'm a surgeon," I remind her.

She scoffs. "How chivalrous of you! There's a pair in the shed over here." She starts toward the corner of the yard and I follow her, nearly tripping over another chicken as it comes right for my ankles.

"Careful, J.J. These chickens are overfed and aggressive. Wouldn't want you rupturing an Achilles. Especially with only hack job doctors around to help," she tells me as she swings open the door of the shed and steps inside.

I step inside behind her, watch in the dark space as she lifts onto her toes and searches the shelves for the gloves. Her shirt lifts as she reaches, revealing an inch of the soft skin around her waistband.

"Where the hell—? I really don't want to be responsible for the destruction of your priceless, delicate phalanges—"

She turns and bumps into me. Her breathing immediately goes ragged, her amber eyes catching the only light that sneaks through a crack in the roof.

"This is a one person shed," she whispers, staring up at me. Her hair has come loose in the search for the gloves. I reach out and push it away from her face, let my fingers linger beneath her ear.

"Do you want me to leave?" I ask.

She pushes her lips together. Shakes her head slowly, her eyes still on me.

"Do you want to talk about what's happening here?" I dip my head lower so that I'm speaking into the space above her shoulder.

She shakes her head again. Then tilts her neck a little to the side, an invitation. I don't hesitate to take it. I let my lips brush against her skin and the sound she makes—like I've just touched her everywhere —makes my entire body throb. I kiss up to her ear, put my hands on her hips, pull her into me so she can feel how much I want her. She whispers my name and my fingers dig into the skin above her jeans—

"Devonnnn!" Her mom's voice breaks the spell like a hot pan dipped in cold water and Devon jumps away from me, knocking a rake off the wall so its handle hits me on the side of the head with a hollow knock. She laughs and covers her mouth as it clatters to the ground.

"Shit," she says, between her hysterical giggles. She pops her head out of the shed. "Yes?"

"What are you doing in there? We need more basil for the sauce. Where's Jeff?"

I move toward the open door and she kicks me in the shin with her good heel.

"I don't know, mother. Maybe Bernice ate him. I'll get the basil," she says, leaning out of the shed with one hand on the door. I rub at my shin and resist the urge to pinch her ass, knowing she'd kill me.

"Bernice wouldn't do that. Would you, Bernie girl?"

"Jesus, Mom. Go inside," Devon orders.

I touch the knot forming on my head. I feel like we are thirteen, and as Devon turns on me, I half expect to see the braces from the picture in the hallway.

"Stay here," she hisses. Her cheeks are flushed the most appealing shade of pink. "I don't—I can't be near you."

"You want me to stay in the shed all night?" I ask, trying not to laugh at how frazzled she is. "You know you are of age to be kissing men in the shed."

"Ew. Just stay there. Count to sixty," she says, trying to shut the door as she steps out into the yard.

"Am I in timeout?"

"Yes," she says simply.

She shuts the shed door with a clang and leaves me in the dark. With a chuckle, I start the count loudly so she can hear, then try not to feel too proud when I hear her giggling outside.

Chapter Twenty-Five

Devon

Lesson 26: Stay out of sheds.

I should have locked Jeff in the shed.

He and my mother have exchanged phone numbers, favorite recipes, and their deepest darkest fears. We are moments away from him braiding her hair. I'm watching him across the table, his face alight as he talks about his family—Jenny and her second-grade class antics, Sammy and her glorious troublemaking, and his mother. Oh, his mother. And all I can think of is how much I want to meet these women.

He meets my gaze across the empty plates smeared with my mom's sauce and reads my mind.

"You'd love them," he says quietly.

I'm nodding like a bobble head doll when I feel Meredith's claws dig into my thigh, reminding me we are at a table of five—not two. I dig *my* claws into *her* thigh, but I don't dare to look at her. I know what I'll see there. And she can't be right. No matter how much I might want her to be.

Kevin swirls his red wine in his glass and asks Jeff about his residency in Chicago. The gold in Kev's hair catches the light from the pendants dangling above and I shift my eyes from him to Jeff. Jeff to him. These two men are so easy to admire. Good looks aside, the way they discuss their patients, the way they care—it's the same tone I use about my students. I don't understand a word they are saying about subdural hematomas, but the tone—the tone I can relate to. The concern etched between Kevin's brows and around Jeff's mouth. That feeling of responsibility. I glance at Meredith and she winks and grins. Immediate regret.

Of course I can't completely understand them—what they face. If I screw up as a teacher, which I do by the minute, someone doesn't die. Worst case scenario for me is a lifelong inability to calculate tax. And who wants to do that anyway?

"Devon, you're doing that thing you do where your face changes with your thoughts," my mom leans in and tells me.

Pfffft. I don't do that.

"You're doing it again."

I turn to her and she pats my head like I'm Brutus, who currently has his head in Jeff's lap waiting for food to drop into or around his mouth.

"Are you all going up to Tara's next weekend?" my mom asks.

She smiles, but it doesn't reach her eyes. It's not that she's not happy for Tara. She's worried. Which is a baseline state for her, a constant piece of motherhood amplified of course by her condition. And there's something else there tucked into the corner of her semi-smile. Regret, maybe? Guilt that she can't be a part of this.

"Unfortunately, I'm at the hospital all weekend," Kevin answers, meeting my gaze. The same regret I just saw on my mother's face frowns back at me from his. Despite the cold hard logic of "he chose this life," I feel badly for him, too. Kev will never stop working to impress his father—Chief of Staff at Lankenau Hospital and Chief of Pricks along the Main Line. But his daddy issues don't stop that small, bitter voice in my head that reminds me of his priorities.

"I can't," Meredith says, softly. But she doesn't glance my way to see my surprise. Mer never misses an opportunity to go to NYC. "I'm on call."

She says it like she's being tortured.

"Will you be going, Jeff?" my mother asks. I go to kick her, but she's already shifted her legs to the side. Clairvoyant bitch.

Jeff looks at me. I look at the table.

"I have an interview in New York City on Saturday, so I'll be up there anyway," he says. If I look up, I know there'll be eight eyes on me—ten if Brutus looks away from the food for once. This is more awkward than a sixth-grade dance.

"Well, that will be nice. I'm sure Tara will be happy to see you. She can't stop talking about how nice it was that you came to Devon's aid that morning."

I lift my gaze and Jeff shrugs, his eyes serious, and on me.

"It was nothing. Whenever—whatever she needs," he murmurs. My cheeks flush under his focus.

My mother's hand reaches out and pats his shoulder and she goes to stand and Kevin and Jeff get up at the same time like we are in Victorian England. Curtsey, Mom!

"We'll do the dishes," Kevin tells her and she puts her hands up in surrender.

"Maybe you two could move in?" my mom suggests.

"Maybe Devon could go fetch the cupcakes from under her bed," Jeff says, lifting his brows at me while he clears my plate.

I narrow my eyes on him. How'd he know my secret spot? I open my mouth to say I have no idea what he's talking about and my mom gives me a look that I have yet to perfect in front of the mirror. It would be so useful during assemblies to have that look in my arsenal.

As I leave the kitchen, I keep my eyes on Jeff to let him know I'm watching him. Gosh forbid he follows me up to my room like he did in the shed. I'd be pregnant by midnight.

I'm like a hormonal teenager around him and I want to chalk it up to my lack of sexy time, but in Syd's words, "denial isn't just a river in South America." Whatever is going on here with Jeff needs fixing. This is not a Katy Perry song and I am not seventeen in my skin-tight jeans—though they do feel a bit tighter after that chicken parm. I'm a grown-ass woman with at least a modicum of self-control.

Ooooh! Cupcakes!

I slide them from beneath my bed and lift the lid, inhaling their sweet, decadent aroma, and stare down at the cream cheese icing that glides across the red-velvet like skis on fresh snow. He even got a few with cookie crumbles on top, just the way I like them. I lift one from its spot in the corner and turn it in my hand. I dab my tongue into the icing. *It's just a cupcake, Devon. Just a perfect, delicious cupcake.*

But no one has ever brought me my favorite cupcakes before. The fact that he even knows my favorite cupcake is making the walls of my chest feel too tight for my heart. This is not good. I've got to do something about this situation—STAT. Shut. It. Down. Before someone, namely me, gets hurt. And ends up with a half-a-dozen fat chickens, terrified to leave the house.

Jeff's a friend. A very kind, very platonic, annoyingly sexy friend. That's all he can be. He proved that when he didn't show up that night for dinner and sent me spiraling into the past like Marty McFly. He has priorities that are not me. Just like my Dad did. And look where that landed us.

I just need to add a few things to my rules and everything can go back to normal, safe, panic-free life. No more sheds. No more balconies. No more anything that architecturally separates us from others. Make-out prevention at its finest.

I open my mouth to take a bite of the cupcake-that-is-just-a-cupcake.

"Devonnnnnn!"

Damn that she-witch.

I yell back. "Comingggg!"

Then I shove the whole cupcake in my mouth.

Dr. Dick

Dr. Dick: What time do you want me to pick you up tomorrow?

Devon: Never. How'd you get my number?

Seriously though, what are you talking about?

Dr. Dick: I'm offering to take you up to Tara's. Remember. I've got an interview at Langone.

Devon: Is Langone a strip club?

Dr. Dick: Langone is a high-priced escort service.

Devon: I'm supposed to be avoiding you.

Dr. Dick: Again? Didn't we already play this game last month?

Devon: Yeah. I lost that round.

Dr. Dick: Do you want the ride or not? I'm sure you could take the train if you are hellbent on winning this month's round.

Devon: Yes. Fine. I'll let you drive me. Out of the goodness of my heart. Pick me up at noon at Mer's.

And Jeff, don't use the line "Do you want a ride or not?" during your escort interview. Women want their gigolos to be subtle and loquacious.

Dr. Dick: Devon, I'd never need to use that line. I know damn well when a woman wants a ride. And I can think of much better things to do with my tongue than be loquacious...

Devon: 🙄

Dr. Dick: See you tomorrow at twelve.

Chapter Twenty-Six

Devon

Lesson 27: Never get in the car with a man who knows Bonnie Tyler lyrics.

I'm standing on the corner of Broad and Passyunk with my tiny capsule wheelie suitcase that Tara gave me specifically for the purpose of visiting her. The lunch hour rush is flooding the sidewalks as people dressed in lawyerly suits or fabulous miniskirts and booties bob and weave into the dozens of delis and steak joints that line this part of town. I'm getting a bit itchy standing here in the crowd, and I'm unsure if it's the waves of strangers jostling my nerves or the impending hours stuck in a tiny robot car with the good doctor.

Jeff's hybrid pulls in front of the fire hydrant near where I'm standing and he hops out, leaving the door open, then rounds the front of the car and gives me a smile as he reaches for my suitcase. I try to focus on the car door, but it's impossible not to glance up at that cursed dimple.

"This is your suitcase? It's the size of a make-up bag," he says, wheeling it toward the trunk.

"Tara insists on traveling light," I tell him. "You really shouldn't leave your door open like that on Broad. You're gonna end up driving a dune buggy."

He stares at me over the roof of his car. His eyes are catching the afternoon sun, glistening with their usual amusement.

I've realized the nerves are not the crowd of people as I glance into his car. It's a tight space and—

"Are you nervous?" he asks, while I duck out of sight and slide into the passenger seat.

I let out a laugh, but it comes out more hysterical than aloof.

"Why would I be nervous?" I ask, studying the window to my right.

"That's exactly what I was wondering, but you're all fidgety and you won't look at me."

I point through the windshield.

"Typically, when you drive you need to look at the road and not the passenger—"

"We are in park."

A car blares its horn and Jeff is forced to shift us out of park and into the flow of traffic. Thank goodness for crazy city drivers. I can tell already by the way his knuckles brush my thigh when he releases the gear shift that he's not going to let me ignore what happened last weekend.

He's going to torture me. And if I must endure him, by Thor, he must endure me.

I scoot to the edge of the seat so I am one with the door and reach for the radio knowing full well that he's going to slap my hand away like he did the last time I messed with his man music on the way to CHOP. But he just lets me fish through the stations. I reprogram his favorite stations and he glances sidelong at my hand but doesn't say a word. I narrow my eyes at the side of his face and settle on the most obnoxious love ballad I can find. "Total Eclipse of the Heart."

My juvenile mutiny backfires, because Jeff's mouth tugs up into that crooked grin and he starts to sing along. I roll my eyes and settle back in my chair, trying not to enjoy Jeff crooning along with Bonnie Tyler.

I think the safest angle here is to pretend to nap. I put my head onto my arm against the side door and I hear the lock press. Even while he's torturing me, he has the foresight to lock the door so I don't fall out of his car. It's a little insane, but sweet.

Somewhere between Jeff's rendition of Celine Dion's "It's All Coming Back to Me Now" and my anxiety/excitement about meeting my future brother-in-law, I pass out with my forehead pressed firmly against the window.

I wake up to the sound of my skull against the glass.

"Sorry," Jeff says, wincing as I try to get my bearings.

"You did that on purpose didn't you?"

I rub at my head and try to surreptitiously wipe the drool from his door handle.

"I'm shocked you can sleep with all of that noise," he tells me.

I look out the window. We're already to exit 9 on the Jersey turnpike. The exit of my alma mater: Rutger's University.

"Your singing was pretty soothing actually," I admit.

"I was talking about your snoring."

"Har. Har."

He lets out a long breath and glances at me for half a second. I lift a brow.

"Devon, we need to talk," he says and every muscle in my body contracts. The last thing we need to do is talk. We need to avoid and deny. Pretend.

"Let's not and say we did," I say. "We were drinking on poker night. And I stumbled in the shed."

His brows pull together and he shakes his head.

"You had a few beers, Devon. I was stone cold sober," he says.

"And you are clumsy as shit, but your balance was perfect in the shed."

I skootch a little closer to the door as if distance will protect me from that dumbass dimple.

"Either way. It was a moment of comforting between friends," I say.

"Mmmhmm."

His smirk is infuriating.

"What aren't you saying, J.J.?" There it is. The deep laugh that I'm used to hearing from him. And all it took was channeling his mother.

"A lot. I'm not saying a lot," he answers. "I think it's time for you to face the inevitable—"

"Sweet Joseph, you are arrogant. Inevitable? Cornering me in the shed does not inevitability make." I cluck and he lets out the breath that I use when my students won't stop saying, "that's what she said."

His cell phone rings from where it's perched on the air conditioning vent and the name Jenny appears with the picture of a beautiful dark-haired woman with an even more beautiful young girl in her lap.

"Shit. I have to answer this," he murmurs. And before I can say of course he's accepted the call on the blue-tooth and the interior of the car is flooded with a smooth but annoyed voice.

"Jesus, Jeff. Fifteen voicemails!"

I smile. Jenny will put his pompous ass in its place. I watch the scenery change outside and pretend not to be listening. The flanks of the highway have shifted from dense forest to industrial factories. The smell of swampy sewer water leaks into the car despite the sealed windows.

"If you had called me back, I wouldn't have needed to leave fifteen voicemails," Jeff bites back.

"Everything is fine over here. Just focus on doctoring and let me handle this," Jenny says.

Jeff's knuckles have lost all color as he grips the wheel. I suddenly have the desire to plug my ears and hum. This conversation isn't for me to hear, but this is the first time I've seen Jeff look so helpless and I'm surprised by how much I want to reach out and cover his hand with mine.

"Jenny, I need you to keep me updated. Stop ignoring me."

A young girl's voice titters in the background and Jenny is no longer listening.

"I've got to go, Jeff. Stop calling. Everything is fine," she says.

"Jenny, don't—"

The other end of the line goes silent and Jeff curses under his breath as he puts his blinker on to head for the Lincoln Tunnel. His shoulders have dropped two inches and his jaw is so tight I can hear his teeth grinding.

"Do you want to talk about it?" I ask softly.

At first, I think he's going to say no. His eyes glaze over as if he's pulled the curtain down between me and his emotions. But then he meets my gaze and his entire face relaxes back into the soft and open Jeff I'm used to seeing.

"My mom is struggling with her finances and my sister refuses to answer my questions. Or let me help." The sentences come out on one breath, like he's been waiting to release them.

"I'm sorry, Jeff. I can't imagine how that must feel to be so far away and so—"

"Useless," he finishes for me.

"I was going to say out of the loop. You are the farthest thing from useless."

"It's maddening. They've never cut me out like this before." His voice is quiet and it's obvious he's no longer with me.

"It seems like your sister has it under control," I point out. "Teacher power."

He nods, but the way he pushes his lips together tells me he doesn't agree.

"Is it just your mom and sister?" I ask.

"Yeah. And Sammy." He hesitates, like he's deciding whether or not to say something else. "My father left us when I was thirteen. And Sammy's father was never in the picture. The men in their lives just keep leaving."

My heart drops onto the floor.

"I hate not being there for her—for them," he whispers.

My heart rolls out the door onto the NJ turnpike.

"I'm so sorry, Jeff," I whisper. My eyes are already glassy. I blink hard and fast.

He looks over at me and I try to look away before he sees the tears.

"Jesus, Devon. Are you crying?"

I shake my head only to let more tears loose.

"I'm an empath," I tell him, voice thick. "And it's sad. Crying is an appropriate reaction."

His hand reaches out and finds mine. I let him curl his fingers between my own.

"You are incredibly kind," he whispers. "Everything will be ok. Thank you, though. For caring."

I should pull my hand away, but the pressure of his fingers on mine is making my head spin. His hands are so strong and warm—skilled hands. Surgeon's hands. I shut my eyes and try to get control of the way my heart is skittering around in my chest.

"It's why we are all so close," he tells me. "Stuff like that brings you closer—ya know?"

I shut my eyes and squeeze his hand harder. I get that. Man, do I get that.

"My mom holds it all together. The riding center. The house. Jenny and Sammy. She's the glue."

He's forgotten I'm in the car, his eyes far away as he stares out the windshield. I watch him chew on the inside of his cheek and I know for my own sake not to push any further. I need to let go of him. The way his thumb is stroking my palm is making me feel like I need to tuck and roll out of the car to save myself. Slowly, I pull my hand from his.

"Your mom must be incredible," I say.

He sighs. I can't take my eyes off of the side of his face. The softness of his expression as he thinks about his family. His vulnerability has my head spinning—a blender filled with compassion and something else—something I need to bury deep before I drown in it. Sirens are blaring in my head and I can't tell if they are coming from the opposite side of the turnpike or from my self-preservation instinct.

"She is," he murmurs.

And she must be if she raised a man like this.

Chapter Twenty-Seven

Jeff

Lesson 28: Nothing like a small car and a long ride to force your hand.

There's no chance in hell Devon is going to talk about what's going on here between us. I've never seen someone so capable of avoidance. Between her and Jenny, I feel like I'm invisible, watching reality unfold, yelling that I'm there, but no one can hear me. Whatever is going on at home is driving me insane. This powerless feeling—it's killing me. I've always been the one my mom and sister turn to in a crisis. Jenny's past aside, their dependence on me is a huge reason why I chose med school—the financial stability and ability to provide. Now they want to shut me out? If it hadn't been for Devon's soft, soothing grip anchoring me back to the car, then I might just be in a bar in the Meadowlands drinking off the burn in my chest.

Which brings us back to the infuriating denial Devon is choosing to wrap around her. If she's going to roll into her shell like an armadillo every time I broach the topic of—whatever this is—I'm just going to have to find another way in.

Tara's voice derails my train of thought and floods the interior of the car, her pitch high, her pace approaching frantic while telling us the quickest route as we crawl up Greenwich Street passing a string of high-end boutiques and art galleries.

"Now what street are you at?" Tara asks, her breathing heavy like she's been chasing her tail for hours.

"Still at tenth," Devon tells her. "You need to breathe."

"I'm setting up the pre-game bar and apps," Tara wheezes.

"And you're sprinting because?"

"You are five blocks away!"

Devon rolls her eyes as the light turns green and we inch forward another ten feet. The traffic is as draining as listening to Tara run a marathon around her apartment.

"I'm going to send Marcello down now. You guys come up and he'll park the car—"

"It's ok. I can find a parking gar—"

"No. You're our guest! I've got all the ingredients for a Sicilian mule waiting for you," she says, and I'm surprised that she remembered our nostalgic-drink conversation from that morning on the way to Jefferson. It was such a tiny blurb, but obviously thoughtfulness runs strong in the Gallagher family blood. I glance over at Devon and she's smiling at me like she knows I'm about to crumple like a coffee filter.

"Alright," I say. "Where should we pull—"

"Marcello's already on his way! See you in five," Tara squeals and hangs up.

"You can't really say no to Tara," Devon says.

I nod. "I can see that. My sister isn't much different," I tell her. But she doesn't need an explanation. She got to witness Jenny's dictatorship firsthand when she refused to tell me what the hell is going on and hung up on me as if I were a telemarketer.

We pull across 13th Street and I'm about to ask her if she's excited to meet this Marcello when there's a frantic banging on the passenger side window and Devon screams and jumps onto the console so that half of her ass is on my right thigh. My foot slips off the brake on impact, but I catch my toe on the grip at the last second and push down hard to keep us from rolling under the pick-up truck in front of us. There's another loud bang and I look to find a very tan, dark-haired man smiling like a lunatic as he presses his palms against Devon's window. At first, I think it's an aggressive homeless person, but Devon lets out a string of curses followed by a chuckle. She shifts back into her seat, reaching for the window button. Before I have the chance to ask her what the hell she's thinking, the window is down and the man is leaning into the car, kissing Devon's cheeks with the enthusiasm of a dog awaiting its long-lost master.

"Marcello," Devon says, when she glances over at me. I must look shocked or confused because she pats my leg and tells me slowly to put the car in park, like she's explaining how to solve a complicated equation to one of her students.

"I knew eet was you from de pictures. Bella sorella," Marcello booms. His voice is rich and velvety, and his teeth are so white I'm hypnotized. "You must be Jeff, no?"

"Yes," I manage to say. It's hard to breathe around this man's energy and the shock of having half a body hovering over Devon's legs.

Marcello nods and slips out of the window frame then starts to walk/bounce around the front of the car. He opens the door for me. People are honking behind us and Marcello barely blinks while he motions with his hands at a man who leans out of his window behind us to scream expletives in our direction. I stand up out of the car and I'm immediately embraced in the most solid man-hug of my life.

"Un piacere," Marcello tells me, patting me on the shoulder. "I am very glad to meet you. I will take it from here. Vai. Enjoy."

He slides into the car as Devon pops out the other side and before I have a chance to even check my pocket for my phone and wallet,

Marcello has screeched away at a speed I didn't know my car could reach.

"Holy shit," Devon whispers. Cars are still honking. We are standing in the middle of the road staring at each other like we just survived a tornado.

I remember how to walk and grab her arm as we play frogger around the cars passing by impatiently. "He's—wow. I mean he's—"

"Perfect for Tara," Devon finishes with a laugh.

And from the little I know about Tara, Devon might just be right. Devon is smiling nearly as wide as Marcello was—if that were anatomically possible. And I can see for the first time how genuinely excited she is for her sister, even if she's crushed at the prospect of the distance that's about to be between them. And terrified for her sister taking such a giant leap of faith.

I find myself needing to touch her as I bear witness to this moment of happiness. I place my hand on her lower back and her eyes close for a moment, her shoulders fall a fraction of an inch. But she doesn't pull away. We slow to a stop in front of a four-story brick apartment building spotted with huge black-rimmed windows. Flower boxes cling to each pane of glass, color spilling from them like melted crayons ready to drip onto the bustling sidewalk below.

She leans forward, presses the shiny silver button at the bottom of the box by the door. I watch the way her eyes crinkle at the sound of Tara's voice over the intercom.

"Come up! Come up! Come up!" Tara sings. Her excitement bleeds out onto Greenwich Street.

I pull the door open and smile down at Devon as she brushes past and stares up at me with narrowed eyes. *Be good.* I know that look well. She's been giving it to me since her full-out verbal assault in the bathroom in July. I grin wider and she lets out a long breath and averts her eyes.

When she's reached the stairs and the feel of her hip against my thigh still tingles pleasantly, I let the door shut behind us and follow.

Chapter Twenty-Eight

Devon

Lesson 29: Leave the man, take the tiramisu.

Tara is on cocaine. I mean—I know she isn't—but the way she flits and flies around the apartment filling my champagne glass, making drinks for Jeff with Marcello, feeding us an array of antipasti, primi piatti, secondi piatti, all the piattis—it's like the two of them are performing some sort of tango they've rehearsed for months. Their infectious bliss keeps shaking something loose inside of me. Hope, maybe? A question floats through my brain like Tara floats atop her three-inch heels. Is this what love looks like? Will I look like Aphrodite on speed if I fall in love?

Doubtful.

Tara slices a cucumber and passes the slivers to Marcello beside her. Whispers of enchanting, vowel-filled, flowing Italian reach me as he presses his lips against my sister's ear while muddling the cucumbers in the copper mule mug. My future brother-in-law cannot look away from Tara. She is impossibly beautiful in her silk slip dress, her curls bouncing around her shoulder like golden springs in a physics experiment run by King Midas. Marcello's eyes are comically wide as he takes her in.

I feel Jeff watching me as I watch them. He's been on his best behavior—thank goodness—sitting as far away from me as physically possible in 1,500 square feet. But, he has barely taken his eyes off of me—a fact that unsettles me in both a worrisome and pleasant way, the latter of which I choose to ignore. I recognize that my hair is sticking to my neck more than bouncing around my shoulders and that my ten-dollar high waisted pencil skirt from the consignment store at home does not send waves of iridescent light off my body like Tara's designer dress. Yet, still, the man stares.

I glance toward him and tilt my head.

"You're being creepy again," I tell him, then point toward the bar. "And Tara's giving you a six count on the vodka. Tread lightly."

"Says the woman holding her seventh glass of Brut."

Shit. Is this seven? I tick away on my fingers and lose count at three, then look back to Jeff.

He nods and I know for a fact that I didn't ask that out loud, because the rim of the glass is pressed to my lips and bubbles are bouncing happily on the front of my tongue like it's a diving board.

"You must drink more quickly, Jeff," Marcello shakes his head firmly and wags a finger at us. "We have many cucumbers left here for you."

Tara lifts up two absurdly large cucumbers to bring the point home. She waggles her brows at me, and I let out a loud sigh. It's difficult to imagine her as a high-power design mogul when she's still making cucumber dick jokes like we did at sixteen.

Tara turns back to overpouring the Grey Goose into Jeff's bronze mug. Her ring catches the white light from the huge crystal chandelier above us and sends a dazzling array of glitter over the far wall of her apartment. These two might be happy and beautiful together behind the bar, but they are dangerously distracted, and Jeff and I will end up as collateral damage if we don't slow down.

"Yo, T. Easy on the Goose," I say.

Tara levels out the bottle and looks away from her fiancé like she's only just remembered I'm there. She smiles at me and I have to laugh. I've seen Tara in love before—giggling, eyes glistening, flirtatious and free, pouring drinks that could down a silver-back. But this is something else. She's lit from within, like Marcello's energy mingles with her own, overloading the circuit breaker. I'm waiting for the lights to flicker around us—for a loud pop to sound and sparks to fly from the outlets.

"Yo, D. Easy on the Brut," Jeff murmurs and I glare.

But I can't maintain the evil eye while he sits tucked into Tara's girl-organ-shaped modern armchair. Watching Jeff figure out how to sit down in that hideous thing was the highlight of my evening. I was with Tara when she purchased it from a furniture gallery four blocks South. I called the chair "The Ovary" when I laid eyes on it amongst the overpriced, pretentious furniture, and since Tara only had one ovary left after having a baseball sized cyst irreparably damage her right female organ at age sixteen, she bought it without even sitting her ass down inside the white ellipsoid, claiming that it would bring balance to her apartment and her reproductive system. Impossibly, Jeff seemed right at home in Tara's Ovary, a fact that she and I giggled about through the first three glasses of champagne every time we glanced over at him.

"Alright, is anyone ready for il dolce?" Tara asks as she sinks beside me on the couch with a fresh glass of champagne. The bubbles trail upward in my glass, happy little golden chains of intoxicating air.

"I'm good for now," I tell her, looping my hand in hers and examining that gorgeous ring for the n-teenth time. I cannot believe my little sister is engaged.

"I wish Mom was here," Tara says softly, and I rub her palm with my thumb.

Jeff catches my eye as he takes a small sip of the drink he just accepted from Marcello and he mouths the number eight at me with his crooked grin. A shudder crawls up my bare legs beneath my pencil skirt. I just need to keep him in Tara's Ovary and I'll be safe.

"You know Mom wishes she were here, too," I tell her, leaning my head on her shoulder.

"I think we drive down Sunday to pay tua madre a visit, no?" Marcello asks and Tara gives him a look that tells me this isn't the first time they've discussed this.

"My therapist says if we continue to enable her, she will have no incentive to step outside of her comfort zone," Tara explains.

"Is your mother agoraphobic?" Jeff asks and I feel my sister tense a little beside me. We haven't used the a-word since Tara confronted my mom two years ago and was thrown out of the house and told not to come back with her "psycho-babble and bullshit." My mother refused treatment in any form, which meant we had to continue to skirt around the obvious while coming up with creative ways to get her outside. Chickens enter stage left.

"Undiagnosed," I tell Jeff who narrows his eyes at me and takes another tentative sip of his mule. The way he's studying me for information makes me want to hide in the couch cushions. We don't talk often about my mom's "issues," mostly because Tara and I can't seem to agree on what to do. I know she needs help, but I refuse to starve her and not buy groceries to try to lure her out into the open. I stand when the weight of Jeff's stare gets to be too much and the Earth tilts right. I sit back down, ignoring Tara's giggle.

"I think it's time for il dolce," Marcello says wisely, winking my way. "The espresso will burn."

"I'll help!" Tara pats my leg and grins at Jeff as she follows her fiancé into the kitchen.

I need to pee.

This time I move slowly, ignoring Dr. Dick's attempt not to laugh.

"Can I help you?" he asks, trying to extricate himself from the egg.

"No!" He freezes. Shakes his head with a breathy laugh. "You cannot help. Sit. Stay."

Good boy.

"Devon, this is absurd. You're—tipsy—and if you hurt that tendon again I'm gonna—"

"Do what? What are you gonna do, you big meathead?" I puff out my chest and he puts both hands up, smiling.

"I don't think I've ever been called that," he says to himself. "Text me when you make it safely to the toilet."

I ignore him and focus on taking my leave slowly. Gracefully. I keep my eyes on Jeff, making sure he doesn't follow, until I hit the hallway wall, literally, and nearly knock a framed drawing of one of Tara's early designs off the mount.

"You ok?" Jeff asks.

"Yup. Just checking for studs."

I've stopped like I always do in front of the sketch of my prom dress. It never ceases to amaze me how talented she was—and is—as I stare at the sleek lines of champagne-colored satin that she created especially for me. She spent hours over my grandmother's old Singer, me reading in bed while she sang along to Black Eyed Peas, moving that gorgeous fabric with her deft, manicured fingers. The gown made me feel like a princess mermaid in a sea of prosecco. The thought of prosecco makes me a little queasy.

I smile through a yawn, reaching out to touch the orange smudgy fingerprint peeking out from the top right corner of the barnwood frame. I was eating hot wings when she showed me, and her outrage at the stain was the first time I remember thinking, "Oh shit, she's going to seriously kill it in fashion." And here we are, nearly a decade of fashion weeks in Paris later, with my little sister taking life (and a hot Milanese man) by the balls just as I'd always known she would.

I glance into Tara's room and take in the heaven that is her bed. It's a cloud backlit by the lights of the city stretching across the windows on the far wall. A puffy, glorious marshmallow that occupies the majority of the master and calls to me like a siren to a sailor. I'm just gonna bounce a little, stroke the silk pillows that keep sis lookin' so fine in the am. I glance behind me like a shoplifter, then sneak inside her boudoir, giving the mattress my best plop. I sink into the quilted comforter and let my cheek cool against the smooth silk. This is magnificent. I don't even have to pee anymore. I'm just going to lay here for a bit. Just to sober up. Shit, is that mascarpone I smell? Mmmmmm. I'll just shut my eyes for a sec—

My mind wakes me and points to my bladder. It's pitch black in my room and I run my hand to my left to find my touch lamp, but instead I feel a lump beneath the blankets. Why am I on the wrong side of my bed? My fingers search some more through the softness, expecting to find the big stuffed llama, Obama, that my dad gave me for my twelfth birthday, but instead they hit something warm, firm, muscular, and smooth—oh shiz.

I sit up too fast. My brain shrivels and shrinks inside my head and I lift my hand away from what I hope was Tara's arm on steroids and press my fingers to my throbbing temples. I'm not home. I'm at Tara's. And what the hell am I wearing? I reach my right hand out into the darkness and come into contact with something cold and gooey. I bring my finger to my nose and sniff. Espresso and—I lick it. Yassss! Tiramisu. I force myself to focus while I lick my hand. I find my phone on the nightstand and press it alive with my wet thumb.

5:15 am. The exact time I get up for school every day. I turn on my flashlight and direct it down at my chest. Black silk tank top that I know isn't mine. I lift the comforter—Tara's comforter, I realize now. Matching black silk shorts with a trim of lace. Fuuuuuck. Slowly I turn the phone light to my left, it fans out like a light house around the room, spinning toward the exact person that I don't want to see.

He's on his stomach, his bare shoulders peeking out from the nine million thread count sheets Tara gifted herself. His hair looks so soft and shiny against the silk pillowcase. The silk worked its magic on him, too. Because he looks fine. He stirs a little when my light hits his insanely thick lashes and I quickly turn it and press it against my braless chest. What—the hell—have I done?

There's no way I slept with him. I wasn't that drunk. I had like three glasses of champagne. Maybe four. I'd remember. I'd definitely remember. And my lady parts don't feel any different. They aren't rejoicing with a chorus or whispering Hallelujah to the sky. I rack my already racked brain for memories of post primi piatti. Shit. I don't remember.

I scurry around the room like a three-footed mouse, grabbing any clothes I can find on the floor, tripping over throw pillows as I go. I've got like three items in my grip, so I snatch up the tiramisu from the nightstand, tiptoe into the hall, and shut the door softly behind me. With the clothes pressed to my chest and the plate of orgasm between my fingers, I walk silently toward the bathroom, my bladder screaming louder than the base drum pounding in my head.

I drop the clothes on the floor, flick on the light switch, squint my eyes enough to survive the onslaught of light, and drop onto the porcelain throne like it might disappear at any moment. As I take care of business and nibble on a ladyfinger drenched in espresso, I force my aching brain to concoct an exit plan. I had one gosh-darned job. Stay away from Jeff Harrison. Yet, somehow, I failed. So, there is only one thing left to do. The mature thing. Run.

When I'm dressed and there is no evidence that the tiramisu ever existed, I make my way down the hall toward the soft orange glow that streams through the wall of glass in Tara's living room. The rising sun turns the skyline black like—

"Buongiorno, bella sorella."

Shit.

"Bon-e—" I stop. Did I just say boner in Italian? I try again, "Bone DiGiorno, Marcello."

"Your blouse—" He points to Jeff's button-down that I scooped off the floor. I look down, realizing I skipped like six buttons.

"Oops," I say, attempting a smile. My lips won't stretch without cracking.

"Let me bring you some espresso," he says, folding the Italian paper he was reading and laying it beside him.

"Marcello, do you think you could help me?"

I have to squint again to protect my eyes from the blinding smile he gives me as he nods emphatically. This man is the literal best.

"Certo. We are family soon, no?" He gestures with his hand for me to go on.

I exhale through my nose. Swallow my pride, nearly choking.

"Will you help me get out of here before Jeff and Tara wake up?"

His eyes twinkle like a Disney princess's and his grin widens.

"I see. I see," he says, nodding. "This is not a problem."

This is definitely a problem. But his words ease my frantic thoughts. The plan was to wait for Jeff until after his interview, drive home together. Maybe have some breakfast with T while he's off wooing a potential future employer. But the plan went out the window the moment I woke up in a negligée and not my "Who runs the world? Girls" t-shirt.

He continues, "You get the espresso. I will get your luggage. I will drive you to the station? When Tara awakens, I will explain."

"Marcello, thank you. You have no idea—"

He holds up his hand and waves me away.

"It is nothing. Niente," he says, patting my shoulder as he passes.

It is everything. Facing Jeff right now—after whatever the hell happened last night—I wouldn't be able to handle that and this hangover. I'm never drinking again—especially in his presence, if I'm ever in his presence again. Every time I think of him, my brain goes fuzzy and my stomach starts bouncing on a trampoline. I'm in way over my head and now I might have tied a brick to my ankle last night.

I pour as much espresso as I can into one of Tara's travel mugs and head for the door, grateful to see Marcello already there with my suitcase and his gleaming white teeth.

"Pronto?" he asks.

I nod even though I have no idea what he said.

"Andiamo, bella sorrella," he tells me, opening the door, and this one I know.

Andiamo, Marcello. Andiamo me the hell out of here—far, far away from the sleeping man-beauty.

Sister, Sister

Devon: I'm sorry I left. Did you get my note?

Tara: You mean the penis drawing you left
on my mirror using shaving cream?

Devon: I folded your panties for you and put
them under the sink.

Tara: Yeah, I found them when I went to get
a tampon. Weird choice.

Why'd you bolt?

Devon: Um. It might be normal for you to
wake up in a stranger's bed wearing Agent
Provacateur, but alas, I just wasn't raised
that way.

Tara: Ew. It's La Perla.

You do know that you were comatose by
the time that stranger brought you a plate of
dessert to check on you when he thought
you fell into another wall.

The stranger then came to fetch me to change you into something more comfortable and insisted he sleep on the couch until I told him I do not allow sleep sweat on my couch.

The stranger is taking us to breakfast right now to thank us for last night.

And the stranger was worried about you all morning because he knows you don't like to travel alone.

Devon: I panicked.

Tara: You don't say.

You should call him.

Devon: I can't.

Tara: I know you're scared. It's scary.

Devon: You are never scared. You are Xena: Warrior Princess. She-rah of Metropolis. Velma Dinkley.

Tara: Who the fuck is Velma Dinkley?

Devon: We are no longer sisters.

Tara: Anyway…

I'm always scared. Everyday. Give the man a chance.

I love you, nutty sister.

Devon: I love you more. I took the rest of the tiramisu from the fridge.

Tell Marcello I'll text him later.

Tara: I told him not to give you his number.

Devon: I got his mom's number, too.

Tara: Stopppppp.

Chapter Twenty-Nine

J eff

Lesson 30: Sometimes Meredith really does know best.

Devon is missing in action. And no one but me seems to think there's any cause for concern. It's been two weeks since Tara's apartment, undoubtedly long enough to nurse a hangover and rest her legs after sprinting full speed out of that bed and out of my life. Hell, she got over national humiliation in less time than this. But she hasn't texted —hasn't shown up for poker night or happy hour—and hasn't gone with us to CHOP to volunteer.

Syd tells me she isn't feeling well, which I believe is code for lying in bed watching *Vampire Diaries* so she doesn't have to see me, but that feels a little egocentric. Last week, Syd and I took a few selfies with the obnoxious positive message latex-free balloons Syd asked me to pick up for the patients, and sent them over to Devon. She sent back a thumbs up on the group chat. Not even a haha or a lol. I mean, I was holding a balloon that says Inhale Good Shit in front of my face and Syd held one that says Exhale Bullshit and all we got was a lousy thumbs up? This is more than just her usual avoidance. This is next level. And I feel a little pathetic, but every day that passes without the sound of her laughter or the sight of her smile makes the ache beneath my ribs spread deeper into my gut. I cannot separate my homesickness from my Devonsickness.

I sit down at the table by the window in the hospital's cafeteria and stare at my phone. It's been two days since I last reached out. Two days of waiting, checking my phone like an infatuated teeny bopper. Oh, and performing surgery, of course. I can feel the acid eating away at my serosa as the worry gnaws through my brain. With Devon m.i.a. and my sister avoiding me, I'm spiraling. Even the intense focus that usually washes over me in the OR is interrupted every so often by someone else's phone pinging and my desperate mind thinking it might be mine. It might be her.

I could just shoot her a quick text. She's teaching anyway, probably doing the Macarena for her eighth graders, wearing her "Surely, Not Everybody Was Kung Fu Fighting" tee shirt. I smile at the image. Lucky kids. They get a 180-day ticket to the Devon Gallagher one-woman show.

"Why are you smiling like that at your soft pretzel?" Kevin asks as he slips into the seat across from me.

I rub a hand over my face.

Kev looks me over and starts to unpack his lunch as his eyes assess.

"I've been meaning to talk to you," he says, opening each of the tiny Tupperware bins he's laid out with a pop. "—about Devon."

My pulse does the double Dutch at the mention of her name, but Kevin's tone tells it to settle the hell down.

"What about Devon?" I rip off a hunk of soft pretzel, count the salt flecks.

Kevin looks around like he's about to tell me the code for a nuclear missile launch. I follow his gaze to the bistro line, where Meredith waits in her white coat, her hands flitting around like humming birds as she chats with Dr. Asario, a senior pathologist.

"Mer would kill me if she knew this," Kev murmurs, "—but the night you had to stay at the hospital—" He lets out a long breath and looks down at the slices of cheese in one of his bins. He's got a goddamned charcuterie in front of him.

I want to interrupt him. Make him feel better, because I know what he's about to say—have known for some time. But it seems like he wants to get this out on his own, so I roll the pretzel between my fingers into a ball and wait.

"I got your message—that night," he breathes. "I got it and I didn't tell Devon and–"

"I know."

His eyes widen. "You know?"

I nod.

"Come on, Kev. You never miss a call. You're one of the most attentive, committed doctors I've ever met."

He shakes his head a little. The flush creeping up his neck stretches upward.

"I'm so sorry, man. I'm an ass. I've loved Devon from the moment she hit me in the testicles with a cornhole bag—but when I saw her have that panic attack and realized I'd caused it—"

It's like every cell in Kevin's body deflates at once. His shoulders fall, his neck seems unable to withstand the weight of his head. I want to tell him that I get it. Love makes us do stupid shit. But he holds up a hand before I can speak and says, "That's not love. You don't hurt the people you love like that. Lie to them. Withhold the truth at their expense—"

"What are you two morons talking about?" Mer asks, plopping her wrapped sandwich onto the table between us. She looks at Kevin and narrows her eyes as he stares down at his fig spread. "You're talking about Devon aren't you?"

I'm suddenly very hungry. I take a huge bite of the pretzel.

"Were you asking Kev why she's ghosting you?"

Kevin gives Mer the look that I give to Jenny whenever I want her to butt the hell out of my business. Meredith ignores him and hones in on me.

"Listen, Jeff. As much as this all started with the 'Great Sex Scare of 2025'—"

I choke a little on the doughy part of the pretzel.

"The great what?"

"—the situation has—evolved." Meredith points a finger and flicks her wrist making a little cyclone. I glance at Kevin for a translation.

"It's the time of year," he adds. "Devon always goes underground in November."

I imagine the glorious little shed having a trapdoor and Devon descending into a bunker with the chickens marching after her in a straight line.

"What do you mean?" I ask.

"November 9th is the anniversary of her dad's death," Kevin says quietly.

And there goes all the air in the room. And with it, my self-respect. I'm such an idiot. "An arrogant, prick," in Devon's words. Here I am obsessing, making this whole situation about me, and she's in pain—mucking through her grief, completely and utterly alone.

"Don't start beating yourself up about it, Jeffery." Meredith sticks a bony elbow into my flank. "She wouldn't want that. Which is why she goes off the grid—to avoid that look on your face."

I fix my face and pretend to listen to Kevin and Meredith as they argue about whether or not to go to the Eagle's game on Sunday, their words drifting past me with the buzz of conversation in the busy cafeteria. I even nod and smile when they direct some of those words at me.

But I don't stop thinking about her.

"Jefffff." Meredith's hand is fluttering in front of my face as she looks down at me from where she stands. She shakes her head and lets out a breath. I look to my right and notice that Kevin has packed up his honey and brie and is talking to the table next to us.

"Listen—," Mer says, sitting back down and dragging the seat towards me so she's uncomfortably close. "If you're this worried about her—"

I open my mouth to speak and she puts her palm against my lips more forcefully than necessary.

"Then you need to just man-up and go after her. Make it so she can't run. Corner her ass."

Of all the things I want to do to her ass, cornering it is not one.

"That doesn't feel right," I say when she slides her fingers away from my mouth. "Maybe she just needs to—"

"Devon *needs* somebody who's gonna show up, Jeff. She takes care of everyone—shows up for everyone else. Her students. Her friends. Her mom. She needs someone who will do the same for her. You gotta trust me on this," she says. She pats my leg. "Besides, it can't get much worse, right? She won't even answer your texts."

Shit. She has a point.

"I'll think about it," I promise.

She rolls her eyes and checks her apple watch.

"Think less. Do more."

And then she's walking away, murmuring something about men being pussies, and I'm stuck looking at the back of her white coat trying to hide just how much I want her to be right.

Chapter Thirty

D evon

Lesson 31: When he shows up, that's a good thing. When he shows up with cupcakes and Hugh Jackman, you're screwed.

Fridays—well Fun Fridays as my students call them—are normally my favorite. Even the sight of my eighth graders wearing the unicorn horns I bought at the dollar store and playing ring toss onto each other's heads after solving fraction problems didn't make me forget. Well, it did when the ring bounced off the Smartboard and hit me directly in the forehead. But that was only because I was stunned stupid for a moment. The second the bell rang and the desks were empty and quiet, I was right back where I started. Trapped in my head, empty and raw.

As I walk across my mom's yard, I see her through her oversized bay window, sitting at the kitchen table gesturing with her hands as her head nods and her lips move. She always keeps her shit together around this time of year for me, the selfless woman that she is. And in return I do the same, waiting till she makes her way to bed to let the mask slip off—let the looping thoughts pull me straight down into the bowels of a restless night.

November blows.

If Mom can fake it, then I can do the same. She's badass for the most part, crippling anxiety about leaving her property notwithstanding, but it is embarrassing that she's talking to Brutus like he's a human being. Her head falls back and she's laughing, and I shake my head, pulling my jacket tighter around my chest as I watch. It's one thing to talk at your dog, but to laugh like your dog is telling you a dirty joke—well I knew my mom had issues, but this is something else.

"Ma, I'm home," I holler as I push through the front door and let my bags schlump to the floor. I cringe at the sound. That's a pile of 127 pre-tests that I stared at during my prep whilst I should have been grading. Four hours worth of grading and sorting to look forward to. This is what comes of breaking your rules.

"Devon, honey. You're early," my mom says in a pitch that makes me wonder if she's been drinking already. Not that I can blame her. I'd have started two hours ago if I hadn't been at my desk.

"It's 4:30—the time I get home every day," I say, stepping into the kitchen. It takes me a moment to process what my eyes are sending to my brain.

Handsome familiar man.

Familiar kitchen setting.

Very familiar woman I call mother.

"Hi," Jeff says as he stands. Brutus doesn't bother to move from where he's sprawled over Jeff's toes.

"Hi," I whisper. I feel like I'm in some awkward scene of a teenage movie. My cheeks feel warm and I turn a little to catch sight of my mom staring at me with this brutal wide-eyed look that says "if you don't jump him, I will." I roll my eyes at her and turn back to Jeff.

"What are you doing here?" I ask, and it comes out too harsh. As usual. But he doesn't flinch. Jeff is used to me by now.

"I wanted to check on you," he says.

"Check on me?" I repeat as I try to shush my heart so he doesn't hear it slamming against my sternum like the Blue Man Group pounding trash can lids. Dumbass heart.

I glance at my mom for answers and she's smiling so big I want to throw something at her.

"You wouldn't answer and I haven't seen you since—I just wanted to make sure you're..."

He trails off and I lift a brow and look him over. He's in jeans and the soft grey tee with the little tear on the sleeve that he seems to live in on the weekends. His hair is damp, and it curls around his ears, no sight of the stubble he usually sports after a day at work. Did he shave for this? I almost ask when I catch my mom looking between us like her neck is on a swivel setting. I clear my throat and tilt my head in a very unsubtle way toward the closest kitchen exit.

She lifts up her hands and submits.

"Lovely speaking to you, Jeff. I do hope you can join us for dinner. And dessert. And maybe break—"

"Mom."

"Alright. Alright. I'll be upstairs. With my beats on, music blaring, not listening to whatever you two—"

"Mom!"

She turns to leave and Jeff calls after her, "Goodnight, Mrs.—"

"Jeff, for the last time, if you don't call me Kathy, I'll make you clean the chicken shit off the deck," Mom says as she ascends.

I wrinkle my nose and shudder. I had to use a window scraper last time.

I shift my focus back to Jeff, whose dimple is in full effect as he watches my mother slide out of the kitchen with Brutus following close behind.

"She has your sense of humor," he says.

"I'm way funnier than her," I tell him. He doesn't look convinced.

"Seriously, you didn't need to come all the way over here. I'm fine. Really."

He lifts a brow. Makes a patronizing noise in the back of his throat. "Fine doesn't go into hiding for weeks at a time," he says.

Who does this man think he is? Telling me I'm not fine. Pffft.

"Don't tell me my business, Dr. Dick. I don't go around telling you who and how to slice and dice."

He slides his hands out of his pockets and leans back against the island.

"As fun as this is, I'm not here to fight with you."

I let my face fall into a pretend pout. "Then why are you here?"

"I'm 'showing up'," he tells me, making air quotes. Like I'm supposed to know what that means.

"Stalking and 'showing up' are two different animals." I air quote right back, but move to the opposite side of the kitchen island for safety reasons. I refold a dishtowel a few times, avoiding the intensity of his gaze.

Meredith told me earlier today that Jeff was worried—that I should call him. But I didn't think he'd "show up" here like this. Looking all kind and concerned and hot AF. I know if I lift his shirt I'll see my best friend's name scrawled across his chest because this has Meredith written all over it. I open the fridge and grab two beers, talking over my shoulder like his presence is not sending my body into hyperdrive.

I slide the beer across the island toward where Jeff is standing, eyeing me like I'm not a sweaty, disheveled mess who played five classes worth of Unicorn Fraction Horn Toss—like my eyes aren't bloodshot and red rimmed and lifeless from sleepless nights of sorrow.

"What's that?" I take a sip of beer and point at the paper bag on the table next to a bunch of DVDs.

Jeff doesn't look away from my face.

"I brought movies," he says smoothly.

"I see that, but why did you go all Fred Flinstone and bring DVDs?"

He shrugs. "I noticed your mom had a DVD player last time I was here."

"Another tally under the stalker column," I murmur into my beer.

"And the other bag is Maggie's," he says in a tone that clearly says I don't deserve it.

Bastard! Cupcakes again? I had a hard enough time rationalizing the last ones. I try to step away, but my hand reaches for the bag like an out of control go-go-gadget arm.

"Am I still a stalker?" he asks, sliding the bag away from me.

"Stalkers aren't always bad," I tell him, gathering control and reaching for one of the DVDs instead. "Take that nice gentleman from *YOU*. Always thinking of her and..." I lose track of my rambling and pull the discs toward me and check the titles.

The Italian Job. Beautiful setting. Beautiful people. Good choice.

I nod and pick up the next.

The Greatest Showman. Love that shit. Musicals are my jam. It's like Jeff can see right into my showtune singing soul.

I reach for the third and he steps between me and the table nearly knocking the beer out of my hand.

"Jeff—" He's so tall. I'm like up to his right nipple and it's so annoying. "Give me the DVD. I just want to see—"

"No. That one was a mistake," he says as he looks down at me.

"Come on. The other ones are perfect. Just let me see."

He shakes his head and I'm staring at the muscle in his neck while I try to reach around his back to grab it out of his hand.

"Devon, trust me," he says, barely having to try to keep it out of my reach.

Our bodies are fully pressed together and I suddenly realize that every inch of me is tingling like I've been massaged for hours. I step back. Stumble a little. Giggle as I catch my balance on the back of a chair. What the hell is wrong with me? I'm delirious. Out of my mind. He smells like he rolled around naked in dryer sheets. I take another slow, deliberate step backward.

"Ok. Jeff. So, what's the plan here. Hypnotize me with Zac Efron and Marky Mark then fill me with sugar until I forget my sorrow?"

He nods, his genuine smile making me forget the sorrow that I'm supposed to be future-forgetting.

"Yeah. Sugar and beer, though," he corrects.

"Sugar and beer," I repeat.

He lifts his brow and waits, like I need to agree to this. Like he didn't already ensure that I'd have to agree to it when he showed up in my mother's kitchen, bewitching her with his charisma and dimple depth. Damn, I just want to say yes. Enjoy this—whatever the hell it is. But I know that's not in the cards. I look down at the nicks in the butcher block counter and probe at one with my finger.

"You know this—" I point between us, "—can't—"

"Devon, did you ever think that this—," he mimics my motion, "—might be something you and I can't control."

"Do you know what an asymptote is, J.J.?" I ask, trying hard not to meet his gaze.

"The curve thing that—"

"The curve is the curve. The asymptote is something else. You are the curve."

He steps around the counter, slowly, like I might bolt again at any moment and I hold up my hand and point. He stops.

"You are the curve," I repeat. "And I am the asymptote. You can get really, really close to the asymptote. But the curve will never touch the asymptote. Are you catching what I'm throwing here, Jeff?"

He looks amused. There is nothing amusing about analytical geometry metaphors.

"You are amazing," he says softly, stepping forward. I freeze.

He runs a finger beneath my chin. I shut my eyes. Focus on the trail of heat he's left across my skin. "Look, asymptote. Curve is touching you."

"That's not what—"

"Besides, I'm not here to touch you," he whispers. "I'm here to help."

My shoulders sag. No touching. Right. Do I need help? I mean, I can't move from this spot, so I might need help with that.

When I open my eyes, he's staring down at me and I feel like I did when I broke mom's car window with a tennis racquet and an acorn. I'm in so much fucking trouble. I could run down the block and hide in the woods like I did when the glass shattered, leaving Tara to take the fall.

"If I throw you out, can I keep the cupcakes?" I ask, my voice too raspy.

"No."

I sigh. "Fine."

I step backwards, hand on the edge of the counter. Maybe he can help. Better this than a night with my mom pretending not to know what day it is. "You can stay. But I need to wash the eighth graders off of me."

He laughs when I crinkle my nose as I process my own words.

"Ew. That came out wrong—"

"Go take a shower, Devon," he says, saving me from myself.

I lift my beer toward him and take my leave, telling my dumdum heart to knock off its shit while I take the steps two at a time.

Chapter Thirty-One

Jeff

Lesson 32: Give her space. Give her cupcakes. But do not give her "Fifty Shades."

I'm tipping the pizza delivery guy when I hear Devon laughing uncontrollably from the kitchen.

"Thanks, man. Drive safe," I say, closing the door between us, trying to wipe the cheesy smile I'm sporting off of my face as I make my way through the living room with the pizzas. Her laughter is pure joy.

"You can't be serious, Jeff," she says, her grin so bright it makes the Edison bulbs above the island look dim. Her hair is wet and pulled into a bun on top of her head, her skin glowing.

Shit. She's holding the third DVD I hid beneath the fruit bowl.

"I told you it was a mistake," I say, placing the pizzas on the table and reaching to snatch the disc out of her hand. She dodges my grab and scurries around to the other side of the island, her oversized sweatpants nearly catching under her feet and making her fall.

"I want to know what you were thinking when you chose '50 Shades' from the machine," she says, her brows merging with her hairline. I'd pick the damn movie again if I got to see her smile like this all night.

I let out a breath. Look to the ceiling.

"Let's call your mom down—"

"To watch soft-core porn with us?"

"To eat the pizza."

She shakes her head.

"Kathy won't be joining us for dinner. She's requested room service," she says, eyes still glittering. "Shame though. She does love herself some S & M."

"You're impossible," I say.

"Impossibly awesome."

Devon slides the DVD across the island to me and winks, then turns to grab some plates from the cabinet. As she lifts onto her toes and reaches upward, her shirt lifts a little exposing the skin at her back. The memory of how soft and warm she was that night on the dance floor makes me grip the edge of the counter. I remind myself why I'm here. To comfort. To listen. Not to ogle.

She turns and meets my gaze, freezes with the plates against her chest. It's like every time she sees me in her kitchen, her brain needs to re-acclimate.

"What do you want to watch first?" she asks, swallowing hard.

"It's your night. Your choice."

"Ok. Efron it is," she says, looking down at her fuzzy pink socks.

"It's a shame I didn't bring anything with Henry Cavill. You know you thought I was him the first night that we met?"

She makes a disbelieving noise and moves toward the pizza boxes. "You didn't actually let my hallucinations go to your head, did you?

Awww. You did. That's sooo—cute?" She tilts her head and gives me an overstated pitying look as she lifts the lid.

This—the teasing and banter—feels too damn good.

"Not everything patients say when the anesthesia wears off is nonsense. In fact, I've heard patients profess their love for people who they never had the guts to tell because of those pesky inhibitions," I tell her. Really, I heard a girl tell a pack of saltines she'd love them forever. But still.

"Mistaking you for Henry Cavill is hardly a declaration of love," she says.

"I didn't say that it was. But it's a declaration of something."

She pulls a slice of pizza onto each plate, narrows one eye at me as she licks the cheese from her fingers.

"You know you are barking up a dead tree—"

"The wrong tree," I correct.

"Yeah, a dead tree is the wrong tree." She takes a bite of pizza, chews slowly, and keeps her eyes on me. "See this shirt." She points to her chest. "It says 'damaged goods'."

It doesn't. It says 'Beer me, bitch.'

"We're all damaged, Devon. Stop trying to push me away and go feed your mom and meet me on the couch."

To my surprise, she doesn't argue. Just lets out a long, uneven breath and picks up a plate, then heads out of the kitchen and up the steps.

I grab the other two slices and a couple of beers from the fridge, and head to the living room, setting it all down on the coffee table in front of the couch. I don't know what I expected to find here, but a laughing, joking Devon was not it. If it weren't for the fact that I've been infatuated with the dancing light in her eyes since that night in recovery, I would never have noticed its absence tonight. But infatuated I am. And so I recognize her humor for what it is. Another coping mechanism—a tool to cover and avoid. She's a world class illusionist.

Confirming my thought, Devon appears from nowhere with a cupcake in one hand and a beer in the other.

"It's Efron time, baby!" she yells in an NFL coach's voice. She lets out a whoop-whoop and does a little fist pump with the cupcake hand, then grabs the DVD and pops it into the player. When she turns and straightens, all of her focus lowers to her cupcake. She rolls her tongue around the top of the icing, and shuts her eyes.

A low sound escapes me before I can swallow it.

"What?" she asks.

Damn it. She hears everything. Teacher senses.

"Nothing," I say.

"That dramatic teenage girl exhale was not nothing. That's the sound Syd makes when I make her focus on pre-calc." She takes another swig of her beer and watches me. I was not thinking of pre-calc.

"Really it was just—it was a cleansing breath."

She takes a step forward, pulls one side of her mouth upward. The white bulbs in the recessed lighting above are sending streaks of copper through her thick hair and I can't stop imagining the way it might feel wrapped around my fingers. Devon seems to see into my mind because a dusting of red spreads across her cheek bones. She lowers her eyes and lets out a breath.

"What?" I ask.

My heart is stuck in this frantic rhythm, the too fast tempo of a song your feet can't keep up with.

"Nothing," she says, but her voice is thicker—warmer. "Just a cleansing breath."

She swallows, the freckle just above her clavicle jumps and settles, then she turns away and plops into the center of the couch.

I stay put, take the time to pull my shit together and stop the tachycardia she's triggered. She needs comfort. And I need to back off. And get my heart rate steady. But I know that all the cleansing breaths in the world aren't going to steady this. I'm fucked. Head-over-heels fucked. And if I really let myself look closely, I know that I have been for a while. Every piece of me is pulling toward her, except that one reasonable part of my brain, saying, "don't be a selfish shit, Jeff." Give her what she needs. Maybe I should head out back and scrape the chicken shit. That'll cool me down.

I take a long swig of my beer and roll my shoulders once, grab onto that reasonable voice in my mind, and get ready to face that cupcake.

Doc, Doc, Goose

Tara: Anyone heard from Devon tonight?

Meredith: She won't text me back either.

Kevin: That's because Jeff went over to
check on her.

Tara: WHATTTTT!

Meredith: About time.

Kevin: He just needed a gentle shove.

Tara: I'm gonna call her.

Meredith: Leave her alone, T! She might
actually be getting laid.

Kevin: There's no way in hell she's going to
sleep with him tonight, of all nights.

Meredith: Is someone jealous?

Tara: I'm with Kevin. Devon won't be able to
get it up tonight.

Meredith: Fine. I give him til' Sunday to close the deal.

Kevin: I'll take that bet. Dev's got on that chastity belt from Robin Hood: Men in Tights.

Tara: I'm still with Kev. Except I don't know what that is.

Meredith: Kevin. You are a fucking nerd. And a hundred dollars Jeff ends Dev's dry spell by sundown on Sunday.

Kevin: I call.

Tara: I'm in.

No outside involvement though.

Meredith: Obviously. It's not like I'm gonna handcuff them together naked or something.

Kevin: Oh man. Here we go.

Tara: Ohhhhhh. I remember! Call the locksmith! haha

Meredith: Please don't humor him, T.

Chapter Thirty-Two

evon

Lesson 33: Be careful with grief. It can push you over the edge.

My emotions are in hyperdrive. I can't keep my leg from bouncing like a sugar-stoned kid on a trampoline. After all those cupcakes, I just might *be* sugar-stoned. And Jeff keeps putting his hand on my thigh to stop it—like that's going to help calm my neurons.

It's not enough that Hugh Jackman and Zac are doing an Irish jig on a bar like they do with less clothes in my dreams twice a week, but Jeff keeps watching me with this adorably cautious expression and asking if I need another cupcake/beer/slice. I want to kiss him so badly that I keep shoving cupcakes in my mouth to keep it occupied. On top of all that, I'm fighting back tears every time something beautiful happens on the screen—and spoiler alert—something beautiful happens every thirty seconds in this goddamned movie. Neither the cupcakes, nor the rapid blinking back of tears is making Jeff's gaze any less tantalizing. And so we are stuck in this vicious, delicious cycle.

I have nothing left to fight whatever the hell is happening here. There's no logic left—just pure, raw emotion. I just keep hearing Meredith's voice in my head. *There's no harm in just one night with him.* A sexual energy purge. I can do just sex. I can. I mean I'm not in college anymore when I had to have Tara paged to the front office of our high school after my first one-night stand so she could comfort me and tell me I was neither pregnant with twins nor infected with trichomoniasis. I'm infinitely more mature now. And I need to take care of this itch before I go insane. I'll still be in control—still be following the rules. Nothing more than sex.

I dab a cookie crumb off the top of my cupcake with the tip of my tongue.

"For chrissakes, Devon. Just eat the darned thing," Jeff murmurs.

"What's your issue with my cupcake?" I ask, lifting it from my lap and taking another swipe at the top with my tongue.

Jeff exhales again and presses pause on the movie. I put him in control of the remote because I didn't want to throw it through the screen at the part where the red-headed woman kisses a married Hugh.

"It's not so much the cupcake I have issue with," Jeff says through gritted teeth. "It's more she who eats it and how she eats it."

My brows fly upward. "Who me?"

He pushes his lips together.

"Yeah, you." He rubs his palms together like he's charging up a defibrillator. We sound like the beginning of *Who Stole the Cookie from the Cookie Jar?* and I can't help but giggle while he adds, "I think you know exactly what you're doing."

Hmmmm. Do I? It's true that I usually don't make a soft moaning sound when I eat a cupcake. I mean, maybe sometimes when they are warm or if I haven't had one in a while, but still. Typically, there's no room in my throat to get sound around the unladylike, masticated lump of cake.

He goes on before I have time to decide what I do or do not know. He leans forward with his elbows on his knees. "I think—maybe you are trying to torture me. Or distract yourself and me from why I'm here." The tendons in his forearm tighten when he makes a fist, but his voice is rough and intense.

I swallow hard past the lingering taste of the icing. Do I want to torture Jeff? I mean he did seem intent on torturing me for a solid part of our ever-evolving relationship. So maybe. Distract myself. Most def.

"I'm just trying to keep my mouth occupied," I say. The truth will set you free. Unfortunately, it also makes Jeff's eyes narrow in on my lips.

"Is that right?" he says, his voice so deep it vibrates inside of me. "What is it you're scared your mouth will do?"

I shrug, lower the cupcake onto the coffee table, and scooch my ass closer to him. He shuts his eyes slowly, his thick lashes leaving a shadow across his cheekbones.

"Devon," he says on an exhale. "You are making doing the right thing impossible—"

"The right thing is overrated," I tell him. He opens his eyes and drinks me in. I want to hand him five straws. Drink away, Jeff.

"I want to be here for you," he says softly. "I know what today is."

And someone just dumped a Gatorade cooler of ice water on me.

"Arghhhhh. Why couldn't you just distract me?" I hiss, sliding my ass back over. "Why!"

He winces. "That's not what you need."

"Jesus, Jeff. Stop telling me what I need!" I stand up and make my way behind the couch, the perfect pacing spot. I'm a tigress at feeding time. And I just want Jeff to stick a finger through the bar. I need to bite. "Do you do this to Jenny and your mom?"

He flinches a little and looks at his hands. I hold my tongue between my teeth to stop myself from lashing out and saying what he knows I'm thinking. *No wonder they aren't calling you back.* It's such a bitchy thing to say that I actually surprise myself with the thought.

"Is it so absurd to just want to forget for a minute?" I ask, softer.

"No, of course not." His voice sounds pained. "But—"

"Then stop being so friggin' noble," I tell him as I head for the wall. Step. Step. Yell. "Stop being Stefan. Be Damon, goddamn it!" Step. Step. Pivot.

His hands are on my shoulders when I turn, and our chests are pressed together, and lordy—his hands—they are so damn big, and I want them to erase all of this anger and grief. I don't want to look up from the soft grey fabric that stretches from shoulder to shoulder, to take my eyes off the way his chest rises against mine and then falls away, making me feel so lonely.

"I'm sorry, Devon. I wish I could take it away," he whispers into my hair, and I lift my gaze slowly, up over the way his pulse jumps against the smooth skin beneath his ear. Over his lips, parted enough that I can feel his warm breath on my hair. Over his eyes where I stop and lose my breath completely. Rational thought has left the building. I'm drowning in this liquid heat that lifts me onto my toes, closes the distance between my mouth and his. I kiss him softly at first, a question whispered from the back row of the class, and for an instant I think he doesn't know the answer, but then, yes, he does. He knows every answer to every question I'll ever ask because the way he kisses me back is unlike anything I've ever felt. It claims me. Tugs me closer. Tells me that there is no close enough. The taste of him—the soft growl he makes when my teeth graze his lower lip. I want him plastered on me like a poster. His tongue finds mine and I forget my name. Holy Christmas. I want all of it. His hands are on my ass. My legs are wrapped around him. I can feel every inch of what he's offering. And the only truth I know is that I want it.

My moan mingles with the sound of my name being prayed against my ear and I realize that he's stopped—my mouth is no longer on his. I feel the wall against my back and try to steady my breath as I register that he's holding me here, that I can still feel him hard against me and all I need in life is to arch into him—get him closer to me. But he's still praying my name and I remind myself I'm not a goddess. I'm just a ball of hot, aching energy that wants to forget whatever it was that I'm supposed to be forgetting.

"Devon. We can't. Not like this."

Yes. We can. Just. Like. This.

I almost whisper please into his mouth, knowing that he's one lick away from giving into anything I ask, but then he pulls back and his eyes meet mine and our breath mingles together between us. The way he's looking at me—so much desire mixed with so much compassion—it breaks me. His pain—the way he seems to be a conduit for everything I'm feeling—wrecks me like a pickaxe slicing through snow. My forehead finds the dip between his pecs and his arms wrap around me and all of the ice and rock I let pile up in layers, those mountains of protective bullshit, the Jenga towers of control, come crumbling down onto Jeff while I shake and sob against him. Somewhere in the background, Hugh Jackman sings about coming alive and I wish it were that easy.

Dr. Hotass—formerly Dr. Dick

Dr. Hotass—formerly Dr. Dick: Can I take you somewhere after CHOP?

Devon: Who's this?

Dr. Hotass—formerly Dr. Dick: The man who carried your snoring ass upstairs and tucked you in last night.

Devon: Oh god. That's creepy as hell.

Thank you for last night. I blame the cupcakes for that crash.

I'm sorry I passed out on you.

And cried on you.

Dr. Hotass—formerly Dr. Dick: And drooled cupcake icing on me.

Devon: To be clear, you are asking me on a date tonight?

Dr. Hotass—formerly Dr. Dick: Do you want it to be a date?

I could invite Kevin and Mer along.

Devon:

Do you want me to bring 50 Shades on our date tonight?

Dr. Hotass—formerly Dr. Dick: Nah. I think we have enough ammunition.

Devon: Do you have a Red Room in that granny apartment of yours?

Dr. Hotass—formerly Dr. Dick: Save some surprises for later, Devon.

Devon: Can I call you, sir?

Dr. Hotass—formerly Dr. Dick: See you soon, Cupcake.

Devon:

Chapter Thirty-Three

J eff

Lesson 34: Beware teenage drivers.

"Tell me which bridge I'm supposed to take home again."

"Syd, honey there's at least four bridges that will take you back to Jersey. And you have the app telling you directions," Devon says, patting Syd's arm.

I can barely hear the two of them over the wind that's attacking me from all angles. When I'd hopped into the convertible this morning and asked Syd why the hell the top was down in November, she'd pointed to the sun and told me she needed all of the vitamin D she could get.

"Ok. You're right. I got this. You two need to be careful though. There's some really bad parts in Philly," Syd yells over the wind as her speedometer needle approaches 70 mph. Like Philly is what's endangering us right now.

We are flying down Christopher Columbus Boulevard at a speed that would surely eject me across the river into Camden if I were stupid enough not to wear a seatbelt and we were to crash.

Devon throws me a look over her shoulder. Despite the adorable protective vibe Syd's got going for Devon and my genuine admiration for Sydney as an overall wonderful human being, I cannot wait to get the hell out of this car. Alive.

Not to mention I'm desperate to get Devon alone again. Volunteering today was rewarding as always, but was a special kind of torture every time our gazes met or our hands accidentally—or not so accidentally—brushed. It was impossible to focus with her in the room. It's impossible to focus when she's not in the room. Because no matter where I go, she's dancing across my brain like it's her stage.

"Syd, slow down," Devon tells her again, hitting the imaginary brake in front of her and grabbing for a nonexistent oh-shit handle.

I need to put an end to this. I lean forward between them. "Alright, we're here," I lie. Better to walk the rest of the way along the waterfront than to die in a Volkswagen Beetle.

Syd screeches to a halt and finds what she thinks is a parking spot but is actually the right turn lane onto Market. I don't correct her and neither does Devon.

"You two be careful tonight. Don't drink and drive," Syd tells us as I climb out over the back of the beetle.

"We don't have a car," Devon points out.

"And remember that the pull-out meth—"

"Byeee, Syd. Text me when you're home safe." Devon shuts the door and points to the line of cars trying to make a right hand turn behind her, their drivers beeping and cursing out their windows. Syd just smiles and gives us a little wave before taking the turn onto Market Street on two wheels.

"Who the hell gave her a license?" I wonder aloud.

"She's worse than Cher from Clueless," Devon answers as the tiny blue bubble disappears from view.

A burst of freezing air rushes up from the river and crosses the busy street, sending Devon's hair across her face. I step toward her, push the soft strands back in place behind her ear as she takes in the sight of the brightly lit Ferris wheel planted on the riverbanks in Penn's Landing. At the base of the wheel, dozens of people slide and spin on ice skates, partaking in the music and laughter that surrounds the outdoor skating rink.

"This is amazing," she says.

"You've never been here?"

I take her hand, lead her to the crosswalk.

"Nah. I've heard Kev and Mer talk about it. They came a lot the year it first opened, but I was in grad school that summer," she explains. She adjusts her grip on my hand so that her fingers slip between mine. "I guess they lost interest."

"Well, Mer does like to mix it up," I point out. "Are you warm enough?"

"I'm fine. She keeps texting me dirty memes today. I don't know what the hell is up with her," she tells me as we dodge the people leaving the landing and make our way around those in line for the carousel. A kid is screaming at his dad that he needs cotton candy. Devon sticks out her lip a little like she's commiserating with the kid —or maybe the dad—who's trying his best to redirect the kid's attention away from the hanging clouds of pink and blue sugar above him.

"Weird. Kevin has been texting me a lot today, too. Giving me unsolicited dating advice," I tell her.

"Who are you dating?"

I blow out a breath, and we both watch it hang above us in the air.

"If I recall correctly, it was you who kept calling tonight a date" I say with a smile. "Kev also wanted to know how you are doing. I told him you're fine."

"Am I?" she asks, stopping in front of the carnival game where you have to fill the toilet with your water gun. Her hands are sunk into her kangaroo pocket. The neon lights dance across her eyes.

"I think so. Or I hope so," I say.

She chews on her bottom lip and looks down at her shoes.

"I wouldn't be, Jeff. If it weren't for you," she says softly. "Usually, I spend this weekend in fetal position every moment that my mom's not around."

My heart clenches in time with my fists.

"Your mom hides it almost as well as you, huh?"

She nods once. "I hear her at night sometimes—when she thinks I'm asleep—"

I reach for her hand in her pocket—squeeze it as I imagine that gut crushing feeling of witnessing your own mother's sorrow.

"But yeah. She hides it well. My dad was the love of her life. He was a liver surgeon at Penn. Constantly getting called in like Kev— saving their lives, leaving his life. And then, one day, he gets a call for a liver harvest—" her mouth turns up at the corner, "just before the call he threw a piece of toast at me and said 'Can't wait to *toast* your mother.' He made the worst dad jokes." She sucks in a breath and looks out over the river.

"Then he left—got in the helicopter with the team to go be a hero like the thousand times before. Did you know they don't use helicopters for procurements anymore? Because of the danger. Of course they figured that out *after*. Too late." She shakes her head and lifts her eyes to the sky. Her voice drops so low that it's nearly carried away in the screams and laughter around us.

"We were celebrating my parents' anniversary with dinner in the city that night and he just—didn't show up. And that was that. End of story," she says.

End of story. The way she says those words makes the bright lights around us dim to grey. Her pain rushes through me, a flash flood that steals the words and breath from my throat. I force myself to ignore it, just like I do when I need to deliver bad news to a family after an operation gone wrong.

"I'm so sorry, Devon," I tell her, tipping her chin back toward me so she knows I mean it. A tear slides down the side of her face and I catch it with my thumb. "His story goes on with you and Tara and your mom. You are his story."

She nods like she knows this, but I can see by the set of her mouth that the words aren't helping.

"I can't help but think—if he'd just been something boring. Sold copy machines or worked at a desk. He'd still be here. My mom would be—"

Shrieking laughter cuts her short when a lone seagull attacks a group of girls behind us and they bump into her as they run for cover, clutching their funnel cakes to their chests.

"Sorry," one girl says as she swats at the bird.

Devon laughs as they retreat, then looks up at me and smiles.

"I'm ok. By Monday, I'll be good as new. Right as rain."

She lifts her brows and tilts her head, asking me to play along. So I do.

"By Monday, you'll be dancing around and singing like Julia Andrews for your students."

She fights a laugh.

"You got a thing for Julia Andrews?" she asks.

"My sister used to make me pretend to be Bert from Mary Poppins."

She chuckles and I feel it warm the air around me.

"I'd love to see a little Chim Chim Cher-ee action. You want a drink, first?" she asks, tilting her head toward a shipping container lined with taps. The lights from the Ferris wheel are spinning in her glassy eyes.

I step toward her, lower my face closer to hers. Her hair smells like the lavender my mom grows along the side of the house. She smells like home. She closes her eyes, her lips part just enough for me to see her tongue and remember how it felt on mine.

"A drink sounds good," I whisper against her ear lobe. She shudders and leans into me. My body responds and I know she feels it from the hitch in her breathing and the flush of her cheeks. I feel buzzed already, no beer required. I plant a soft kiss on her cheekbone and tear myself away to grab some liquid distraction.

When I return with two plastic pints, she's talking to the little boy who'd been screaming for cotton candy, the Dad smiling at her while she hands the kid one of her blue multi-stringed bracelets that she wears around her wrist. The little boy is clearly smitten. I don't blame him because Devon is giving him the most dazzling smile in her arsenal and telling him that the bracelet grants whoever wears it the power to change the world. She has lots of these little string bracelets, a collection of causes that she supports.

I wait until the little boy runs off pretending to shoot web from the new gift on his wrist, his father close behind yelling thank you over his shoulder, then I close the distance and hand her the drink.

"Why don't you teach elementary school?" I ask.

She thanks me for the beer and gives me a look that say Oh-Fuck-No.

"I'm serious. You're obviously great with younger kids."

We start to walk along the boardwalk, sipping our beers as the sky over the river begins to bleed and burn with layers of red and orange. The sun dips lower between the towering buildings to the west and the reflection of the lights hanging in the trees around us swims and glitters along the surface of the dark water. The sweet smell of funnel cake mingles with fried steak and I watch Devon check out every food vendor that we pass.

"I love kids. They can sense that. But middle schoolers are where it's at," she tells me.

Interesting. From what I understand of adolescence, "middle schooler" is the least beloved stage of development.

"I don't think everyone would agree with you," I point out, adding on, "you want something to eat?" When I see her eyes widen at the sight of a taco truck, I know her answer.

"Everyone who doesn't agree is wrong," she tells me. "And hell yes."

We fall in line with the people awaiting their turn to order their tacos and burritos. Devon is taking in every person who passes with open curiosity and a smile. I can't stop staring at her mouth.

"Basically, what I've realized," she tells me, and I try to remember what we were talking about. "Is that everyone needs to be educated about those years of life. The psychology behind them is pivotal for raising mentally healthy people. But no one, not even most educators, feel equipped to handle what these kids are going through. And, believe me, the teachers ask for training, but they are rarely given what they need. No one wants to watch these kids suffer. So that age gets a bad rep. It's just not fair. They shouldn't have to feel the weight of other people's ignorance."

I think back to what it was like to watch Jenny struggle at that age. I remember the comments. *Why don't you just make her eat? She's thirteen. She's just doing this for attention.*

Ignorance didn't even begin to cover it.

"How do we educate that many people?" I ask.

Devon looks at me like she's forgotten I was beside her, hanging on her every word.

"Doctors would be a good start. Partnering with educators to ensure that there's mental health curriculum in the schools. Training teachers how to make the students feel safe. There's an amazing professor from Stanford who's trailblazing this agenda. Dr. Basantis. She's been out in front for years, teaching college level classes, launching studies on student mental health, and hacking at the bull-shit red tape that comes with mental health."

She's obviously given this a lot of thought and research.

"Why don't you call her? Or contact the APA?"

She shakes her head.

"I've spoken to the American Psychological Association. They are pulled so thin that a union with the education system is like asking to see a leprechaun riding a unicorn. And I'm sure the last thing Dr. Basantis needs is some middle school math teacher up her ass. This woman is far too busy fighting the good fight," she says.

"Maybe she needs foot soldiers. Or maybe you need to go at it from the inside—approach your district and school board."

She gives a humorless laugh.

"Oh, I've tried. I teach in an area more concerned with appearances and standardized test scores than mental health. My district's number one item is protecting their asses from lawsuits, so no one wants to talk about the scars on Suzy's thigh or Kayla dropping pounds like they're going out of style. They want to hide that shit, so other parents don't complain."

Ah. I nod. I know these areas. I grew up in one as well.

"Unbelievable," I murmur.

"But unfortunately, true," she says. "I almost lost Syd because of their bullshit. My principal told me not to call her mom. That the school nurse had sent the information about her weight in the yearly physical. Syd was nearing crisis, so I went to the guidance counselor, who happens to be a good friend of mine, and ignored him. It could have gone badly. But Syd's mom was at her wit's end and just wanted to save her daughter, so we were met with gratitude instead of defensiveness. Thank goodness."

"Syd is amazing," I tell her.

She beams at me like I've just complimented her instead of her old student, then steps up to the counter to give her order. As much as I feel the frustration pouring out of her when she discusses the shortcomings of her school system, I love how her free hand flutters and flies when she talks about this. Her passion is so intense I can feel it buzzing over her skin, waiting to jolt anyone who needs a wake-up call. I order and pay, then step to the side to wait for our food with her. She's obviously deep in thought as she sips at her beer.

"Sydney is like a little sister to me," she explains. "Most teachers and definitely all administrators think it's crazy to have a relationship like that with a former student."

"And you? What do you think?"

She takes a long sip of her beer, swallows, pushes her hair back over the top of her ear.

"I think it saves lives," she says. Her tone is so certain that I can't imagine the fools who keep her from doing what she believes is right.

Our order slides out toward us on the counter and I grab it while Devon shoves packets of hot sauce in her pocket, then I lead the way toward the floating garden. Of all of the amazing things this city has to offer, this barge is high on my list of favorites. We walk around the hollowed-out rectangle that juts out into the river and I watch Devon's eyes widen as she takes in the drifting pads of live greenery that float around in the watery middle. I let her take it in, feeling lucky Kev and Mer never brought her here. I get to witness the way she lights from within, releasing a nervous soft giggle, when she sees what's waiting for us at the far end of the barge. I motion for her to sit.

"What the hell is this?" she asks with a laugh.

"It's a net, Sherlock."

She looks at the people in the net beside the one in front of us, then scans the entire row of net loungers. Our neighbors have their legs outstretched toward the railing, relaxing on their elbows, a blanket wrapped around their shoulders, staring out at the darkening sky behind the huge Battleship stationed permanently across the water. She leans over the net and looks down into the dark sloshing water that runs beneath it.

"Are there sharks?" She sticks her toe out toward the net lounge and looks at me as if I've asked her to go skydiving.

"In the river?"

She points to the baseball park across the water. "Camden Riversharks."

She's dead serious. I try not to laugh.

"You want me to sit on this?" she asks again, toeing the rope.

I laugh and step out onto the ropes, carefully balancing the two baskets of food in one hand and my beer in the other. I lower myself to a crouch and hold out the tacos like bait.

"If you want your tacos, you'll have to."

"Holding tacos hostage is low, Jeff. Even for you." She steps out onto the net and uses the top of my head to steady herself when she tips to the side a little.

"You are so insanely graceful."

She plops down beside me and gives me the finger before grabbing her taco basket from my lap.

"Motor skills were never my forte," she says before taking a huge bite of the softshell brimming with meat and cheese.

"That explains the injury," I tell her. The carne asada smells almost as amazing as her hair. "What is your forte?"

She chews slowly, her eyes closed while she savors the meat and cheese. I'm reminded of the goddamned cupcakes.

"Not this again," I murmur to the sky.

She licks her lips and chuckles, then answers my question.

"I'm sure you've picked up on my many strengths." She puts her fingers out and starts to tic them off. "Rule-making. Chicken husbandry. Classroom pageantry. Algebra. Karaoke—"

"That last one was a surprise to me," I tell her around another bite.

She freezes, processing what I'm saying.

"Oh commmme on." She drops her taco in the basket. Puts a hand over her face. "You saw the video?"

"Many, mannny times," I tell her. "You were really good. You know. Until you weren't."

"Fucking Tara. I was about to hit that running man so hard," she whispers. She looks over at me and matches my grin. I take a sip of my beer, watching her over the rim of the cup. The streak of pink along her cheekbones deepens a shade to crimson and her bottom lip pulls between her teeth. Her wide eyes water in the breeze. She looks so innocent.

"Jeff," she starts, leaning closer so that her arm is pressed against mine. "Can we have sex tonight?"

I spit out my beer. The two men beside us lift their heads and look our way. Devon laughs and winks at me.

"Direct communication. Another forte," she says, reaching out to push my jaw upward. "I've just been thinking that this," she points between us just like she did last night, "really needs an outlet. You know, to get out of our systems before we fry from the inside."

Ah. She thinks this is just some sexual tension then. Can't pretend that doesn't hurt. I push my lips together, study her very serious expression. She's all business right now. If that's what she wants to tell herself, I'll let her have it. For now.

"So, can we have--?"

I press my mouth to hers and I'm immediately rewarded by a soft moan as she lies back into the net. Kissing her makes everything around us fade away; the soft sloshing of water against the pylons beneath us falls beneath the amazing sound she makes when I deepen the kiss. When her half-eaten taco basket tilts off her lap and plops into the water below, I go to pull away, but she puts both hands in my hair and whispers "Fuck the tacos" into my mouth. I've never wanted anything like I want her right now and if we don't get off this net there's a solid chance of this PDA becoming something illegal.

I move my lips to her neck and ask her if she's ready.

"How far?" she breathes.

"Four blocks."

I nibble at her ear and she hisses.

"Get an Uber and we can have an epic makeout sesh in the back," she says with a wide smile.

My phone is out, Uber app open and ready, before she even has a chance to swipe my carne asada and take a bite.

Chapter Thirty-Four

D evon

Lesson 35: Never underestimate the hands of a surgeon.

This Uber is absurd. If I lay flat in the backseat, I'd barely be able to touch the far side of the car with my arms outstretched overhead. It's a bear den. I know my echo will bounce around the interior, but I decide not to test it as I count the steps it takes for Jeff to slip between the bucket seats and sit beside me in the third row.

"Is this an XXXL?" I whisper.

He shrugs as the sliding door shuts behind him and the lights go off.

"Figured you'd want privacy," he tells me in my ear. "Since you promised an 'epic make-out sesh'."

I giggle. It sounds ridiculous when he says it. When I say it, it sounds amazing, mature, and sexy.

"You have like four minutes until we arr—"

I cut him off with my mouth and am immediately rewarded with a light growl from the back of his throat. I try to undo my seatbelt so I can straddle him, but he grabs my wrist and makes it clear he will make no such allowance as he continues to kiss me senseless. The car might as well be on autopilot. No driver exists. My entire world is the pressure of his lips, the light caress of his tongue, and the need to have him closer. So much closer.

"You're fulfilling like eight of my ultimate teenage fantasies right now," he says after breaking the kiss. His voice is in my ear, which obviously leads straight down south because the sound of those words makes everything below clench tight. Then his teeth graze my ear lobe and I know my anatomy teacher knew nothing. He moves lower, his lips barely touching my neck and softly landing beside my clavicle, his tongue finds the bare skin there. I wrap my fingers in his hair and stifle a moan.

"I want to hear them—the fantasies—but I need your mouth to keep doing that," I say. I'm breathless and I need to feel more of him. I trail my free hand down his chest, toward his waist, but he catches my wrist again before I can reach what I want.

His mouth is back hovering over mine, our breath mingling between us and I'm aching. I'm in actual pain. That's how bad I want this—him.

"You stopped," I whisper, watching the light from the passing bars and restaurants reflect off his pupils.

"Devon, when we get back to my place, there isn't going to be an inch of your body that my mouth won't cover."

Holy.

Shit.

I swallow.

"Promise?"

He laughs. Kisses me softly this time. And the car stops. The Uber driver clears his throat. Four blocks have sadly come and gone. Part of me never wants to leave this backseat—but with his promise still freshly bouncing off the headrest of the bucket seat in front of me, I let go of his hair. Jeff seems to be in about as much pain as me when the interior light comes on and I catch his lower lip between my teeth before he pulls away to commence our exit. The Uber driver grins at me and I keep my eyes on Jeff's ass. Which does nothing to ease my desperate need.

"How fast can you get us upstairs?" I ask from behind him as he twists the key in the thousandth lock.

He pushes the door open and turns sideways so I can pass. I step up into his foyer and flick on the switch.

"I can get upstairs fast. But you need to take it slow. Last thing we need is for you to stumble and reinjure yourself—end up in the imaging center at Jefferson again."

"I'm not sure if I find this offensive or endearing," I tell him, holding onto the handrail with caution. I really don't want to go to the imaging center right now.

"You can decide after," he says from behind me.

"After what?"

"After we do all the things I've been thinking about since I met you."

His hands are on my hips now, guiding me forward. As I reach the top of his steps, his fingers dip under my sweatshirt and push firmly into my lower back.

"All the things." I nod. "Since we met? Like at the bar? Or when I was stoned in recovery. Because I'm pretty sure that violates all sorts of patient/doctor rules—"

I forget how to make words when we reach the side of the couch and he pulls me backward so that every inch of my backside is pressed against his front. He's warm and hard—everywhere—and the thought of feeling him inside of me makes my legs go all wobbly.

He tilts my head to the side and breaths against my neck. I can feel his smile. I love his smile.

"Both. You aren't my patient. I'm allowed to picture you bent over this couch." His lips press against the skin behind my ear and I let out a soft helpless sound. I push my ass into him and the sound he makes is just as desperate.

"Jeff?"

He's still pressing kisses along the side of my neck, sucking and nibbling as he goes.

"Hmmm?"

The vibration of the sound tightens my skin like a guitar string.

"I need you to take your clothes off," I tell him.

And I really do. I need to feel every inch of what's pressed against me through our jeans. Wrap my hands around it and drive him as crazy as he's driving me.

"I'm going to turn you around now, Devon. This sweatshirt—" he slides his fingers under the hem and lifts the soft grey cotton, "while I love it immensely—it needs to go. Then I'm going to kiss you into the bedroom. Lay you down, pull off your jeans, and make you cum in my mouth. Okay?"

Jesus H. Christ. Okay? What is the superlative of okay?

"Can you explain the plan again?"

I'm not joking—I really want to hear the plan again, especially that last part—but he grants me a throaty chuckle then turns me slowly. Every second that he looks down at me feels like hours—the most glorious and infuriating torture. Then my hoodie is being lifted up, up and away and I'm momentarily blind, but I can hear the appreciative sound he makes at the sight of me topless. I took more time with my undergarments than I did with my outfit, and when I see the way he's looking at my bra, the hard line of his jaw so tense it might snap, it makes the effort I made so worthwhile.

"You're insanely beautiful," he whispers.

"Half of that might be right," I tell him. I want his hands back on me. But he's still admiring me like I'm hanging on the wall of the Louvre. I loop my arms around his neck, tangle my fingers in his soft, thick hair, pull him down so his lips are just over mine.

He throws the balled-up hoodie across the room and it knocks over one of the gold-plated cat statues that line the top shelf of the built-ins.

"Your landlady, Betsy Ross, is going to be pissed if you break her antiques," I tell him while he runs a slow trail along the black lace at the top of my bra.

He ignores me, too focused on his fingers circling and teasing around my nipple that's pushing out at him, screaming to be touched.

When he finally gives in, the feel of his fingertips through the lace makes my head go back. I gasp and barely have time to recover before his mouth crashes down onto mine. And this—this out of control but perfect colliding of his lips and tongue and mine—this single moment is filled with more want and desire than the entirety of my womanhood. A distant voice in the back of my mind wonders what the hell I was doing all that time following dumbass rules while I could have been doing this, but Jeff's hands beneath my lace bra silence even that.

I only realize that he's moved me to the bedroom when the feel of the cool comforter pushes against my back. He's still kissing me, softer now, as he deftly unbuttons my jeans. Oh, the benefits of bedding a surgeon.

"What?" he asks.

Shit. Did I say that out loud?

"Nothing. It's your hands. Good hands. I like hands."

That's all I can manage to get from my brain to my mouth right now, because he's slowly making his way over my breasts, pulling the lace down beneath them, proving that his lips and tongue are just as likeable and skilled as his hands. When the trail leads down below my navel, I squirm, and he stops. He smiles up at me and I want to grab hold of his shirt and pull him down against me and take over, wipe that smile off his face, but he's got one hand still keeping me down, fingers splayed across my abdomen while he slides the denim off of me. He keeps his eyes on mine until he can't. Then all of his attention goes to the lace between my legs.

I nearly wore my "Don't open 'til Christmas" undies, but I'm eternally grateful for my choice because of the look he's giving them. That focus—the way his chest stops rising and falling as he drinks me in—it sends so much heat down over me that five alarms sound in my fuzzy brain. His fingers trail from my knee upward and stop just before the lace. I suddenly hate the lace. I hate every scrap of it, every inch that keeps his fingers from where I need them to be.

"Jeff, please."

He looks up into my eyes, lifts his brows. Pretends not to know what I want. I was right. He's Satan.

He lowers his head.

"Jeff, please what?" he asks, his lips whisper over the inside of my knee. He kisses my inner thigh.

"I'm going to make you pay for—"

His finger dips beneath the lace and there's nothing left on the planet besides that feeling—the pooling warmth—the demanding pressure building beneath his touch. He slides a finger into me and his smile melts away.

"Fuck, Devon. You are so wet."

I arch up against his touch, my body screaming for more. I say his name again. And when I meet his gaze, I can tell he's done playing with me. He wants what I want.

He curses, slips off the lace, and dips his head between my legs. When his mouth joins his hand, the pressure of his lips and tongue exactly where I need it, I cry out—shatter against him—crash into a thousand pieces—a hammer against the thinnest pane of glass. He doesn't let up and I'm breaking over and over—wave after wave of pleasure coursing through me—a new drug that I'll never have enough of. Every ounce of built-up need flows over and into Jeff, who takes it like a gift, his eyes alight and fixed on my face.

"Jeff," I whisper, tearing my gaze away from him to the sweetly spinning ceiling.

He murmurs a "what?" against me and the pleasant sensitivity of the movement catches my breath.

"Can you take your clothes off now?" I ask, my fingers still woven through his hair as he lifts from my new favorite place for him, and joins me in the pillows, elbow bent, head in hand.

"Just relax," he tells me, stroking lazy circles over my stomach. "We have all night."

I turn onto my side, press myself up next to him.

"And I plan to use the whole night. But right now, I need you to ditch the clothes."

I use all of the strength to lift my leg over his hip and roll him over and under me. I'm sure he's astounded by my grace, but he doesn't comment because he's looking up at me with that look again.

That's the look I give to the cupcakes.

I slip my hands under his shirt and shut my eyes at the feel of him, silently counting the number of ab muscles my fingertips encounter.

"What are you doing?" he asks, as I get to six.

"Counting."

"Counting what?"

"My blessings."

His laughter sends a shot of heat back down below and I tug him upward so I can get his goddamned shirt off. He helps me through the struggle, then props himself on his elbows so that I can look him over.

"How do you have time to make these?" I ask, running my hand up between his pecs. It is a rhetorical question, but he answers.

"Steroids."

I smile. Jeff is getting funnier. But I'm not telling him that because he already has every advantage over me. No way I'm giving him humor, too.

I shake my head. "Can't be steroids. They cause ED." I reach behind me and rub him through his jeans. His head falls back and the sight of him vulnerable just from that one small gesture makes me want to push further. I lower my mouth over his, sip at his bottom lip.

"So obviously it's not steroids," I tell him.

"You're killing me," he says, kissing beneath my chin.

I slide myself back out of reach between his legs and fold my knees beneath me as I start to work the buttons and slide off the denim almost as smoothly as he did it. Almost. He watches me lift a bit off the mattress to get some leverage as I tug, and where I expect amusement, I find something else altogether. Something that makes me feel warm and gooey—cookie dough in its second minute in the oven. And the feeling isn't just in my core. It fills my chest too. Scares the ever-loving shit out of me.

Jeff must sense that I need some help because he sits up as I toss the jeans to the side, and pulls me back to him, pushes my hair back with both hands and holds my face in his palms.

"Why do you suddenly look scared—like you've discovered I'm a vampire?" he asks.

"I wish." I laugh. "Fear and ecstasy are two different animals, buddy. If I call you Damon will you be upset?"

His dimple appears then disappears all too soon.

"Seriously, do you need to slow down?" His eyes are slightly narrowed, his mouth a firm line while he tries to read me. I squeeze my thighs tighter around his hips and rock against him. And I think he knows my answer because the sound he makes tells me there will be no slowing down now. He grabs my hips with his hands and pushes against me, just one last pesky layer of cotton between me and what I want. Before the soft moan even escapes my lips, I'm flipped onto my back with his weight back on top of me, his mouth back on mine. He stands, grabs each ankle and pulls me to the edge of the bed then looks down at me and says.

"Stay here."

Where am I going to go, Jeff? Across the street for some pizza? Around the corner for a flat white?

He smiles like he's got a direct line to my sarcastic thoughts then turns and disappears into the bathroom, assumedly to grab protection. When he reappears in the square of light that surrounds him from the open door, I breathe deeply and sit-up a little so I can fully experience the sight of his slow walk back, the way he steps out of his boxer-briefs, pauses to let me take him all in for the first time—it is the sweetest, most painful anticipation I've ever felt.

He watches me the entire time he rolls on the condom and I feel an irrational surge of jealousy towards that layer of latex. I want to be around him. I reach for him, close each of my fingers around what I want and his eyes close, and I stroke him slowly, until he lets out a low growl and grabs my busy hand. He snakes his fingers between mine and pushes me back into the mattress, pinning the hand he claimed over my head. I push my ass up off the bed, needing to be closer, and he fills me in one slow thrust. I squeeze my knees tighter, never wanting to let go of this—of him inside of me. All I know for certain in this world is that the heavy, tingling need is rising up again, more insistent this time.

I hook my ankles behind his back and move to feed that need, slowly at first, then faster, harder as Jeff's voice sends spirals of heat down over my body. His wants and desires are emptying into my ear and every one makes the feeling intensify and grow. What he's going to do to me—how long he's wanted this—every word is like spraying hairspray on an open flame and the images that are playing through my head make me greedy and wild. I clutch his shoulder with my free hand and rock until I'm teetering on the edge again.

"Let go, Devon. I want to feel you let go around me—"

His rhythm picks up, his free hand pulling my hips down toward him so he's so deep that I cry out as the pleasure spikes and sends me tumbling into the delicious release. Jeff lets go as I fall, my name on his lips against my neck, his fingers still threaded through mine and clutching my hip. When the final pulse of relief pours out of us, he looks down at me, his eyes dark and serious, a dangerous smile teasing his mouth and says,

"You only called me Damon once. Not too bad."

I laugh until his mouth makes me forget what's so funny.

Chapter Thirty-Five

J eff

Lesson 36: See lesson 23 and raise it to hide all care packages from Donna.

I watch her tiptoe across my bedroom, the morning sun streaming through the blinds, sending streaks of light reaching toward her. I can't blame the light. I want to reach for her, too. Pull her back in bed and tuck her up against me so that time can freeze around last night. Her effort to not wake me is both endearing and comical as she steps in the middle of a wire hanger and gets it stuck on her foot.

"I'm awake," I tell her before she kills herself. I lift myself up onto my elbow.

She jumps, then rushes into the open bathroom and scoots behind the door so I can only see her face and rumpled hair.

"Devon, are you seriously trying to hide your body from me? I just spent the better part of ten hours doing things to you that—"

"That was under the haze of first sex."

"And second sex. Third sex. Fourth—"

"I can count, Jeff. Math teacher. You just don't need to see the details of my ass at the butt crack of dawn. No pun intended."

"You have two freckles on the left cheek and a beauty mark directly beneath the right."

She rolls her eyes and shuts the bathroom door. I lay my head back onto the pillow. Thirty-four years lived and the last twenty-four hours are by far the most fun I've had in all of that time. My abs actually hurt from laughing. And obviously the rest of me is pleasantly sore from everything else. There are no words to describe the 'everything else.'

"Jeffffff," I hear her voice over the running water. She pulls open the door, a toothbrush hanging out the side of her mouth. She's wrapped in one of my black and white towels. Before I have a chance to ask her where the hell she got a toothbrush from, she lifts the giant box of condoms my mom sent me my first week here.

"Should I be concerned by the sheer quantity of condoms you have here?" she asks before turning and spitting into the sink.

"Why would you be?" I ask, sitting up against the headboard.

She rinses her mouth, taps the toothbrush, then puts it down.

"Ummmm. Well, typically you don't buy the oversized value pack unless you're planning on having lots of random sex," she explains, lifting a chain of the packaged condoms up and letting it fall like an accordion back into the box.

"And?" I lift my brows and watch her put the condoms back on the counter where I'd left them last night.

She takes a few steps back into the room, sidestepping the hanger from before.

"Anddd, I guess I'm asking if you're having lots of random sex." She wrinkles her nose, as if she's sorry she even asked. "I'm sorry.

This is none of my business. You can say it is none of your business, Devon. This is just sex, so—"

I cut her off before she twists the knife further into my gut. "Thanks for the permission, but it is your business."

She sits on the end of the bed so her back is to me. Still just sex to her? I'm tempted to draw this out. Torture and tease her to make up for the fact that she's using my heart like a speed bag. But the truth is I can't even bear the thought of her feeling like she's second fiddle. Not after the pain I witnessed the other night.

"There are exactly four condoms missing from that box. Figure out what that means, math teacher."

She plops backward onto the mattress. Her hair fans out around her head and she narrows her eyes at the ceiling. I know she's not still processing the information. She's moved on to the next thought. I interrupt whatever she's stewing on.

"They're from my mom, by the way."

She chokes on a laugh.

"What?" Her entire face lights up.

"The condoms are from my mother. One of her goofy care package items," I explain.

Devon purses her lips and nods. She's holding back. I can tell by the set of her jaw that she wants to bust my balls and is biting her tongue. Probably because it has to do with my mother. And she knows how worried I am about what's going on back home with the finances.

"You can go there. I can see that brain of yours coming up with like a dozen mom jokes," I say.

She scrubs her palms over her face and shakes her head.

"That's not true. I have nothing to say about your mother encouraging you to be a man-whore—a safe and protected man-whore. I think that's a really lovely sentiment. I'm just wondering—"

I lean forward a little so I can reach out and touch her hair, twirl it around a finger. She's smirking up at me, her feet dangling and kicking over the edge of the bed. Seeing her like this, wrapped up in my towel, comfortable in my bed, makes me happier than it should. Too much joy is a dangerous thing. Especially if you're not sure if the other person feels the joy the same way.

"Again, none of my business," she starts, "but you are a really good-looking guy—"

"Thank you."

"And you are a foot doctor."

"An orthopedic surgeon."

"Right. That's what I said." She smiles. "And you've been here for like almost five months, right?"

"Is there a point coming soon?" I ask, tugging a little at the piece of hair I have and then releasing it.

She flips over, puts her chin in her palms, and props herself up on her elbows.

"I guess I'm just asking why. Why haven't you used more condoms?" she asks.

I see a slight flush creep up her cheeks from her neck. This is interesting. Not only is it apparent that she cares about my answer from the way she's studying my face, but it is fascinating that she's clueless enough to even ask.

She doesn't let me answer before she starts to babble. "I mean I've seen the way women respond to you and Kev told me that the nurses had a pool on who would get you in bed first. There can't be a shortage of—"

"I wanted you," I interrupt. That simple.

Her lip quirks up on one side.

"The whole time?"

Now she's just fishing.

I nod. "The whole time."

And the truth is worth the dazzler she gives me. She crawls up the bed, puts one knee on either side of me so that the towel rides up, exposing just enough of her to get me hard. She kisses me sweetly and I slip a hand up the towel, move my hand against her in the way I know she likes. She whimpers. Pushes down against me.

"Devon," I say in her ear.

"Hmmm?" Her eyes are closed as she grinds against my touch.

"It was worth the wait," I tell her. Her eyes open and soften as she dips her forehead to mine.

"There are still ninety-six condoms left in that box," she says. "Makes me think of that beer bottle song."

She starts to hum.

I flip her over into the pillows and the towel comes loose around her, opening up so I can see everything. She lets me look this time and when I meet her gaze again, I tell her, "I'm sure we can put a dent in that."

Chapter Thirty-Six

Devon

Lesson 37: Always double check the shrooms.

Tara is more excited about Jeff coming to dinner than she was about her own engagement. Which says a lot considering the way she and Marcello sparkle when they're together. She's dancing around, filling my prosecco glass after every sip, smiling like a lunatic while my mother works on the spaghetti squash that survived the massacre the deer unleashed on the garden last night. Believe it or not, the screeching chickens, a five-foot fence, and an overweight golden retriever are not enough to deter the greedy beasties. But my mom barely batted a lash when she noticed the pumpkin entrails spread across the soil this morning, murmuring something about the circle of life to me as I left for school. Apparently, we were having a

Mufasa/Simba moment while I wiped at the coffee I spilled on my jeans—a daily, unpreventable mishap.

"Top off!" Tara sings as she pours me more bubbly.

I stare up at her.

"You need to calm down."

She touches my shoulder. Her nails are painted a striking shade of navy with a blush half-moon along the bottom cuticle. No chips. I look at my fingers and make a note to take off the remnants of last month's polish. Woman-ing is hard.

"Do I?" she asks, sinking back into her seat.

I lift my brows and she waves my advice away. She really does need to calm down. She's been begging me for details all afternoon, stealing the two hours of quiet I require on Fridays after school to recharge. I love her to death, but this school year is a pile of shit, with Principal Dickhead and his inability to stand up for what's right and another week of watching Jessica fade away without any response from her mother, madam school-board president. On top of that, rumors have begun to circulate about my legendary defiance of admin's orders to take my posters down. God knows who leaked that little tidbit, because I certainly didn't. And I know my favorite guidance counselor, Elizabeth Stanton, didn't.

"I'm just saying—don't make a bigger deal of this than it is," I tell her again.

She flicks her wrist, shooing my concerns into the ether. She makes a noise with her teeth that makes me want to lick my finger and smear her perfect eyeliner.

"Are you still pretending this is just sex? Jesus, Devon. I've seen the way—"

Saved by the bell. The ring echoes around us. Tara and I both stand, exchange a look, and take off for the door like we are eight again, pushing and grabbing at each other to get there first.

"Devon! No hair," she hollers when I grab a curl. Brutus is barking from where he lies in the kitchen and my mom is yelling for us to grow up.

"I didn't want to touch the designer silk," I laugh, using my ass to block her as I twist the doorknob and pull open the door letting a rush of cold air into the house.

The late afternoon sun hovers just above the tree line. Its light frames Jeff like a paper cutout, his wide shoulders blocking the pinks and purples stretching across the sky behind him. When I blink hard, my eyes focus on his warm and easy smile, the one that makes me feel like I've just won the lottery. He looks so natural on my mom's welcome mat. Like he grew up next door. And came to dinner every Sunday.

"You two ok?" he asks with a laugh, and I feel Tara still pulling on the hood of my sweatshirt while I stick my ass out to keep her back—box her out like I'm LeBron.

"Why wouldn't we be?" I ask.

Tara ducks under my arms to give him a hug. My hug. I look on helplessly while she tugs him past me, his eyes bright as he kisses my head on the brush past, into the kitchen where my mom greets him and takes the bakery box and bottle of red wine out of his hands.

"You know, Jeff. You don't need to keep bringing dessert," my mom ensures him.

"Yeah he does," I say. Jeff winks over my mother's head. The cupcakes are a living, breathing part of our relationship at this point. Jeff enjoys me eating them. I enjoy me eating them. Win win.

"Beer?" I ask him on my way to the fridge.

"Please," he says, before asking my mom if she needs help. She shoos him away and he takes a seat beside Tara at the table. Brutus immediately shuffles over and falls onto his feet with a harumph.

Tara is in full swing by the time the poor guy can crack open the lager.

"So, obviously I have a rigorous interview process for anyone who dates my sister," Tara says, her voice low like I'm not standing right behind Jeff as she talks to him.

"Oooh, careful with the d-word. She's got rules," Jeff says with a crooked grin my way.

"Can we not?" I say, giving Tara a look as I make my way to my seat.

Tara ignores me.

"But then she told me you and she were just—" She steeples her fingers together and taps a few times, her brows waggling suggestively.

"Building a teepee?" I ask.

She ignores me again.

"Which by the way lost me and Kev a hundred bucks each—"

"You bet on your sister's sex life?" my mom asks from where she's chopping.

That's right, Mom, you tell her.

"And you didn't think to loop me in?" she adds.

What the—?

"Next time, Ma. Anyway, Jeff, you pass inspection—based on the conversations you and I have had," Tara finishes. She gives Jeff a meaningful look, but he doesn't see it because he's watching me across the table, his lips pressed together while his eyes crinkle in the corner. Is he enjoying Tara's blindness to boundaries? Or is he pleading for me to make it stop? I would try to help, but now I'm curious.

"What conversations?" I probe.

He lets out a breath and my sister turns to me like she's just realized I'm at the table.

"Private conversations." She tips the dregs of the prosecco bottle into my already full flute. I have to bend over the table and sip it so that it doesn't overflow.

"Mmmhmmm. Private. It's funny how you define private, T," I murmur.

"Tara basically pointed out the fact that I was infatuated with you long before you became—available to me," Jeff says.

I feel that little hiccup in my heart that he keeps giving me every time he says something sweet or looks at me like this—like I'm a gift.

"Infatuated, eh?" I carefully lift my drink to my mouth.

Jeff just lifts a brow in response. I'll take infatuated. Even if it does feel a little temporary. I'm sure he's not analyzing his vocab choices right now with my mom buzzing around us like a thirsty mosquito.

"Jeff, dear, do you like mushrooms?" my mom asks, putting her fingers on Jeff's shoulder. His shoulders are my new favorite. They're firm like a melon rind and there's a sharp dip between his blade that I like to trail my nails—

"Devonnnn," my mom drags out my name like she's been calling it for several minutes.

"What?"

"Can you go grab some mushrooms from the log?"

Mushrooms. Log. Got it.

I stand and tell Tara to be good. Then grab a knife and head outside toward the shiitake mushroom log I'd ordered from Terrain last year. The deer luckily can't get into the makeshift greenhouse my mom crafted on the deck. As I cut the stems flush against the log trying not to let my shivering cause a slip and finger loss, I watch Tara and Jeff through the window. She's talking excitedly with her hands in a way that makes me think she'll fit right into her new home in Milan. The countdown to her departure has been a bittersweet murmur I hear every so often beneath the laughter and other sounds that Jeff and I have been making these last few weeks. If I weren't three hundred percent sure that Marcello is going to work his ass off to make her happy, this ache would be a hell of a lot worse. But watching her fingers flutter through the air while Jeff's deep laugh reaches me through the thick glass reminds me that Tara wasn't made to stay still. She's supposed to be out there. Working her magic on the world. While I grow fungus in a log with Mom.

By the time I arrive back at the table, Tara has slid her chair closer to Jeff and is looking at pictures of his niece, Sammy, sitting atop a huge Clydesdale. I've had the pleasure of talking to her quite a few times in the past weeks as she frequently calls Jeff to sneakily report the goings on out West. Though her intel isn't exactly trustworthy, since she told us last weekend that Grandma had gotten a check for a million dollars in the mail and she believed her mother had a date with John Stamos. Sammy has a tendency to hear what she wants to hear, coupled with a superb imagination. Either way, while listening to Jeff's conversations with her as she hid in the coat closet from Jenny, who was obviously avoiding his calls at all costs, it became very apparent that Sammy and Jeff are close. And that he adores her. Which in turn makes him more adorable.

"She's so beautiful, Jeff," my sister tells him.

"Thanks," he says, smiling at the screen.

He misses his family. He doesn't try to hide it. In fact, he tells me quite often.

"I'd love to have a niece," she says wistfully while I snort the prosecco that's risen into my sinus cavity. Jeff laughs as my eyes tear up and my mother does a mediocre job of coming to my rescue.

"Are you going home next weekend for Thanksgiving, Jeff?" my mom asks from across the kitchen island.

Jeff presses his screen blank and looks up at me. His face is open, but unreadable.

"I'm not sure if I can," he says simply.

I almost ask why not. He's been dying to get home and figure out the finances and see his women-kin. Then I realize that I might be biting off more than I want to chew. Is he waiting to see what happens with me? With us? I take another sip of prosecco. It's clear that this has risen a bit above my "just sex" rule, but turkey-sharing is some next-level shit. It's only been a few weeks. Barely long enough for a tattoo to heal.

I give myself a mental bitch-slap to calm down just as he adds, "I'm scheduled to work, but I've been trying to get coverage."

Ok. So it's not me he's waiting for. It's work. Maybe he's not ready for turkey sharing, either. I should be relieved. But that drop in my stomach is a lot more like cold, hard, disappointment.

I ignore it and ask my mom, "You ready for help?"

"Yes," she says, dumping the meal from her oversized sauté pan into a bowl. I wipe the drool with my sleeve when the steam sends delicious clouds of garlic and browned butter toward me. Even Brutus lifts his head.

"That smells amazing, Kathy." Jeff stands and helps us grab the bowls and utensils from the island.

"Butter and garlic. Few things in the world that smell better than that," my mom says, taking her seat beside me.

I want to argue that Jeff's aftershave lotion smells better than that. But I settle for a smile across the table at him.

"Alright, glasses up," my mom directs. We lift our drinks. "To Tara's adventures abroad. May they bring her the happiness and love that she deserves!"

"Salute!" Tara adds. She's beaming as we tilt our glasses together. Her smile is lit with all of the anticipation of a school in June.

"Dig in," Mom says, spooning a huge plate for herself.

The sound of silverware clinking against plates dominates the room for a few minutes, interrupted only by sounds of appreciation and praise we throw Mom's way. The mushrooms melt against my tongue, earthy and savory. There's something so peaceful about the four of us quietly enjoying the meal. The week from hell fades into the distant background of my brain along with Tara's departure next week. I'm just so happy to be here. Now. With my family. With the people I love.

Love. The thought settles so lightly—a butterfly touching down on a leaf—that at first, I don't feel its weight. It tickles my brain, tiptoes gently across the surface, then slides down into a crack, somewhere deeper where I can't bat it away. Jeff meets my gaze and gives me a crooked smile around a mouthful of food. This feeling—the contentment—this cannot be linked to Jeff.

"Shit."

All heads turn my way. Jeff presses his lips together like he wants to laugh.

"What, honey?" Mom asks.

I open my mouth. Close it.

"The mushrooms. I was saying, '*Shiit*-ake mushrooms are so good.' Mmmmm."

I stare back down at my plate and ignore the looks I'm getting. It's the prosecco. These ridiculous conclusions are from Tara's heavy-handed bartending again. Or maybe these aren't shiitakes. Terrain sent the wrong mushrooms. I could be tripping balls.

I feel the warmth in my chest and neck when Jeff laughs at something my mom says, and I try to focus on the words floating around the kitchen. But I'm being assaulted by the clicking pieces of a puzzle I don't want to look at. I am not feeling this. I *can't* be feeling this. I am not—I swallow past the lump in my throat. I am not falling for Jeff.

"So, I have a little bit of a surprise for you, Dev," Tara starts.

I force myself to focus on her lips, repeating the words in my brain so I can follow along without getting pulled back into the troubling tornado my mind is swept away in.

"Marcello bought you two tickets to Milan for the week of spring break," she finishes.

Her eyes are narrowed on me.

"Two tickets?" I whisper.

She nods. I look to mom. She laughs and shakes her head. Of course, she's not going to come to Milan with me. She won't go to the grocery store with me let alone a foreign country. I look back to Tara and she leans toward Jeff before I can stop her. Before I can reach out and dig my fingers into her skinny thighs to tell her not to speak. Not to throw me a rope-less anchor while I'm already flailing in Jeff-infested waters.

"Do you think you could get off work for a few days?" she asks him.

To his credit, he doesn't respond. He turns my way, studies my face, possibly recognizes the panic that has me in its grips.

"I think, maybe—Devon will want to talk about that," he answers.

Good, Jeff. Good answer. We'll talk—about that.

It is the perfect response. I force myself to smile and hope I don't look as crazy as I feel. Be calm and eat more squash. Everything is fine. I'm fine. Just got caught up in the moment, that's all. Squash is obviously an aphrodisiac.

I let out a deep, cleansing breath and pull my shit together.

I am so not in love with Jeff.

Chapter Thirty-Seven

J^{eff}

Lesson 38: Some things are worth waiting for.

I'm in love with Devon.

But that's not what scares me. She's curled up in fetal position beside me, the hem of her t-shirt hitched up above her navel so that I can see the way her stomach falls and rises with every breath. It's one of those rare times when she's not snoring, and it makes every thought in my head too loud to ignore. I need to talk to her—see if she might be in the same boat as me. Shit, I'd take the same ocean at this point.

There's a lot to sort through here even if she feels how I feel. I have six months left in this fellowship—six months until I return home for good to start my career and do what I set out to do. But the thought of broaching this topic with her makes my pulse skyrocket. She's like a feral cat that has started to come around—

rubbing against my leg, maybe even letting me scratch behind her ears. But I know the second I start talking about feelings and a future, there's a large chance she's gonna bolt back out into the woods.

One of Devon's eyes opens slowly, and she blinks fast against the streak of light sneaking in between the blinds. She wrinkles her nose and turns her face into the pillow.

"It's so creepy when you watch me sleep." Her voice is muffled but I can hear her smile.

"Is it?"

"Yeah. It is." She turns back toward me and I touch her cheek. There's a line there from how she slept on the pillow. "It makes me think you're planning to make a skin-suit out of me."

I laugh and trail my finger down her neck.

"You do have nice skin."

"If I wake up to you moisturizing me, I'm done," she says.

"I'll have to be more careful." I pull her closer, but she giggles and squirms away, sliding down beneath the comforter. I watch the lump move toward the foot of the bed and then disappear when Devon empties onto the ground with a thump.

"You alright down there?"

She pops up.

"All good," she says.

I focus on her bare legs stretching from beneath the tee she's stolen from me. She claims she's had it since she was sixteen, even has a story about Tara finding it at Macy's in a nearby mall that has since been leveled for business offices. She has similar stories for two of my hoodies and half of my store of scrubs. Apparently, her mall had a scrub supply store called "Doctor Duds." The creative effort involved in her lies is disturbingly impressive.

She makes her way into the bathroom and reappears with the toothbrush she's claimed as her own hanging out the side of her mouth. She talks through the foam on her teeth and tongue.

"Before I come back there and you distract me with your hands," she starts, shifting the toothbrush to the other side of her mouth. "We have some things to discuss."

I nod and sit up against the headboard to give her my full attention. This is my chance to come clean—to tell her how I'm feeling and hope she doesn't scratch my cheek, hiss and run. I watch her retreat back to the sink. She spits, rinses, and reappears with her best attempt at a serious face. And I'm suddenly more nervous than my first sitting for the Boards.

"Item one," she begins. "I know that you and my mother have been texting."

I let my face go blank. Pretend not to know what she's talking about.

"I know this because every time I catch her texting you, she tells me to mind my business and I'm fairly certain that there is nothing in this world that's more 'my business' than my mom and my boyfriend. You two think you're so sneaky, but you should know that I'm totally fine with—"

"Can you back up?"

She takes two steps backward. Smart ass.

"What did you say after 'my business'?" I ask, folding my hands behind my head.

She blushes, a soft slow spread of pink, and for a gut-wrenching moment I think it was just a slip of the tongue. An old habit. But then she smiles. Shyly. An adverb that rarely follows any action Devon takes.

"My mom?" she tries.

"No, no. After that," I say.

I'm working hard to keep my face neutral—not let her see how a simple possessive pronoun and a label have just set fireworks off in my chest.

She walks to the edge of the bed and sits, folding her knees beneath her.

"You mean the part where I called you my boyfriend?" she asks, tilting her head so her hair falls to one side. She's stunning. And she has no idea.

"Yup. That part."

She purses her lips to the side, pretends to be thinking.

"Maybe, that was the wrong word. Maybe you'd prefer the term 'side piece'? Wait no! 'Fuck-buddy'?"

I reach out and grab her around the hips, toss her back onto the pillows so that she's beneath me.

"I'll take boyfriend," I say, barely able to get the words out from beneath the happiness lumped in my throat. "So you aren't running away?"

She leans up, kisses me until my tongue tingles from the minty toothpaste.

"Nope. Since you screwed up my Achilles, it's hard to run. But you might after I ask you about item two on the list," she says when we break apart to catch our breath.

"Can it wait?"

She wraps her legs around my hips and twists so that she's on top. Her eyes narrow on my mouth and if I hadn't woken up hard just from being beside her, that look alone would do it.

"Will you be my chaperone in Milan? Because all of my suitors have been asking to go with me and I just can't hold them off any longer."

She pulls her bottom lip into her mouth and two tiny ski marks appear between her brows. Is she honestly worried that I'd say no? I want to tell her she should never worry. That whatever she asks me, the answer is yes. I want to tell her everything. But instead I say, "I'll agree to that, if you'll come home with me for a few days before Christmas. I know you'll want to be back with your mom by Christmas eve—"

She puts her fingers to my lips, leans over me, her perfect mouth hovering just over mine, her hair falling around my face like a curtain. This isn't our first holiday, if you consider the hour I spent with her in the on-call room eating leftovers on Thanksgiving night when I got off my shift. On-call room holidays—she'd said it was a tradition her father had started with them when they were little. She'd said it just felt right. Still, her silence is starting to scare me.

"You should know I'm not a great traveler. And last time I went somewhere, I ended up in the ER, spilling my guts to some satanic stranger."

I bite her finger. She yelps and pulls it away.

"I'll just keep you away from microphones and we should be good."

"And stages."

"Those, too." I kiss beneath her chin. She rocks her hips the smallest bit and I'm senseless.

"Well, now that that's all settled, we can handle item three."

She moves against me and her mouth meets mine, eager and insistent, and I know without a fraction of a doubt that my own items are going to have to wait. Because there's nothing else in this world beside Devon and item three.

Chapter Thirty-Eight

D evon

Lesson 39: Just keep chipping away.

"I volunteer as tribute!"

My eyes find Dana standing in the middle of her group in the back left corner of the room. She's trying to pretend she hasn't been swept into the tide of my glorious pre-holiday break fun, Algebra Hunger Games, but her smile tugs at her lips as I hold three fingers up in the air—the *Hunger Games* salute. My minions follow suit. My hair is in a high ponytail with a fuzzy scrunchy I borrowed from Syd, and my shirt has a picture of Jennifer Lawrence in full mockingjay costume. Go big or go home.

"Then so you shall be tribute, Dana Vilario. The sixth member of the twenty-fifth annual Algebra Hunger Games—"

"Damnnnn, Ms. G. You're old!"

"She made the number up. The books weren't even out then, Sam. Jesus!" Maddie throws a piece of crumpled paper at him.

"What's that Samuel? You'd like to take Dana's spot as tribute?" I ask.

The kids laugh as Sam shakes his head like his hair's on fire.

"So as I was saying. Tribute Vilario of District Six, take your place in the arena." I gesture toward the duct tape that spells out arena at the center of the room. Dana picks up the nerf gun suction cup bow and arrow that I bought for obvious reasons and holds it upside down, then adjusts. She narrows her eyes at the whiteboard where I drew a target filled with different point values. "Tributes, are you ready?"

Everyone in the class hoots and hollers and a few people in my hallway shut their doors to block out what is surely recognized as great-times-in-Gallagher's-class by all but a few teachers I've yet to win over. Just give me one more decade.

"Ready! Aimmmmm. Fire!"

She unleashes the arrow and it hits the board with a pop right in the center of the bullseye.

"Katnisssssss Everdeen. Five points! Go, go, go."

I press the next page button on the Acitvboard and an equation appears on the screen. The sound of furious scribbling in notebooks is so loud that I barely hear the ping from my cell on my desk.

As I move toward my phone, I watch the class. All heads are bent toward their work, sans two. One is Joseph Flint. He is melting in his chair like he might have just eaten a weed brownie in the bathroom. In reality, his ADHD meds are probably out of stock again. The shortages are wreaking havoc on these poor kids. And of course, Jessica Stoner. She is staring into space, her hoodie pulled up over her thinning hair. I bite my cheek and wake up my screen. A flight check-in reminder pops up and my stomach launches into a triple axel. I felt a lot of feels before my last trip to Chicago, but this is different. Less dread, more top of a rollercoaster with my hands in the air. I touch the toe of my flat to the hard outer casing of my luggage beneath my desk.

"Done!" Dana yells as she stands up, her cheeks flushed from the effort. Two more tributes announce that they're done and stand up.

"District Six. District Three. District One. In that order. Keep solving, you never know—"

The bell cuts me off and there is a unanimous groan. I make a heart with my hands and they roll their eyes at me. But I heard the groan! They don't want to leave math.

"Tributes submit your answer to the reaping basket. We will announce this year's winner next year! Have an amazing break and a happy New Year! Go forward. Be brave! Take a Starburst."

Ravenous beasts hold up their hands while I toss candy in their direction. It's like a piñata bursting at a toddler's birthday. Except they're thirteen.

"Bye, Ms. G! Happy Holidays! Thank you!"

I feed them sugar like a good teacher and wave them off as I head toward Jess kneeling to pick up her books from the floor.

"You ready for the break, Jess?"

She shakes her head and stands up, steadying herself on the corner of her desk. Her knuckles protrude from her hand like a range of mountains. She stares at her Air Force Ones.

"Jess," I start. But then I stop. Wait for her to look up and meet my gaze. It takes a full ten count of silence, but I hold out. "How can I help?"

She shakes her head and the hoodie slides back a little.

"You can't." She pulls her shoulders back. "I'm fine," she says.

Fine. I know that lie.

"I can. And I will. There are ways around your—"

"I'm ok, Ms. G. Really. My mom's right. This is just a phase."

Oh fuck this. A phase?

"Jessica, what if we had a code phrase? Something you could use when you just feel like you can't—when you need it."

A tear escapes from the corner of her bloodshot eye.

"Ok," she says softly.

"Ok."

I nod my head, pluck a Post-it from a basket nearby and scribble on the paper with a pen from her desk.

"That's my email, Jess. And that's the phrase. You type that to me —any time. And help is on its way."

She takes the Post-it and by-god she smiles a little when she reads the words.

"What the heck is a Shadow Daddy?" she asks.

"It's a bit inappropriate actually, maybe we should change it—to something less—"

"No. Shadow Daddy is perfect." She folds the pink paper and tucks it into her pencil case.

"See you next year?" I ask.

"See you next year," she says.

I watch her shuffle out of the room before making my way to the phone by the door. I need to call Nurse Amy—and Elizabeth in guidance. Hopefully they haven't fled with the wave of children running out of school. As I lift the receiver to my ear, cursing Jessica Stoner's mother, there's movement to my right and I turn to find my own definition of male paradise leaning against my door jamb, equipped with a visitor name tag on his left pec that reads Dr. Dick.

"For the love of Pete! You did not walk through the halls with that on your name tag." I laugh.

He looks down, his eyes wide.

"Who wrote that?" he asks looking behind him.

"Five minutes earlier and you would have made every one of my students' TikTok feeds."

He snaps away his disappointment and steps forward.

"You ok?"

I fix my face.

"Yeah. It's just that girl I told you about—"

"Jessica?" And there's the crease between his brows.

I nod and smooth his lines with my thumb. This man. I want to package him up and send him to every woman on Earth. The ultimate gift that keeps on giving. Heart of gold, brain of a surgeon, body of a Hemsworth.

"I just have to call guidance and the nurse, then I'm good to go."

He nods and walks around my room, taking it all in. I watch him pick up the nerf bow and shake his head with a smile as he sees the arrow still stuck to the target on the white board. I leave a message for Amy and update Lizzie, then approach him while he studies my mental health posters.

"I wonder how many kids you've saved—just by letting them know you see them," he says to the poster Syd gave me.

He turns and looks me over, his eyes filled with something that makes every cell in my body tense up and freeze. That look—it makes me feel like Wonder Woman—unstoppable and invincible. I shudder and he puts his hands on my shoulders, his thumbs circling the base of my neck.

"You ready for this?"

No. No. A thousand times no.

"Yup," I whisper.

He laughs at me and pats my head like I'm Brutus, then lowers his mouth over mine, stops just before our lips touch.

"Get your bag, liar," he says into my mouth.

His lips find mine and his arms wrap around me and just like that, the shell of my lie cracks and crumbles while a new truth pecks its way out into the light. Am I ready for this? I'm ready for anything if he's here beside me.

Chapter Thirty-Nine

J^{eff}

Lesson 40: Tell her.

Devon is doing remarkably well for an un-drugged, self-proclaimed "terrible traveler." Though it could be the upgraded business class seats—excuse me, cabins—that are keeping her somewhat serene. I wanted this experience to be less stressful for her and it was worth it to see her reaction as she blinked back tears and told me I shouldn't have. But as amazing as the seats are with their lie-flat feature, private stocked mini-bar, and widescreen TVs, there is an unfortunate divider between our "cabins" that prevents Devon from curling into my side for the two-and-a-half-hour flight.

She's been unusually quiet since I showed up in her classroom. Devon is many things, but silent is rarely one of them. Her foot is tapping against the plastic that separates us, the only sign of her nerves that I can find while she listens to something through the plush noise-cancelling headphones the airline provided. She nods and shuts her eyes, agreeing with whoever is speaking in her ears. She pulls her lip between her teeth, chews on it thoughtfully. I nearly climb over the divider.

Her eyes open and she meets my gaze. Slides her headphones back around her neck.

"Hi," she whispers.

"Hey."

She reaches her hand over the partition and I take it, playing with the bracelets that dangle at her wrist.

"Who's talking to you over there?" I ask.

She lifts her phone off her lap and presses the screen, so her Coursera app pops up. It's not the first time I've caught her taking courses. She's told me how much she loves to learn. This time it's a Science of Happiness series.

"Doctor Eleanor Basantis," I read. "She's the one you mentioned on our first not-a-date."

She nods.

I wait for her to go on. She knocks on the partition. Sits up on her knees so she can see me completely over top of it.

"Can you get the stewardess to remove this thing?" she asks.

I smile as she grips the divider and gives it a shake, like she might be able to loosen it and lift it from between us. A flight attendant passes and gives Devon a strange look. She lifts her palms upward in surrender.

"Tell me about the lecture before you get us thrown off the plane," I tell her.

"Could they do that?"

"Yup."

"Ok. Well, this woman I told you about—Dr. Basantis—saw a spike in mental health issues in her high-achieving students some years back and recognized a need for something new. Something that would benefit her pupils for the long run." Her hands are flying as she speaks, her eyes bright and alive. "So, she designed this course that basically reinvents the way you think. It challenges all the norms that society has traditionally accepted about happiness. It's had the highest enrollment in the history of her school. She's incredible."

"And what science is she using?" I ask. I could listen to her talk about this for hours. The way every word is infused with her passion for the subject. I've grown accustomed to her fire. It warms me.

"Neuroscience. Studies from UCLA. Harvard. Princeton. NIMH. Ummmm. Other major research facilities. Do you want to listen with me?"

Her lips are parted while she waits, brows lifted like she's just asked me to take her to prom.

"Yeah. I do," I tell her. And she actually bounces a little in her seat. Even if I wasn't interested—which I am—that reaction would have been enough to sit through hours of tedium.

She starts to root around her purse for her splitter, muttering into the bag at her feet. "You're coming into the game a little late; I'm nearing the end of her lessons. Top of the fifth inning—"

"Bottom of the ninth," I correct.

"Mmmhmm. So basically, what you've missed is that she's disproving the concept of more money, more happiness. There's a threshold. A Goldilocks-just-right number." She pops back up from rootling through her bag and holds out her hand for my headphone cord. I place it in her palm and let my hand linger on hers. She meets my gaze and smiles.

"I'm really excited to share this with you. Is that weird?" she asks. Her smile falters for a moment, self-conscious.

I lift my hand from hers, trail my finger along the side of her perfect face.

"I want you to share everything with me," I tell her.

She presses her lips together and my chest tightens. Too much? Is she searching for a parachute? Her eyes glisten in the overhead cabin light that I've kept on to read the legal thriller I grabbed at the newsstand at the airport. Then she smiles again, and I see what I've been hoping for. She's happy. Tears-in-her-eyes and all-choked-up happy. The kind of happiness I want to see on her always.

"I think I'd like that," she whispers, leaning over the divider. There's so much relief at hearing her say that.

I kiss her until the plastic between us becomes unbearable against my ribs.

"You ready?" she asks breathlessly, her thumb hovering over the play button.

I'm ready, Devon. Ready for anything you ask of me.

I match her grin and nod. She sits back in her chair. Her eyes close as Dr. Basantis's voice fills my head. And though I give the lecture my full attention, listening closely to the documented studies about how much money is optimal for contentment, I can still hear the sound of that nagging voice in my head, reminding me that Devon and I need to talk.

"A study at Princeton University did show a positive correlation between happiness and wealth, but only to the threshold of $75,000..."

But did this study take into account if your mother was about to lose her business or her home?

Devon's hand finds me over the partition and she wraps her fingers in mine and squeezes. I shut my eyes and lean my head back. I need to tell her how I feel about her. I need to tell her about my interview on Saturday and that this is the job I want.

"A similar study in the UK saw that doubling someone's pay increased their happiness by less than 0.2 while having a partner saw a happiness rise of 0.6 and a close relationship with family saw a rise of 0.4..."

I don't need to choose between the three. We will make this work. I can get the 0.2, the 0.6, and the 0.4. I just need to tell her. I picture Meredith shaking her head at me, telling me to woman-up and do what needs to be done. I look over at Devon, her eyes narrowed at the window as she nods along to the lecture.

Tonight. I'll tell her tonight.

Chapter Forty

Devon

Lesson 41: There's something about farm-raised men.

Jeff has driven us straight through a Norman Rockwell painting and into a dream. There are farms in South Jersey, plenty in fact, but this is something different. It's snowing and Jeff is driving like a grandma, but it gives me the chance to stare out at the white, rolling acres—so untouched I can hear the crisp crunch of the first step in the snow. The thought of someone stepping on it makes my molars grind. It's pristine. Like a fresh sheet of notebook paper on the first day of school. We pass a stone house wrapped in oversized colored lights and I feel as if I'm at the center of a snow globe. I put down my window and lean a little, breathe it in, ignoring the fat, wet flakes that slap my cheeks.

"Are you going to stick your head out like a dog?" Jeff asks. His hand skims the inside of my thigh and I'm grateful for the cool air rushing in.

"I might." I stick out my tongue to catch some snow and he laughs. "You said you lived in Chicago. Are you driving me out to a murder site? Is it skin-suit time?"

"I say Chicago because no one knows where the hell Wayne, Illinois is," he explains.

Impossibly, Jeff slows down. The blinker clicks on and we turn onto a drive that I can feel is unpaved from the way the tires grind beneath us. Two lines of bare-branched oaks lead and follow us on either side as we crawl up the path.

"I'm nervous!"

It comes out too loud and I turn to see his grin illuminated by the dashboard lights.

"You want me to pull over and we can sleep in the rental car?" He eases on the brake and turns the wheel a little to the right.

"We'd freeze to death and your mom would find us naked in the back seat—a nude, eight-limbed popsicle. She'd never recover—"

"Why would we be naked?"

"That's what you do when you're cold. Body heat. Basic survival. And also because we'd want to get in one last quickie before we died."

He laughs.

"Maybe you could teach me more survival tactics later—"

"Hell no. That's rule number twelve. No sex in your mom's house."

We are currently driving over a little wooden bridge and I ignore Jeff's tsking sound to hear the sound of running water beneath the engine. Over the river, and through the woods, to—

"That rule is unfounded and hypocritical. We've had sex at your mom's house. Remember?"

I smile. Remember? Ha! Um, yeah, Jeff. I remember. I could write a dissertation on every time he's touched me. But I just nod and enjoy the distress my booty probation is causing him. Like I could possibly uphold this rule if Jeff and I are in the same vicinity for 24 hours.

"Outside structures aren't mentioned in the rule, so sheds don't count. And I live there..."

My voice trails off as Jeff's childhood home appears before us like the only star on a cloudless night. The one-story rancher is wrapped in white light, so warm and inviting I think for a second I can smell freshly baked cookies. Our headlights fill the covered porch that hugs the entire front and I see them, two dark-haired women standing, bundled in real winter coats, the rocking chairs they just occupied still tilting back and forth behind them, and Sammy bouncing up and down, moving at impressive speeds as she bounds down the steps toward us.

Jeff squeezes my thigh and kills the ignition. He's out of the car before I have a chance to exhale. He lifts Sammy in his arms and spins. She's stuck in his orbit. Welcome to the club, Sammy girl.

I open the door to the scent of burning cedar, a smell that makes me think of the huge chest at my grandmother's house where she kept her favorite sweaters and hid her chocolates from my mom. But never me. Jeff carries Sammy over and her smile melts what's left of my already gooey insides. She opens her arms for me to join the hug and I do.

"Do you think I could be your flower girl, Devon?" she asks into my hair.

I choke on my spit and then smoothly play it off as a laugh. Jeff rubs my back.

"Sammy, are you planning J.J.'s wedding again? I told you that's my job."

I let go of Sammy and Jeff and find myself face to face with the woman, the myth, the legend.

"Thank you so much for inviting me, Mrs. Harrison. And thank you for the salmon you sent me and my mom!"

I'm happy to say that I have made it in this world as I am now the proud recipient of Donna Harrison care packages. Last week she sent me ten pounds of Alaskan salmon. My mother and I had to clear the freezer we never use in the garage. No one could possibly ingest that much salmon. Not even a grizzly.

She waves away my thanks and puts her arm around my shoulder and steers me toward the house. There's a Griswold-sized Christmas tree in the front window, home to at least four squirrels.

"Devon, we're so happy you came. J.J. has brought home one girl in all of his life and she was forced to partner with him on a group project on ancient Etruscan aqueducts," she explains, leading me up the path toward Jenny. She is an exact replica of her older brother, but her chin is softer, her eyes a lighter shade in the twinkling light. She's smiling at the memory, one trademark Harrison dimple indenting her right cheek.

"I remember that project because we had piles of toilet paper all over the house when J.J. took the rolls for his architecture," Jenny adds. She opens her arms to me and I step inside. She hugs like her brother. I nearly sigh, but then realize this isn't Jeff squeezing me.

"I want all the stories," I tell her and she pats my back.

"I'll write them down for you," she promises as her mom tugs me away.

"Could you two please not scare her away? I just got her to hold still." Jeff's voice reaches me through the front door as I'm ushered through a living space with the biggest couch known to man and a stone fireplace that reaches from floor to ceiling. I will live here.

I blink away the fantasy of curling up on that couch as I'm pulled into the kitchen where a huge farmhouse table is covered in cheese and bread and wine. It's nearly midnight, but the smell of marinara sauce coming from the crock pot at the center reminds me I've had nothing to eat since the nasty, stale soft pretzel at the Philly airport.

"Are you hungry, honey?"

My stomach answers with a Chewbacca sound and Jeff's mom laughs.

"Sit. Eat. Drink," she says, pulling out the bench for me so I'm across from the huge bay window that frames the back of the space.

Donna catches me staring out at the moonlit silver land that cannot be called a backyard. A back world? It goes on forever, a huge blanket of snow, the fences separating the space like stitches on a quilt. And in the center of it all sits a red barn, the lanterns on its outer walls illuminating what must be fresh paint. The red is so bright, they must have painted it yesterday—to welcome me. I giggle to myself.

"It's beautiful isn't it?" Mrs. Harrison says softly. I look up to find her taking in the scenery with the same awe that just swept over me. But there's sadness tucked in the corner of her gaze.

"It is. What a place to grow up," I say. Imagining Jeff out there, chasing his sister across the grass, hiding in the barn, riding a horse— Oh Mylanta—adult Jeff atop a horse might make me orgasm on the spot. I swallow hard just as Jenny appears in the large doorway that's framed with weathered barnwood.

"You have a small amount of catching up to do," she tells me as she pours wine into my glass. "I gotta put Sam to bed, but I'll be back to drink with you."

Sam appears beside her, her eyes wide but weary. "Goodnight, Devon! I'll see you in the morning for Pancake Pile-up."

"That sounds amazing!" I tell her and her smile widens.

"You'll see," she says wisely.

Jeff appears behind her, puts his hands on her shoulders.

"I'm gonna read to Sammy. You ok?" he asks.

I'm more than ok. There's so much excitement and love in this kitchen that I already feel drunk.

"I'm good. It'll give me time to hear your mom's version of all your most humiliating stories—so we can even the score," I tell him, lifting my wine glass.

His mom sits across from me and raises her own wine glass.

"To evening the score," she repeats.

We clink our rims and sip.

"Oh shit," Jeff murmurs.

"Yup. You're in a shitload of trouble," Sammy says, grinning up at him.

"Samantha!"

From the mouth of babes. I'm in a shitload of trouble, too, Samantha.

I meet Jeff's eyes across the space and memorize every detail of the moment—the way my cheeks hurt because I'm smiling so wide, the smell of the red sauce mingling with the burning cedar in the other room, the sound of crackling wood and Donna's soft laughter as she ladles me a huge plate of meatballs, and the light in Jeff's eyes as he takes it all in. I want to remember this exact scene so I can tell my grandkids about the first time I knew I was in love.

Chapter Forty-One

J eff

Lesson 42: Childhood posters should be removed at the age of eighteen and stored for safekeeping.

Devon is sprawled out on my bed like a starfish. A starfish who sounds like she has seawater stuck in her lungs.

Despite the awful knot in my gut from the news my mother just gave me, being back in my room feels exactly as it should. Right. Like chicken noodle soup in a mug on a sick day. And it feels even more complete with the gorgeous snoring creature taking up all the room in my bed. She fits here, amongst my dusty basketball trophies and posters of Kelly Kapowski—which makes her explode into giggles every time she looks at it. I sit down on the edge of the bed as softly as I can, but she stirs and flings an arm over her head.

Jenny and Sammy are still fast asleep, my mother still downstairs at the table covered in unpaid bills and lists of needed items. We spent an hour in the pre-dawn light pouring over the numbers, trying to figure out how to prevent what my mother tells me is inevitable.

"J.J. The therapy center is outdated. We need equipment and some of the horses need to retire. I refuse to take the money you have yet to even make. We're at the tipping point. It's sell the farm and give up the business or lose the house."

The business is her passion. And the house? The house is as much a part of this family as Jenny or I.

We argued for what felt like an eternity after that, but all I got out of her was the promise that she'd hear me out after my interview tomorrow. The woman is stubborn, no doubt, but her heart is in the right place.

I'm exhausted and the day has not begun. I let out a breath and slide Devon's bad foot into my lap then softly press my fingers below her calf. I saw her limping yesterday, when she went to brush her teeth before bed. She refuses to complain or admit it, but I know the travel has put some strain on her Achilles.

I run my thumb gently along the tendon and find the small knot in her muscle near her ankle, she groans.

"I'm gonna kick you in the face again," she says thickly.

I laugh.

"You need to get this knot out or it's going to get worse."

"Are we doing this again? You need to sleep." She rubs at her eyes and then blinks a few times and focuses on me.

"Where would you like me to sleep?"

She looks around the bed, notices that she's covering every square inch, then smiles to herself.

"I just wanted to touch all of it," she says, sliding her foot off my lap and leaning up against the wooden headboard. "Every little section of where teenage Jeff used to make love to himself while looking at Kelly Kapowski."

"Are you jealous? Because I can take her down." I stand and start to walk over to the poster.

"No!"

My fingers slide beneath the corner of the smooth paper. I lift a brow.

"You want her to stay?" I ask.

She nods. "You can't change a thing in here. It's like a shrine. To Little Jeff."

"Are you calling my penis Little Jeff?"

The laughter pops out of her like a cork. "I mean Young Jeff," she corrects.

I slide back into the bed next to her and pull her alongside of me so that we are laying face to face.

"Good. Because I wouldn't want to have to spend all day in bed with you proving you wrong about that," I say, running my hand down her side over her hip.

She makes a soft sound as I lower my lips over hers.

"Jeff," she whispers into my mouth.

"Hmm?"

I kiss along her chin. Then down her neck. She arches into me and I grab her perfect ass and keep her there.

"I heard you and your mom talking this morning. Is everything ok?"

I let my hand slide back up to a more decent place to rest as I pull back and look down into her eyes.

"The therapy center is bringing in less and less every year. It doesn't help that Donna pretends to forget to charge some of the families who can't handle the payments," I explain.

"Will they have to move? This place—it's magic. Sammy is so happy here."

I lift her chin toward me. Two little lines are etched between her brows. I run my thumb over each of them, but they stay. Persistent little worries. "It'll be ok."

She shakes her head a little and smiles. "I'm supposed to be comforting you and here you are trying to soothe me. Why are you so —*you*?"

"Years of therapy?"

She laughs, then realizes there's truth in my words. There's no judgment. No surprise really, either. In fact, the set of her lips and small breath she releases tells me that what I'm telling her makes perfect sense. I kiss the tip of her nose.

"I need to tell you something," she says against my chin, tilting her head back so I can have an unobstructed view of her full mouth.

"I'm listening."

She puts her hands around my face, wraps her fingers in my hair and pulls me back an inch, away from her, forces me to be still. Her cheeks are flushed, her eyes so wide I could dive into them.

"I'm in love with your mom's meatballs," she says and I let out the breath stuck in my throat. She smiles. "And also you. I'm in love with you. I tried really hard not to be. But my dumdum heart won't listen."

My mouth fills with words. All the words. Too many to sort through as they use my tongue as a trampoline, all bouncing around making chaos. I focus on the way the gold in her eyes starts to swim as she blinks hard and fast. I open my mouth to speak. Close it again. She's so beautiful. So soft and still so strong. She's just jumped off a cliff—broken all of her rules—with nothing but the hope that I'll catch her.

"Your heart is a genius," I say, and the smile she gives me makes me want to say more. To say everything. There's too much to tell her. So much she needs to know. I'll start with the good, because there is so much good. Then tell her the rest. We'll make it work.

"I've loved you since—"

Her lips crush against mine and she steals the breath from my lungs. She kisses me with so much urgency I have no choice but to roll her over so she's on top of me—give in to every ounce of her iron strong will. Not that I'm complaining.

When her mouth finally leaves mine, I can barely think let alone speak.

"Should we go out to the barn?" I manage.

"And miss my chance to claim you with Miss Bayside watching? Hell no."

She giggles then looks down at me with a crooked smile and a wicked gleam in her eyes.

"Tell Little Jeff we are gonna break rule twelve."

I don't need to. He already knows.

Chapter Forty-Two

Devon

Lesson 43: Comfort should be handled carefully—or you'll get too comfortable.

Sammy has painted every one of my fingernails at least fifteen times. And I use the word fingernail loosely to include the tip of my finger, my cuticles, and in some instances, all finger skin above the knuckle.

"She never was one to stay inside the lines," Jenny says over my shoulder.

I chuckle and Sammy looks up at me with Jeff's eyes. She's got me wrapped around her sloppily painted little finger.

"Do you like them?" she asks, eyebrows lifted to her widow's peak. My hair is in fifteen ponytails, spraying from all regions of my skull like a demented dinosaur. And my eyeshadow came straight off of Debbie Gibson's first album cover. Jenny warned me about a

Samantha make-over—even showed me pictures of Jeff with lipstick on his eyelids and pink streaks in his hair. But this just made me want to step up to the gauntlet.

"What's not to like? You are the Van Gogh of nails!" I twinkle my fingers in her face and she giggles. Her giggle is like running through watermelon-flavored bubbles. But it's cut short by a random thought. She wrinkles her nose and tilts her head.

"Isn't that the guy with the ear?" she asks.

I press my lips together and nod. "He did have an ear."

"No, no." She rolls her eyes. Her eye rolls rival Syd's in depth and tone. "He cut one off!" she says.

I look at her seriously. Touch my blue finger to her nose.

"Sometimes genius comes at a cost."

Sammy blinks twice.

"Are you a genius?" she asks.

Finally, I've been recognized. Jenny laughs at my expression from where she's piling like five hundred peanut butter and jelly sandwiches.

"You'll have to ask Uncle J.J. that question," I tell her, and she lights up at the prospect of just speaking to her uncle. I look up to find Jenny eyeing me from where she swipes at a generous glob of jelly with her butter knife. She smiles.

"You two have the exact same delighted expression at the mention of my brother," she says pointing the knife between us.

I look to Sammy and realize we are both smiling like we've been gifted baby guinea pigs. I lift my fist out to Sammy for a fist bump. Ain't no shame in loving Jeff.

"Mom, what time are Jeff and Grams coming home?" Sammy asks, checking all of the caps to the nail polish then placing them in her Caboodles. Man, I miss my Caboodles. The square footage of storage is absolutely astounding. I should keep one on my desk at school.

Jenny lowers her eyes back to the bread and shakes her head.

"Soon, sweetie."

If I didn't have these incredible woman senses, I'd miss the letdown of her shoulders and the puff of air escaping her flared nostrils. Jeff and Donna are out on a financial planning mission. I imagine them at the Old Savings and Loan downtown talking out their options with someone hopefully more like George Bailey than old Mr. Potter. But it's obvious that Jenny feels guilty somehow. Like she's responsible for this situation because she couldn't hold down the fort while her brother was off mastering footery.

"Are we trying to break a pb&j record?" I ask, grabbing some wheat bread.

Jenny laughs and pushes the peanut butter my way.

"You know I live with my mom, too," I tell her.

"J.J. mentioned that."

"Yup. She's the greatest. Just like your mom. But she's got her issues." I lift a giant mound of creamy peanut butter onto the bread and Jenny eyes me like she might regret letting me help.

"Don't we all?" she murmurs.

Hells yes. If there's anything I learned about mental health, it's that the spectrum is long and wide. With plenty of room for all of us to pull up a seat.

"I guess what I'm trying to say is that we can't always feel responsible for them—our moms. Especially when one has her own children to think of."

Jenny stares at me with her mother's eyes. I've stalked all the family pictures in the house and have analyzed the genetic gifts of each child—drawn up a picture of Jeff's missing father with his dark greenies in my mind. He also has a dastardly mustache.

Sammy is pushing her way between us at the counter, wielding a butter knife of her own."Uh oh, are you pulling a Van Gogh? No one wants ear in their sandwich, girl," I say, poking her in the ribs with my finger.

She squirms away towards her mom only to be met with a swipe of peanut butter on the nose. Her beautiful eyes widen, outraged at the assault.

"Oh my gosh. You didn't!" Sammy says.

I laugh and she slowly turns on me. I'm a traitor.

"You two are supposed to be grown-ups!"

This makes us laugh even harder while Sammy slowly and primly pulls the glob of peanut butter off of her nose. She wags her knife at me. Narrows her eyes.

"Just you wait til' Uncle J.J. gets home from his interview. Then it'll be even," Sammy says, flinging the peanut butter from her finger onto the wax paper with a thud.

Jenny's eyes meet mine over Sammy's dark head.

"Interview?"

I'm not sure if I've asked it out loud until Jenny nods a few seconds later, her eyes scanning my face for something.

Interview. For what? A maid? For a dog walker? No. He doesn't have a dog. I know what kind of interview it is, and my stomach is suddenly pulling my bellybutton inside out. I try to talk myself out of the pit that I'm sliding headfirst into. I mean he's been on lots of interviews these past few weeks. They don't mean anything. Obviously, he's a hot commodity. People are going to want him.

I want him.

If Jeff were thinking of taking a job across the country, I'm sure he would have told me. It's not like he would tell me he loves me and then decide to move to Chicago twelve hours later. That makes no sense. Unless he'd already decided. Unless he assumed I understood.

My head feels a little woozy and I realize I haven't breathed in some time. Jenny's hand finds my shoulder. I look down at her unpainted fingers. There's no need to jump to conclusions. Jeff will have a plan. He always has a plan.

"He'll be home soon," Jenny whispers.

And I know it's meant to make me feel better. But suddenly I'm dreading the moment Jeff walks through the door, because that's one moment closer to getting answers to the questions that are now tugging at the corners of my brain like guy lines on a tent. Naturally, the universe gives zero shits about what I want, because before the dread reaches my toes, I hear the front screen door creak open and slam shut. Sammy takes off like a terrier greeting her long-lost owner, leaving the knife to clatter on the countertop between the mountains of sandwiches. And Jeff's voice reaches me, warm and smooth as the peanut butter I'm spreading.

"Honeys, we're home."

Chapter Forty-Three

J^{eff}

Lesson 44: The smell of peanut butter will never be the same.

Sammy's dangling off my back like an orangutan as I walk into the kitchen. She smells like peanut butter—the whole house does—and there's nail polish all over her hands and wrists like she was accosted by a deranged manicurist.

"Hey," Devon says from behind a pile of sandwiches.

She looks like a pop-star Medusa from the eighties. I want to tease her. To laugh and tell her the good news, that I got my dream position at Chicago Central. That the sudden nature of the vacancy allowed me to negotiate my contract like I was on *Shark Tank*. That the signing bonus for starting sooner than I'd planned and leaving my fellowship without my specialty covered the entire mortgage debt, the new therapy equipment, and then some. That my attending was so happy to have me back, he gave me every weekend off in January and February to adjust and visit Devon. Everything is going to be ok. Better than ok. But I can tell immediately from the set of her mouth and the way she looks down at the bread in her hand that something isn't right.

I look to Jenny who gives me a sad smile and a nod to confirm what I already know.

Devon knows that I was interviewing. And she's not happy that I didn't tell her.

It's a lame excuse to say that I didn't lie—that it really was a financial mission after accepting the job and taking my mother straight to the bank. At this point, I know that the conversation we are about to have is so far overdue that the library would have just made me pay for the book. I untangle Sammy's arms from my neck and kiss her on the cheek, place her back on her own two feet.

"You wanna do a trail ride in a little?" I ask.

She lights up. The insanely bushy Christmas tree that sits behind her has nothing on that smile.

"That's a great idea, J.J. We'll get the horses tacked up. You two join us when you're ready." My mom lifts on her toes and kisses my temple then heads straight for Devon and puts her hands on each of her shoulders. "You will ride Athena. You share a spirit."

I half expect Devon to decline—spout off some rule about horseback riding—but she just tilts her head and smiles.

"Sounds like fun," she says. And my mom folds her in a hug then motions for Jenny to get the hell out of dodge.

"I gotta talk to Devon and then we can go," I tell Sammy.

Three of the four women of my life scatter from the kitchen and I'm left to face the conversation I've been dreading for so long. Devon loves me. And I love her. Now that we know, we can handle a little distance.

I walk around the island and wrap my arms around her hips, kiss the side of her neck. She doesn't tilt her head the way she usually does.

"I'm sorry," I start.

Devon keeps swiping at the bread.

"What are you sorry for, Jeff?" she says.

I put my hands on top of her arms, stilling her movement.

"We have enough sandwiches. Can you look at me?"

Her shoulders drop as she lets go of her butter knife.

"I don't know if I can look at you." Her voice is thick. "I'm scared to see something I think I should've seen a while ago."

I spin her around and twine my fingers in hers, noticing that her hands are spattered with color like she was shot with paintballs. I hold them up between us.

"No future in cosmetology," I whisper. But Devon doesn't laugh. And the absence of that sound is what scares me the most.

"You took the job, didn't you?" she asks.

Shit. We are doing this.

"Devon," I tilt her face up toward mine and a tear leaks out of the corner of her left eye, streams back toward her ear. "This was always the plan. My family needs—"

She nods and her fifteen ponytails all swing in different directions.

"I think I knew. I always knew. I just hoped. I let myself hope. When? How long?"

She's biting her lip so hard that I think she might be breaking skin. I try to brush my thumb against her lip and she turns her face.

"Right away. After the new year—" Her eyes shut slowly, blocking me out. "We can make this work. I'll fly out to Philly the first eight weekends then twice a month and you can fly here the weekends I'm on call," I say. It's not unreasonable. Until we can come up with a better solution.

"I can't do long distance."

She meets my gaze. Her eyes have hardened. The usual liquid irises look like the block of amber from Jurassic Park. And I'm the mosquito suspended in it.

"It's not long distance when I'm there and you're here."

"You know what I mean. I can't do it."

I stare down at her and wait. You don't get to make statements like that and not explain. She stares right back, every inch of softness I saw last night gone from her face.

"I can't be sitting at the table with your empty seat," she hesitates, possibly considering if she can leave it there. When she looks up at me, she must see that she can't. "I know you need to be here. I know you have to choose your career—your family. I just can't—do this again. My dad—he could never show up, Jeff. Every holiday. Every big event. We could never be his first priority. It broke us. It broke me."

I run my thumb beneath her cheekbone, through the path a tear left shimmering in the light from the pendant hanging over the island. She lets me. I wait for her to tilt her cheek into my hand. She does not.

"You aren't broken. And I'm not your father. I went into orthopedics so I could have a life—be with my family—be with you," I tell her. "I'm choosing you, Devon. I just need you to choose me." She stiffens under my touch.

"What you're asking of me is exactly what he asked of my mother. Sit around and wait—be ok with the empty seat. I can barely get her into the backyard, Jeff. It ruined her."

She tugs her hand from mine, steps back, and I swallow.

"That's not us, Devon."

"You can't promise that. Shit happens, Jeff. Just like it did that night you didn't show up for dinner."

I study her face, the way her lips tremble as she tries to breathe. The way her arms cross in front of her to protect herself—from me? I think of the scar tissue you have to cut through when you open up a joint that's been previously operated on. That's what I need to do. I've got to press a little harder.

"Move here. Come with me," I whisper. A hail Mary straight down the middle of the field.

She narrows her eyes.

"Really, Jeff? Just leave my life? Do you expect a dowry, too?"

Shit. Interception.

"What do you want from me?" I ask.

And though I really want her to answer—to give me her honest picture of a future—she looks like the question punched her in the gut. She puts a hand on the edge of the sink behind her. Shakes her head too hard.

"I can't ask it and you can't give it."

I step forward and she puts her hand up to stop me. This is the moment where you either push harder and hope for the best or find a way around the scar. I'm not trained for this. And there's no attending I can call to help.

"You need to be here for your family," she says. "And I need to be there. My students. My mom. My life is there."

"Which leaves us where, Devon?" I can't keep the anger out of my voice as I take in the stubborn set of her jaw. "You're just going to let this go and give up? That easily?"

"It's not giving up. It's saving us both from getting hurt later down the line." She looks up at the ceiling then back at me. "This is what we have to do. This is the only way."

She says it with such firmness that it feels like she's slapped me across the face. I narrow my eyes at her. It's not the only way. There is always a way. She doesn't blink. And the tears have stopped. This is what she wants. To let it crash before it's taken off, just to minimize the damage. Damage that might never happen.

"This is bullshit," I tell her. She flinches.

"You don't know what it was like. I can't do it again."

"I know what it's like to lose, Devon. And that's what this is. A loss. But worse, because you're choosing it."

She shakes her head. If only she could use some of her misguided stubbornness to fight for this. For us. *That's not what she wants.*

"It's over," she whispers. And I can't tell if she's saying it to me or to herself. But it doesn't matter because either way the words are spoken.

I need to get out of this kitchen. Away from the smell of peanut butter that normally comforts me but is now turning my stomach. I give Devon a stiff nod and turn my back on her, the buzzing in my ears so loud that I can barely hear my heart yelling at me to fight while my mind says let her go.

Five minutes ago, everything was falling into place. And yet here I am, striding out of the house and then letting the front door shut with a bang, leaving a huge chunk of my heart shattered on my mother's kitchen floor.

Sometimes the scars are so thick that there's no way around. And if you press too hard, you could end up doing more harm than good.

Chapter Forty-Four

D^{evon}

Lesson 45: Eat your meatballs before TSA.

Why does hugging Jenny and Donna goodbye feel as awful as holding on to the back of Tara's cashmere sweater when I dropped her at JFK to fly across the world to her new home? And why the hell does the pressure of Sammy's arms around my back—her face pressed into my chest in a way that normally would be uncomfortable—make me want to yank her through airport security and face criminal charges?

Jeff is last. And if I hadn't sobbed through the entire night in his bed, clutching his sheets like a stalker under the watchful eye of Bayside's most popular girl while Jeff slept downstairs on the heaven couch, so close but a world away, I'd probably break down in tears just looking at him. But I'm all dried up. Empty and brittle. One little poke could crack me open.

This hurts like a bitch. But I'd take it over the inevitability of Jeff giving up on us a year from now, when he realizes that the distance could never work. That the flights are affecting his performance as a surgeon and I'm to blame. That he barely has time with his family because of me. Or worse than all of these combined, the unthinkable could happen. Like it has before.

I meet Jeff's gaze and put a hand on my chest to keep from splitting in two.

Jenny tugs Sammy toward an airport souvenir shop, pointing toward some sort of chocolate sculpture of Wrigley Field and Donna puts her hand over her heart then passes me a vat of meatballs before following after her daughter. I hug it to my chest like it's a stuffed animal. There's nothing but silence between Jeff and me, and it's not the comfortable kind we're used to. I keep thinking about his back when he walked away from me yesterday. The set of his shoulders. *Better now than later*—my new mantra to get me through this. All I have to do is remember my mother's empty stare as I drove her to the police station from the restaurant that night—my sister sobbing silently in the back seat. Things would only hurt more down the line—with more history and memories—more to lose.

"You'll text me when you land?" he asks. His eyes are bloodshot, and I'd almost consider taking it all back just to see him smile. To see that dimple.

"I'll text Jenny."

He shuts his eyes and lets out a breath.

"Right. No contact," he says with an exhausted shake of his head.

"It'll make it easier," I say.

But I'm talking out of my ass. Nothing will make this easier. Not even the soft, rolling fog of too much wine. I tried that last night. Jenny kept it flowing for me, even sat beside me and rubbed my back while I drunk cried on her and ate five bars of Cracker Barrel.

"Nothing will make this easier," he says, and I want to laugh.

He's still reading my mind even when I'm pushing him away with all my might.

"We're doing the right thing."

He stares at me like I'm standing on a soapbox screaming that the world is flat.

"If this is the right thing, Devon, why does it feel so damn wrong?"

I look over my shoulder at the insanely long line through security. Christmas Eve flight was a poor choice. I just need to get through those metal detectors, then I can't turn back. And he can't follow me without inciting the wrath of TSA.

"Sometimes the hardest thing and the right thing are the same," I say.

"Isn't that a poster in your classroom?"

I smile. He doesn't.

I don't look up at him when I put down the meatballs and rush him like a linebacker, wrapping my arms around his waist to hug him tight. I can't not hug him goodbye. I put everything I have into that hug. Leave it all there for him to soak up and hold onto as he presses his face into my hair.

"Devon—"

Oh god, Jeff. Please don't. I slip from his grip and hurry away. I don't dare to look back as I dip in between the crowd, hurrying away from the soul-crushing pain like it's stuck to that place. It's not.

The pain shuffles beside me as I make my way around the three hundred turns of the security-check line. I cling to my meatballs. Maybe, I'll freeze them. Keep them forever.

"Ma'am, is there liquid in that container?"

I turn toward the voice and a young woman in uniform points to the two-quart Rubbermaid clutched to my bosom. I twist away a little, but the sauce sloshes and she lifts her brows.

"Very little sauce. Mostly meat," I lie. These are the sauciest.

"I'm sorry, but you're going to have to dump those in—"

"I can't! I need them for—I'm anemic! Low iron."

Shit. People are now staring. The TSA guard pulls her walkie from her waist and goes to lift it to her mouth. I imagine five officers yanking the meatballs from my frozen grip, searching my cavities for smuggled extras.

"Ok. Ok. I'll dump it," I tell her as she presses the button, the static from her walkie pushing me toward the trash can. I could just eat one before I go. I turn to the person beside me and whisper, "Do you have a fork?"

The woman pulls her kids behind her and steps away from me.

Just dump the meatballs, Devon. Let them go.

Better now than later.

I pop off the lid and give them one last look, turn my face away, and drop them into the depths of the shiny black plastic-lined bin.

J.J.—formerly Dr. Hotass— formerly formerly Dr. Dick

J.J.—formerly Dr. Hotass—formerly formerly Dr. Dick: I know you said no contact, but I wanted to let you know I'll be in Philly this weekend to pack up.

Brunch at Traversa on Saturday at eleven with Mer and Kev.

Then the ED ward in the afternoon with Syd. I'm taking her for dinner after.

I know Syd would love it if you could come.

I'd like it, too.

...

Chapter Forty-Five

J^{eff}

Lesson 46: Never underestimate the wrath of a loyal teen.

Sydney is so angry at me that she's barely touched the sourdough grilled cheese hiding in the basket of fries before her.

"How can two highly educated adults be so stupid? Masters plus doctorate equals pair of dumdums."

I let her rant and take a sip of my water as she twists at her eyebrow ring. Her hair is a new shade of red, a deep rich crimson that makes everyone passing our table glance her way. She never glances back.

"I don't know, Syd. People get hurt and then they shut down. Defense mechanisms and all that."

I reach for a fry in her basket and she smacks my hand away.

"You need to text her again. This is the last time you'll be in

Philly and she needs to get her ass in here and say goodbye," she rants. "And she's been ghosting me all week. Tell her that she doesn't get to break up with me, too."

I shrug and she sighs, lifts her sandwich to her mouth, and takes a huge bite. A line of cheese drips down her chin and she swipes it away with her napkin, then continues to glare at me.

"We had our goodbye and I can't text her again. Once was already an infraction to her no contact rule. And I'm sure she'll text you as soon as she can. We aren't having a custody battle over you," I say, attempting a small smile. It hurts my mouth, so I stop. It's like Devon took that with her, too.

My apartment on Washington Square is entirely cleared out. My patients are divvied up and under the care of capable interns and residents. Syd and I made our rounds at the children's hospital ED ward—sans Devon of course. Mer and Kev agreed not to mention her again when I threatened to leave Traversa today. They have booked flights out to visit in June and we've said our goodbye-for-nows. All the loose ends are tied and knotted. It's like I was never even here.

The drive back to Chicago is going to be a bitch—alone with my thoughts of her. I downloaded all of the lectures in the Dr. Basantis series Devon had me listening to. That should help me keep my mind off of her.

"Why do you look like I just punched you in the gut?" she asks. Another line of cheese stretches from the sandwich to her mouth.

"I think that might just be my face now."

She karate chops the cheese with her knife and shakes her head.

"I just don't get it. If you love each other why the hell aren't you over there—"

"Beneath her window with a boombox?" I interrupt.

She lifts her nose.

"What the fuck is a boombox?"

Apparently it's embarrassing to be born in the nineties. I've seen Sammy give me this exact face before. She slurps at her soda.

"You know, I really hope you don't curse like this at your interview next month," I say, reaching for the ketchup bottle.

She narrows her eyes at me.

"What interview?"

I shrug, untwist the ketchup bottle.

"I spoke to some friends at the Pediatric Center at Northwestern—"

She's around the table so fast I barely have time to release the Heinz. Her arms wrap around me and I wait until she's done squeezing me before I reach into my pocket and hand her the plane ticket. I wish Devon were here for this.

She looks down at it, the tiny diamond in her left brow reflects off the tears that fill her eyes.

"I'll never get into Northwestern," she whispers, still staring at the dark block lettering on the ticket.

I've seen Devon manage Syd's self-doubts a thousand times. Always the same dialogue, like they're reading from a script they wrote together. I find the words. Channel my inner-Devon.

"Who was that?" I ask.

She meets my gaze. Lifts a brow. Then finally gives into her role.

"Self-doubt," she tells me.

She knows this routine. And though she rolls her eyes every time, she always smiles at the end.

"What do we do with self-doubt?" I picture Devon lifting her hand into Syd's face, getting ready to tick off the answers.

"Acknowledge, accept, and restructure," Syd answers in an overly chipper tone.

I forget the next part, because I'm always too focused on Devon's smiling face.

Syd elbows me and says, "Now you tell me to 'prove it' in an obnoxious frat boy voice."

"Prove it," I say too loudly. Someone in the booth next to us clears their throat.

And there's that smile. I see a waiter nearly drop his tray while he stares at it in my periphery.

Syd doesn't see it—doesn't know she stops people in their tracks with that dazzler.

She's focused on her part of Devon's script.

"Hey, self-doubt. You're ok sometimes. But right now, you aren't as loud as my purpose. I will help kids. I will become a pediatric psychiatrist."

She looks right into my eyes as she says it. And I know she's right. There's no stopping her. Silence passes between us and Syd slides the plane ticket off the table and chews on her lip.

"I know she loves you," she tells me.

I nod. I know it, too.

"And you love her," she says.

I nod again. Open my mouth to speak and close it again, unsure if what I'm about to say might ruin this young girl—no young woman— for life. But she needs to know.

I swallow and tell her the truth.

"Sometimes that's not enough."

Syd tilts her head and makes the sound my mom makes some- times with her teeth. She looks me over like I've just told her the wrong answer to the easiest question in the world. Then she pats my shoulder twice and goes back to her side of the table where she polishes off her sandwich, leaving me to wonder who just schooled who.

Chapter Forty-Six

D^{evon}

Lesson 47: Heartbreak is not an equation you can solve.

"Each group has been given three systems of equations. To date, you've all become masters at solving them—finding the point that makes both of the equations true—like genius detectives—"

"Or master thieves cracking the safe code!" Logan interrupts me. Not surprising.

"Yes, if you'd rather be sociopaths in this simile, by all means." I give him a thumbs up while I circulate, a few well-read kids giggling to themselves at my joke. Normally that sound would fill me with that warm, gooey feeling, but it falls short. I'm much harder to fill these days.

"Anywho," I continue. "You might run into something you've never seen before with these systems. Your job is to use your teammates, your brains, and any of the resources I've placed at your tables to figure out the answers to these three systems—if you can. Mwahaha."

I steeple my fingers and do my best evil laugh. They just stare at me like I'm their mother wiping something off their chin.

Danielle's hand goes up in the back. Her acrylics are filed to points. She looks badass. "Can we use the graph?" she asks.

"Is it at your table?" I ask back.

"Yes."

I lift my brows and Danielle nods. Inference making skills. Check.

"Alright, are you ready, teams?"

A chorus of yeses smacks me from all angles. And one hell yes. I shake my head at the latter.

"Go!"

Twenty-five heads bend toward their task. Four stay still and stare at my X-men poster across the room. I'll take that percentage.

I head for my desk and set the timer on my phone, barely resisting the temptation to read Jeff's texts about being in the area last Saturday for the hundredth time. The dot dot dot had been like three quick shots to the heart. Boom. Pow. Bang. And they'd lasted there for almost an hour before they disappeared. What did he write that he never sent? I'd thought of every possible text. *I love you and I'm outside your window with a boombox.* Or, *I'm moving my family and career to New Jersey to be with you.* My imagination could be so selfish. I've reread those six bubbles a thousand times; touched the screen like I could feel him through it. Thank goodness for school and my students. They are the only thing left distracting me from this awful gaping hole in my gut. I picture it as Miss Pac-Man swallowing all the little balls of joy that she can get her greedy lips around.

"Eight minutes, sleuths and thieves," I announce, holding up my phone screen.

I love team discovery math. They are always so engaged, excited to arrive at the knowledge. The scratching of pencils on notebook paper soothes me for a moment before it gets gobbled up.

I've been texting with Jenny—a dangerous pastime, I know, based on my desperate need to escape all things Jeffish. But my dumdum heart has to check in on his mother and Sammy. And indirectly, Jeff.

It seems things are moving along as expected. They have paid off everything they needed to. And Jeff is starting his new position at Chicago Central. Life is moving on for them. Moving forward. Making progress.

Sydney will be flying out at the end of January and staying with his family. When she told me what Jeff did for her, I cried. There was joy in those tears—excitement for her incredible future—and so much pride. After everything that girl has been through, she's not tethered by her past or her self-doubt. She's a goddamned trailblazer.

But there was also something else inside me when I pictured the Harrison's home, Sammy sitting on the ginormous couch with her little feet out on the worn leather ottoman, the fire in front of her crackling beneath her family's laughter. Nostalgia, maybe? Or envy? As embarrassing as that is to admit.

None of it lasted for long. All of the emotions were swallowed whole before I had a good chance to look too closely.

"Four minutes, my people!"

"That's a lifetime!" Savannah says looking up at me. I wink. Usually I turn off timers for her because she has anxiety. But we've been working on her saying something positive every time her brain starts to become overwhelmed by the clock. She still sounds sarcastic every time she blurts out the positive thought, but at least it gets her through the panic.

My phone vibrates in my hand. Another text from Meredith. I swipe the alert up and off the screen. If it's not Meredith, it's Tara—not Tara, it's Kev and so on and so forth. The lot of them have been up my ass like they're teaming up to give me a colonoscopy. Tara with her well-intentioned reminders that she'll see me over spring break and Meredith with her absurd attempts to get me out of the house. *Your mother called. They are professionally cleaning the house so you can't go home. The chickens got into the fridge and there's bird shit everywhere. Airborne Salmonella and E.coli.* This one says *My photographer friend from South Street is doing a naked educator shoot. He wants you at his apartment by noon on Saturday. It'll be tasteful, I promise.* She's relentless and ridiculous. But appreciated.

"This is the final countdown. Duna-na-na-na. Duna-na-na-na!" I sing.

The kids take over, continuing the duna-na-na's while the clock ticks away the last minute. How I wish I could be in their desks, occupying my mind with six linear equations, discovering the answers to the unknown instead of knowing.

"Ok. Pencils up or down or whatever," I say as I turn off the awful beeping alarm. "Who wants to start?"

They look at each other. Some nudge a person in their group. Some are still staring at the X-men poster.

"I will." Danielle strums her badass nails on the desk. "Can I hang up these graphs?"

"My board es tu board," I tell her. "Magnets are in the bin over there by Jimmy."

Jimmy looks away from the poster wall.

"What?" he asks.

Kid's either stoned or stayed up all night playing video games. I point to the magnets behind him and he hands them to Danielle. She tells him thanks then whips her dark ponytail back around so she can focus on hanging up the graphs.

"Alright, so my group chose to graph these linear equations to try to get a picture of what we were dealing with."

I squint at their work. I've had these graphs blown up with my own money because there's never enough room in the budget, but I still need to get pretty close. The y-intercept is off on one of the lines, but it won't matter. They'll still be able to get to the right conclusion.

Danielle uses an expo marker and whacks the first graph so that all the heads in the classroom turn toward her. She's a goddamned natural.

"This graph shows that the two lines intersect. Which is what we've been seeing with all of the systems we've solved so far. So, they have one point in common. One x and y value that works in both of the equations. One solution." She smiles at her friend from her group then slides to the next graph. "Butttttt, this one was weird. Because when you graph the lines, they are exactly the same." She runs her expo marker over the single line on the graph. "So, they share every point—every x and y value. This must be infinite solutions."

A few ahhs and ohhs sound from the crowd. I won't even have to teach anything if Danielle keeps going at this rate.

"And what about that last one, Danielle? What did your group find?" I ask, sliding beside Jimmy to block his view of the recycling bin that he's zoning out on.

"Oh, this graph is sad," Danielle starts, pushing her bottom lip out. "These lines never meet. They are like two soulmates who will never end up together. They share nothing. There is no solution."

Two soulmates who will never end up together.

Danielle has struck a nerve. No. All the nerves. And I'm vibrating from the blow.

"Ms. G?"

She steps toward me and I try to swallow, but my throat is so thick.

This is silly. Pull yourself together. I give myself a mental bitch slap, but it barely tingles. My mind keeps returning to that graph.

It doesn't matter how long those lines go on for. They could stretch off the graph in both directions, up and down over that wall where they hang, out and away into the sky—into the universe and deep into the Earth's crust. Nothing could change their course. Nothing.

Even a thirteen-year-old can see there is no solution.

"Are you ok?"

I shake my head, then recover with a slow clap that the other students immediately jump upon. Young adults cannot resist a slow clap.

"I'm just awestruck. Well done Danielle's group!" I say over the noise.

The bell rings and they forget all about the slow clap as they stampede toward the door. I yell goodbye to them and start to straighten the desks into rows for tomorrow, nice and neat and orderly, unlike my insides. My eye catches on something hot pink in the back of the room and I make my way toward it, bend and pluck the post-it off the floor between my fingertips. I turn it over and read what's clearly a child's handwriting.

Shadow Daddy

And just like that, my own Ms. Pacman is swallowed whole by Jessica's pain.

Chapter Forty-Seven

J^{eff}

Lesson 48: Excision is never easy. Excision from the heart can be deadly.

I hate removing hardware from the human body. Obviously, it comes with the job, just as implanting the hardware does, but there is always a greater risk the second time you open someone up. The tissue is more scarred. Vessels and nerves are at greater risk than the original surgery. And the incision is always bigger the second time around. The surgery I just performed, my last of the day, was no exception to this general rule.

All in all, the removal was not as clean as I'd have liked—far more difficult than I expected.

Much like my removal of Devon from my life. Except more difficult doesn't cover it. Devon isn't a screw that I can pull from my bone. She's the marrow itself.

Of course, it might not hurt as much if I were to restrain myself from the contact I have with her mom and Tara; not to mention Mer, Kev, and Syd. I feel like every text and phone call between us is just covered in Devon even though the only one to come right out and mention her name is Sydney. She refuses to let it go. Even if Devon has told her a hundred times that it's over.

Last Saturday she told me that Devon saw the sunflowers and cards I'd sent the teens at the ED ward and had immediately teared up and left for the bathroom. The goal was to make her smile, not cry. But Syd insists that these little breakdowns are steps in the right direction. I'm just unsure what the right direction is.

My own family isn't much help, either. They do nothing to skirt around the fact that they've been in contact with her. My traitorous mother even sent out a care package, procured and put together by my sister. I, on the other hand, have been given no such care. In fact, one of the first things my mother said to me after we'd sealed and stamped the final check to the mortgage company, was "Go get her, you idiot."

It's so cold in Chicago, the moment I step outside the hospital doors, I can't feel my face. Sirens squeal in the distance on their way toward where I just left, and I send a silent wish that everything turns out ok for whoever needs that awful sound. I bite off my glove and shake out my fingers as I hurry toward Lake Shore Drive. The closer I get to the water, the windier it gets, and when I pull my phone from my pocket, a few snowflakes float through the blueish light of my screen and make tiny wet dots on the glass. I swipe them away and dial Jenny.

"Hey," she says. Sammy's voice squeals in the background that she has Gin Rummy.

"What do you guys want to eat?" I ask her.

"Pizza is fine."

Sammy claps in the background and starts a "Pizza" chant. I hear my mother join in and almost smile.

"We had pizza last night," I remind her.

"Fan favorite," Jenny says.

She tells Sammy to deal again. The kid is a card shark thanks to hours with Grams.

"Alright, be over in about an hour. I have somewhere to go first."

Jenny is silent for a moment, perhaps debating whether or not to ask where I'm headed. A gust of wind steals my breath as I step onto the walking path along Lake Michigan and then Jenny's soft voice fills my ear again.

"Love you, J.J."

"Love you, too."

I hear everyone in the background yell their love for me and then the line goes silent. All of that love and somehow my chest still aches with every frigid breath I take.

I keep my eyes focused on the white stone turrets of Northwestern University that try to reach up toward the glass skyscrapers along Michigan Ave. A modicum of warmth flows through me at the thought of Sydney's upcoming visit next week. She's going to knock the socks off of this admissions interviewer. The man she's scheduled with doesn't know what he's in for. Her personal essay was so moving —vulnerable and inspiring—I could barely speak for an hour after reading it.

I head through the tree-lined commons area, passing the college students in their boots and mittens on their way to whatever party or bar is least likely to check IDs. I follow the signs for the path toward Feinberg School of Medicine and push through the heavy wooden doors beneath the arched entryway.

There's a guest lecturer tonight, and I have an appointment to talk to her directly after her presentation. Which ended five minutes ago. I hurry toward the auditorium as students and doctors file past me, shrugging on coats and wrapping on scarves as they go. They are discussing the lecture, commenting on the power of positive thinking and on the studies that surprised them most. I get to the open doors just as the last student pushes out.

The woman who is in the center of the semicircular lecture hall surprises me with how young she is and I can hear Devon's voice reprimanding me for being an ageist or sexist or both. She's bent over her computer at the table in the center pit, adjusting the text on a slide about body image that is mirrored on the huge projection screen behind her. I clear my throat and start down the steps. She pauses what she's doing and looks up at me, pushing her glasses up into her dark hair.

"You must be Dr. Harrison," she says with a smile.

I reach my hand out over the table and she shakes it with a firm grip.

"Thank you so much for meeting with me, Dr. Basantis. When I saw that you'd set up camp in town, it seemed too good to be true," I tell her.

She waves the flattery away.

"I should be thanking you," she says, snapping her laptop shut. "I've been looking for someone like this for over a year now."

I nod. "She's very special." I swallow hard. Special doesn't cover it. "She's passionate about her students' mental health and about education. I'd love for you to talk to her."

She slides her laptop into her messenger bag. Her dark eyes crinkle at the corners and she tilts her head like she can see right into my mind.

"Let's get a coffee and you can tell me all about this Ms. Gallagher."

I nod and let her lead the way.

Chapter Forty-Eight

D^{evon}

Lesson 49: Ambushes can be helpful.

"Mom!" I shout up the staircase as I yank off my jacket and hang it on the hook in the hallway. "You are not going to believe how shitty my day was."

Silence meets my somewhat whiny voice that I reserve only for conversations with the woman who is forced to love me by genetics.

"Mom?"

I hold still in the hallway, halting my progress toward the Friday-post-shitty-week beer that has my name on it. I listen for her snores. Another lucky inheritance for me.

Nothing.

"Kathy?" I try again, turning back toward the front of the house to check for her car.

As I pull back the curtain, something like hope courses through me. But it's swallowed quickly. The old hunk of junk sits unmoved in the driveway. Why wouldn't it be? She must be out back with the chickens—socializing.

Just before I let the heavy fabric slip from my fingers, the puttering of an engine fills the living room space and a hunter green sedan bumps its way up our long driveway between the leafless trees. I stare, wondering who the hell is visiting my mother or myself on a Friday afternoon. Well, really, on any afternoon. We don't entertain often.

I hit my forehead on the glass trying to get a better look at the driver—a woman in glasses who I've never seen in my life. But my focus is interrupted when my mother slips out of the passenger seat and slams the car door behind her, yelling and waving her goodbyes as the stranger reverses back from where she came. I'm rubbing the place where I smacked my head, sure to be a horn within the hour, as my mother sort of skips up the porch and stops when she sees me staring out the window.

She lifts her hand in greeting, but I can't find my muscles. I just stare at her, my mind muddled with impossible explanations. *She was kidnapped. Then returned by the FBI.* Didn't my phone ping a silver alert today? My mother shrugs the shoulders of her sherpa-lined coat and pushes through the front door so that I'm left staring at the snow dust whipping around our front yard like ghosts.

"Hi, honey," she says.

I turn slowly. Lift a brow.

"How was your day?" she asks.

I laugh. She rolls her eyes and hangs her coat beside mine.

"My day was shit. Principal Dickhead is still angry at me for initiating the crisis protocol for that student I told you about and then on top of that, he removed all of my mental health posters from my room."

I feel rage about all of this—the insanity of being told not to save a child in the way I've been trained. Jessica is where she belongs now thanks to that training—that protocol put in place to protect. But none of that matters to the powers that be. What matters is that I've cracked the ice Jess was trapped under, and while she can finally breathe, the cracks in the district's veneer are now visible to everyone looking on.

I let out my anger on a breath and focus on my mother. "But none of that matters because I believe someone else had a good day. I believe someone has been hiding something from their favorite daughter."

She moves toward the kitchen and I follow her.

"Hiding is a strong word, dear," she tells me as she opens the fridge and takes out my Friday-post-shitty-week beer. "And I hide nothing from Tara."

Low blow. But I shan't be distracted.

"Is it? I just saw you sitting shotgun in an ugly green Taurus. You haven't been in a car since I dragged you into my back seat when your appendix burst."

I point to the beer and she slides it across the counter.

"I've been seeing a cognitive behavioral therapist," she tells me.

We both twist open our drinks at the same time. The sound of released pressure pops and then fizzes in the space between us.

So many questions. But first, a sweet punch of joy. This is the biggest win since the Phillies took the pennant. My mother not only left the house, she left the house with a goddamned licensed professional.

"This is amazing news," I tell her.

She nods and gives me a small smile.

"I've gotten to the 7-11 by the old Blockbuster," she murmurs.

"Inside of it!?"

Another small nod.

"Holy shit, Mom. I'm so proud of you." I lift my beer and she lets out a breath and clinks the rim against mine.

"My goal is to get to Tara's with you in the spring," she tells me, and I notice the glassy determination in her eyes for the first time.

"When did—how did you find this cognitive—?"

She walks away, cutting me off midsentence, and calls over her shoulder, "Gotta get changed!"

And just like that I know. I know how she found help—or how help found her.

This was Jeff's doing.

I run after her, my clumsy footsteps stumbling up the stairs as she doesn't even miss a beat.

"Jeff sent her, didn't he?"

My mom's hands go up.

"Mom, just tell me—"

She whirls on me.

"Why don't you ask him yourself, Devon? You're a big girl. And he's obviously worth the text message."

Uh oh. She's using the same tone she used on me when she found cigarettes in my Altoid tin in ninth grade. Ingenious hiding spot, I know.

I look down at the grey carpet that runs through the upstairs hallway. I can't.

"I can't," I whisper at my feet.

I can feel her staring at me like two hot pokers are being stuck into the top of my head.

"You can't," she repeats. But there is no anger this time. Her arms go around me and I let myself sink into her hug. She gives the best mom hugs. "You know, I *can't* leave the house, but I just tasted all the Slurpee flavors at 7-11. So sometimes can't just isn't the right word."

I sigh into her shoulder. Mom wisdom is the worst. I'm about to ask her if they had blue raspberry when I hear the front door open and close below us.

"Mrs. G, we're heeeerrrreeee," Syd yells.

I push out of my hug and look up at my mother.

"What else are you keeping from me, woman?" I ask.

She smiles and my hair stands up.

"Go downstairs and greet our guests. I've gotta change my shirt."

She points to a red blotch on the hemline and I imagine her beneath the cherry Slurpee nozzle, mouth open, head back.

Guests? Syd doesn't count as a guest. I crane my neck around the hallway corner and try to see down the stairs as I navigate downward, but they've moved on. I arrive in the kitchen just in time to hear Meredith telling Syd that she had to saw through a sternum today. Syd's eyes are so wide. Awe is dripping from her bottom lip.

"Devon!" Syd wraps her arms around me then releases just as quickly and barks, "Sit!"

Kevin stands and gives me a look that I got from my teacher in elementary school when I put the chicks in the class toilet to go for a swim. I'm in trouble. I swerve for the fridge and grab another beer before circling back around and heading to the chair Kev pulled out between him and Mer. My mother's seat at the head of the table is left empty and waiting. The queen's chair. I slide into the pauper's chair and meet Kev's clear blue gaze for a long second before he looks away and pats me on the back. A pity pat.

"So, to what do I owe the pleasure of this little visit? Saturday dinners usually happen on a Saturday not a—"

"Alright, so first, thank you all for coming," my mother says as she breezes into the kitchen and slips into her throne. "I promise to wine and dine you after this—"

"What is *this*?" My voice no longer belies my suspicion, and Meredith's hand gives my thigh a reassuring squeeze. Which makes my suspicion worse.

"This is your idea, honey."

I have many great ideas. Edible Chapstick. Magnetic wallpaper. Disposable vibrators. I can't keep track.

Luckily, Syd clarifies, "An emotional intervention."

I shake my head. "Firstly, I did not come up with the idea of emotional interventions. And secondly, aw hell no." I start to stand.

"Sit down, Devon Michelle."

Ugh. The middle name. I sit with a juvenile harrumph. Syd mouths my middle name to Meredith who nods sadly.

"Mr. Gallagher had a thing for Grease 2 and Michelle Pfeiffer," Mer explains.

My mother begins, "So, we are gathered here today—"

"You forgot 'dearly beloved.' Can we get a bottle of wine opened first?" I sip my beer.

"—to help Devon understand that she has a problem. And, hopefully, give her a plan to move forward."

Sweet Giuseppe. We are doing this.

"Who would like to start?" my mother asks.

I raise my hand. She ignores me and chooses Mer. I note how that feels so I don't do it to my students. Meredith swivels in her chair so she is looking right at me. My heart skitters left then swerves right.

"Alright, here we go. Devon—" She pushes her lips together, and I can see her mouth rebelling against whatever she's about to say. "You are my dearest friend and I love you very, very much. So you need to stop being a complete ass—"

"Remember, Mer. 'I' statements," my mother corrects.

"Right. I can no longer sit by and watch you be a complete ass."

I lift my brows waiting for my mother to correct her obvious misuse of an I statement. Mom just folds her hand in front of her and nods.

"You have found someone who you want to sleep with more than four times," Mer continues. I give her a warning look and incline my head toward Syd. Young ears. Syd rolls her eyes. "And you are pissing it away because of your fear."

"I statements—"

"I feel like you need to stop being a little bi—"

"Ok, thank you Meredith. Kevin, would you like to go next?" my mother asks.

He nods. Grants me a small smile.

"Devon, it's hard for me to say this—we've always shared so much and I've been in love with you for so long—"

What in the? Who's loving who, now?

"Until I saw you and Jeff together and recognized that there was something more. The way you look at him—that's what I want. I want someone to light up like you do when Jeff walks into a room. And I want to laugh at her dumb jokes."

"My jokes are not—"

He lifts a hand. "I still love you—just less pathetic-stalker and more hoe-bro."

My lips move, repeating the term hoe-bro quietly. Trying it on for size, while Kev races on, "I love you the right amount. And I want you to have all of that stuff I mentioned. I want you to have your Jeff."

My Jeff. I stop saying hoe-bro to myself and try to take in the whole monologue.

"That's a lot to process," I whisper.

"Well said, Kevin," Mom says.

Kevin smiles like he's just received a compliment from the chief of surgery.

My mom doesn't seem to give a shit about processing time because she already has her own spiel waterfalling out of her mouth and into my tired brain. I might run. My amygdala wants me to run. Meredith pulls my chair around the corner of the table, closer to her and my amygdala sends a smoke signal to the ether. Trapped.

I tune into Mom's voice, realizing I've done that Charlie Brown thing where her words sound like the announcements in school.

"Devon, I know you want to run right now. You've got that frantic look you had when you 'overdosed' on pot and thought the SWAT team had the house surrounded."

Shittttt. That was intense.

"I need you to take a breath and make sure you aren't tuning me out. This is important. And I've been working on it with my therapist for months."

"Months?"

She nods at me.

"October 13th," she tells me, her eyes scanning my face for recognition.

That's the Monday after Jeff met her. The Monday after the

shed. Long before I even thought about allowing him near my box-o'love—well—maybe, I'd thought of it. But, still. It was before. Before us.

Something about this fact has lodged itself in my throat and refused to budge—a little throat-squatter.

"I met your dad at a co-ed wedding shower for one of my college professors. He told me he had no idea who any of the people at the party were—that he was just there for the free brunch and booze. He was arrogant. Third year in med school. Better looking than even Kevin." She throws Kev a wink and I watch her eyes fill with watery starlight before the next part. The next part is my favorite. "But he sat through that whole shower making me laugh despite my attempts to ignore him and then before I went to leave, I watched him help clean up with the couple's mom and pack every gift that they'd received into their car. That was it."

"He did pack a mean car," I muse, remembering the way he would make us leave all of our luggage on the curb and then play a mental game of Tetris while we all piled in to fight over the music or the temperature or whatever the hell we thought was important then.

"Your father was a doctor, Devon. He was a surgeon and he cared a lot about his patients. But he cared more about you. About us. Surgery wasn't everything that he was. And I think we forget that sometimes. That we blame that part of him even though it was just a piece of his puzzle. A part that we loved before—just as much as all the other parts."

She flattens her palms on the table surface and meets my gaze. A million memories are assaulting me, the sound of his bad jokes and my laughter as we sat here—at this table. The look of pure joy on his face every time I walked into the hospital on the day after a call to bring him leftovers. The feel of his calloused fingers wrapped around my hand—the smell of soap always following him because he'd scrub them raw to keep us from getting sick. I reach across Meredith's lap and grab my mother's hand from the table. It's softer than his was.

"The accident wrecked us, Devon. But, it was an accident. It wasn't written in stone somewhere. It wasn't his choice. And it certainly wasn't something any of us could control. I don't want to be counted in the wreckage anymore, hun. And he wouldn't want that, either."

Fat, salty tears are making their way over my cheeks and into Mer's lap. To her credit, she doesn't seem to care. She's rubbing my back as I'm still sprawled out across her.

"That was one hell of a speech," I manage.

Everyone around the table nods. I look to Syd, fiddling with her eyebrow ring.

"Tough act to follow, kid," I say.

Syd just smiles and slides a folded piece of paper across the table. There's smudges and thumb prints all over it and when I reach for it, the paper is feather thin, soft from being handled, the creases so deep I could fall in them.

"What's this?" I ask.

Syd shrugs and pushes her lips together while I unfold the paper that appears to have been ripped out of a binding. My sloppy cursive is the first thing I recognize.

Dearest Sydney Rae,

What a year. Girl, you went through it. But look at you. June 21st, and here you are in front of me, an 8th grader for one more endless day, trying to peek at what I'm writing even though I told you to get away from my desk and go sit down.

You never listen. You were born to defy—in the most annoying but amazing way.

Whenever that voice comes back, Syd—whenever it tells you who you are or what you can and cannot be. I want you to defy. No more restrictions. No more stopping the world from giving you what you deserve. DEFY.

Because you deserve everything. All of it. All the love. All the food. All the fun. The best that life has to offer. And if you restrict yourself from any of it, you could miss out on all of it.

When you forget that, you just reach out. I'll be there to remind you what a defiant pain-in-the-what you can be.

All my love,

Ms. G

I look up from the note that I wrote in her yearbook—the note that she ripped out and obviously has carried in her wallet/pocket/heart for the past four years. Syd's smile widens and I press the words to my chest hoping they brand me.

"If you restrict yourself from any of it, you could miss out on all of it," she recites.

I want to stand, fold her in my arms, but I don't get the chance. Before I can even push back in my chair, I'm attacked by all of them in an epic group hug.

Through the heap of bodies and the smothering love, Tara's voice reaches me from the phone sitting in the middle of the table.

"Ummm, guys. I'm still here…"

Chapter Forty-Nine

D evon

Lesson 50: Sometimes the only way forward is to grab that microphone —again.

I'm sweating like I've been sitting in a steam room for an hour. I've told myself repeatedly that this would be just like Back-to-School Night—that I would say my spiel, get my point across with a smile and some well-placed humor, then get the heck out. But the truth is, this is nothing like BTSN. This is nothing less than the most important thing I've ever done.

The cafeteria at our middle school is packed with parents and teachers and administrators. Seven school board members sit at a string of long tables on the stage, my superintendent, Dr. Franklin, amongst them. Five of them are bent over their cellphones looking particularly bored by the chatter and laughter bouncing off the metal walls of our auditorium. When Dr. Franklin approaches the micro-phone, the speakers flanking the stage release an ear-splitting sound that I now believe is done on purpose to shut people up. It works. The crowd shuffles and slides into their seats and Dr. Franklin pushes his glasses up higher on his nose and begins.

"Hopefully, you all grabbed a copy of the agenda as you came in. Let me first start by thanking you for coming out here tonight in this awful weather." He pauses and gives the audience a practiced smile. "You probably noticed that we're starting with open microphone tonight, so that you folks can get home earlier and get warm."

Bullshit. They start with open mic so the parents can miss the political nonsense they pass at the end of the meeting. If they aren't here to hear it, then they can't fight it.

"So, let's take attendance and then open it up to you fine people."

He begins to call the names of the remaining school board members, who barely look up from their phones in order to stand and give a small wave. He ends with the president, a middle-aged blonde woman who I recognize immediately when she stands from the president's seat and looks out at the crowd for the first time. My pulse races. It's Mrs. Stoner. And she looks tired. Defeated. My heart crumples a little for her. Jessica is doing well in her inpatient treatment, but she'll be at the facility for weeks to come. And I'm not a mother, but I can imagine that none of this is easy for her.

The temptation to tuck tail and make a beeline for the double doors is so strong that I have to grip the edge of my seat. *Remember who you are doing this for.*

"Alright, all present and accounted for. The floor is officially open for concerns, suggestions, and questions," Dr. Franklin tells us before he turns and heads back to his seat.

I stand—force my feet to move—as I whisper "excuse me" to the people I squeeze by, ignoring their curious and perhaps judgmental looks as I make my way to the podium placed in the middle of the cafeteria floor that faces the board of ed. I have no notecards—no speech written on paper—just the words burned into my heart. The words my friends and family helped me find.

I stand behind the podium and send a silent thank you to Tara for the pair of heels I found left in her closet. Even with them, I have to lower the microphone to meet my needs, and it shrieks its protest, as expected. But the room was already silent.

I stare at the black bulb I'm meant to speak into and take a deep breath. It wasn't so long ago that a microphone turned on me and attacked like a cobra. But if it hadn't, I'd never have met Jeff. And that's an alternate universe I'd never want to consider.

"Good evening parents, fellow teachers, administrators, and board members," I begin, my voice as shaky as my hands. I take a deep breath and look around the room. Find my school guidance counselor, Elizabeth, and focus on her smiling face—take strength from it.

"I'm Devon Gallagher and I've been lucky enough to teach eighth grade math in this district for the past ten years."

As I shift my gaze from Lizzie, I notice more familiar faces—parents of students past and present. Families that have touched my life and sent kind words that I too have touched theirs.

I stand a bit straighter.

"It's with a heavy heart that I stand here tonight to give my notice of resignation from my position." My voice does not shake this time.

The room fills with hushed whispers and Dr. Franklin looks around, stands, and makes his way to the microphone.

"Ms. Gallagher first let me thank you for your service to our community these past ten years. I've had your name pass my desk on several occasions and always in midst of accolades and gratitude," he says. He pauses, meeting my gaze. "You do know that a simple letter of resignation would suffice—"

I lift a hand.

"I apologize, Dr. Franklin, but in this case, it would not."

He lifts his grey eyebrows and opens his mouth to speak again, but then thinks better of it and nods before returning to his seat beside the school board president. She is staring at me with an expression I cannot read—and perhaps don't want to.

"The reason I'm speaking here tonight is to remind us all of our district's mission statement: 'We seek to create an equitable education for all students to ensure that they are fully respected and respect—"

"Ms. Gallagher, I believe we all know our district's mission statement, as we end each board meeting with it," says a woman at the end of the table. The brown plaque in front of her reads Mrs. Graham. Not a familiar name.

I shake my head. If only she would listen to those words.

"We all may know the words, Mrs. Graham, but sometimes we need a reminder of what they mean."

She sits back, lets out a long breath that hits the microphone and makes a deep static. And I continue.

"These words have always been easy for me to live by—to respect every individual no matter what they believe, look like, who they love or identify as—no matter what they battle silently in their minds. And, believe me, they battle. More than any of us could ever imagine. Every student who has passed through my class has felt respected in every possible way, despite the difficulties this district has presented in making that happen."

Dr. Franklin shifts his weight and his metal chair makes a screeching sound on the stage. I stare right at him.

"Five years ago, I was told not to discuss mental health in my classroom. Against all of my better judgement and every National Mental Health Organization's expert advice, I was quieted about a subject that should be discussed openly and often. I was told it is not my area of expertise. I was told to 'stay in my lane.'

"After several months of confusion, silence, and frustrated tears, I decided to make mental health my lane. I went back to school, received a master's in adolescent psychology, all so I could uphold this district's mission statement. And despite our contracted tuition reimbursement program for teachers' continuing education, I was denied. 'Irrelevant subject continuity.' Irrelevant? Is there anything more relevant in this world than your children's mental health?" I meet the gazes of the parents I recognize.

A low murmur breaks out across the auditorium and I see Dr. Franklin go to stand up. But just then, the auditorium doors open, and there is Sydney with that smile. She steps to the side and holds the door, ushering in dozens of current and past students, some older than I'd care to admit. I can feel my eyes fill up at the sight of them as they make their way down the center aisle to stand behind me. My people.

"I didn't quit then. I couldn't. I needed to be here for them—" I wave my arm toward the group behind me. Goodness, there must be fifty of them. Syd did her job well. I motion to her to make her way up onto the stage.

"Sydney, one of my former students, and now a lifetime part of my family is going to show you a poster."

Syd makes her way up the steps onto the stage, gives a little head nod to each of the board members, then turns and unrolls my crisis hotline poster.

"Many of you have seen this before. Maybe you even have one where you work, but for those who don't know, it's a piece of paper that has saved many lives. Some lives that happen to be in this room today. This poster has been hanging in my room for many years. This year, I was asked to take it down by someone who has promised to uphold this district's mission statement. I refused, and months later, along with my power to help children the best way I know how, it disappeared from my room."

The murmurs erupt into full blown chatter and Dr. Franklin moves swiftly to stand beside Sydney on the stage.

"Surely you aren't accusing an administrator of stealing your posters, Ms. Gallagher," he says.

I shake my head.

"I'm not. I'm not here to make accusations. I'm here to advocate for my students—to remind you that, despite your beliefs, they have the right to feel safe and respected. To get help when they need it."

I turn to the young adults behind me and nod. One by one, they approach the wall of the auditorium and hang up the signs and posters they made. The gentle clicking of their magnets connecting with the wall sounds like someone banging away on a typewriter. Some of them are exact replicas of the ones stolen from my room and some are more personal. Statements of who they are—who they love —what they face every day. When the last magnet clicks into place, and the final student turns and meets my gaze, I let the tears fall silently as I take them in. Then I nod, turn to the microphone, and say, "Thank you for these ten amazing years. I wish all of your children the best."

I turn, walk down the center aisle between the metal seats, eyeing the black cord that runs along the path. But this time I make it without humiliation, my focus so singular that I barely hear the sound of murmured thank yous and growing applause as I push through the auditorium door. I just want to get out without incident—get home to my mother to celebrate the call I received from Dr. Basantis—to even out the adrenaline now pumping through my system with a nice cold beer. But I hear my name being called as I step out into the miserable wet chill and I stop wrestling with my jacket and slow my pace.

"Please, Ms. Gallagher. I need—"

I stop, swallow down a freezing gulp of wind, and turn to find Mrs. Stoner staring at me—her face red from the chase. Or from anger.

"Ms. Gallagher. We need to talk."

I shut my eyes, ready to be berated for my role in her daughter's treatment. She needs someone to blame, and here I am, wet and cold and ripe for the picking. But no angry words hit me. I open one eye to see where they could have hit instead to find Jessica Stoner's mother trying hard to wipe the tears from her cheeks with the palm of her hand.

"I'm sorry, Ms. Gallagher. There's no—I should have—I didn't know." She lets out a low sound, a mix between a sob and a whimper and her pain shakes me so hard I feel it in my teeth. "That's wrong. I knew. I knew something was going on. I was too scared to act. Jessica had always been so bright. So together. I couldn't believe it. I didn't know where to turn. And now—"

Her words are cut off by her hands covering her face as another howl of icy wind slices through the parking lot between us.

"I understand, Mrs. Stoner." And as I look at her fall apart before me, thinking of my own mother, I do. I'm not a mom, but I can feel the guilt radiating off of her like it's heat. "There's no handbook for this. No training for being a mom."

She slides her hands off her face and lets out a breath.

"You saved her life," she whispers, she puts both hands out in front of her. "Thank you. Thank you so much."

I take her hands and squeeze, then put everything I have into what I tell her.

"None of this is your fault. It's no one's fault. Jessica will be ok."

She holds my gaze for what feels like an eternity. Then she nods, thanks me again, and makes her way back through the doors that I passed through for 185 days of every year for the last decade of my life.

Chapter Fifty

Jeff

Lesson 51: The greatest things happen in recovery.

I'm spent. I need about ten hours of sleep and 64 ounces of caffeine to get ready for Sydney's arrival tonight, but I only have time for the latter. I slip off my white coat and hang it on the back of my office chair. I'm grabbing my parka off the hook on the door when it pushes open and I need to slide out of the way or get pinned.

"Oh, I'm so sorry Dr. Harrison," Danny says, wincing. "I know you want to get out of here, but there's a patient in recovery that might need you."

"Whose patient is it?" I ask, less annoyed than surprised that one of my colleagues would not be around to help after they operated.

Danny shrugs and lifts up his palms to let me know he's just the messenger.

"Alright. I'll be right there."

I go to thank Danny for letting me know, but he's already slipped back out into the hall, headed toward the nurses' bay. I hang the parka back on the hook and shrug the white coat back on. Syd will kill me if I'm late to pick her up. Or worse, she'll ask me if she can drive my car.

I slip my phone out of my pocket and check the time. I've got forty-five minutes to get out to O'Hare—an impossible task if it weren't rush hour in Chicago. I blow out a frustrated breath and press on Devon's video for the thousandth time today. Her clear voice bounces off the tile floor of the hospital hallway. I've memorized every word of this speech—every movement of her hands and tilt of her head. She's a warrior. An angel of vengeance. And apparently, I'm only one of three million viewers who finds her fascinating.

I feel every ounce of respect and love that's visible in the students' eyes as they look to Devon from where they stand. Was I ever that brave? To stand for something like these kids did that night? No, I wasn't. But I didn't have Devon Gallagher to lead me. And Syd. Well, I'm not surprised by her anymore. She could hand me the moon and I would think, "makes sense."

It's been two weeks since this video surfaced and went viral. And still no contact.

I was stupid to believe this changed anything—that maybe Devon's decision meant we stood a chance. I texted her against all instincts for self-preservation and—crickets. The silence has just added a second layer of heartbreak. Even Sydney has stopped pushing me to make some grand gesture. If Syd gives up, you know it's hopeless.

The heels of my boots click through my self-pity as I approach recovery. It is eerily empty. No sign of the nurses who work tirelessly to keep our patients alive and well. Maybe Danny had it wrong. But then I hear murmuring behind a closed curtain. I take in a strengthening breath and make my way toward the blue plastic, stopping when I hear Syd's familiar voice.

"Just put your hair down. Try to look a little sexy—"

There's the sound of someone slapping skin, then a familiar giggle.

My fingers close around the edge and I pull back the curtain, listening hard over the messy clattering sound the metal rings make against the rod.

I freeze, curtain still in hand.

Syd is reaching around Devon's head, trying to get at her hair band and Devon is smacking her hands away, much like she had when I tried to inspect her Achilles.

"Hi," she says from beneath Syd's armpit.

That smile. I forget to breathe.

Syd spins, smiles at me, and says, "I'll be waiting in the men's locker room," then brushes past and leaves me to take in what I've been missing.

She's sitting on the table with her legs up and her shoes off so that I can see the bottom of her socks where there's a little picture of an open can labeled whoop ass.

My tongue is so thick, I'm going to choke on it. Her cheeks redden a little and she pulls her bottom lip into her mouth. Talk, Jeff. Move. But I can't even think past the moron screaming in my brain. *She's here. She's here.*

No shit.

She looks down at her lap. The smile that blinded me when I opened the curtain has crumbled at the edges as she rambles. "I came with Syd. For moral support—not that she needs it—and I'm in town to meet Dr. Basantis about a job offer—but I'm sure you know all about that."

I nod.

"Jeff—" she starts then stops. She slides her ass to the edge of the table and reaches her toes toward the tile that's still a stretch away.

"Don't stand up," I tell her.

She narrows her eyes.

"Just give me a second to think. And to figure out this isn't my reoccurring dream," I say.

Her smile unfolds, slow but certain.

She scoots back onto the table and bends her legs beneath her.

Her voice is a whisper. "What you did for Syd. No. What you did for my mother. For me."

I take a step closer. Reach out to touch her foot, then pull back.

"It's no different than what you've done for every student in your classroom."

She shrugs and says, "It was nothing."

"We both know it's not nothing."

"Fine, it's something." She looks up at the hospital lights and chuckles. "You know your mom sent me a care-package."

"I'd heard—made Jenny go pick up whatever the hell it was—"

"It was a vibrator," she laughs.

Oh, mother. What the hell am I going to do with that woman?

"With a note—a poem really—*while you're away without my son, bought you this for a bit of fun.*"

I nod. "Clever."

"Very," Devon agrees.

"So, why are you here?" I ask.

I catch her eyeing my white jacket and dip my head lower to interrupt her gaze.

"In the hospital?" she murmurs.

I nod.

"I think you messed something up when you—"

"Operated? Because we've been over this."

She shakes her head and pushes her lips together.

"I think you messed something up when you let me leave Chicago," she finishes.

The moron in my brain stops screaming. And the chorus starts to sing.

"Could you repeat that?"

"Sure. You messed up," she says, then lifts a brow.

Like I give two shits who we blame this on. As long as she's here —with me.

"So, this time, I'm to keep you here with me? No matter what you say?"

I sit on the edge of the table, wrap my fingers around her good ankle.

"Exactly. I brought that DVD in case you need pointers. I give you permission to shackle and chain if necessary." She waggles her brows and I chuckle as she leans forward so that her eyes are even with mine, lips a breath away. "But I promise it won't be necessary. I want to be where you are."

I bite down on a smile.

"And the Basantis job has nothing to do with this? Heading up a non-profit that educates educators about mental health? What is it again—outreach advocate?"

"Fringe benny," she whispers into my mouth. "And it's awareness ambassador."

I yank her ankle so it's in my lap and catch her head with my hand in her hair.

"I'm scared," she whispers.

I pull her closer. Press my head to hers.

"I'd be nervous if you weren't," I tell her. "Were you scared when you took on a school board?"

She nods and her lips brush against mine.

"It was worth it," she says. "Just like this."

She kisses me with so much force I nearly fall backward off the recovery bed. Every cell in my body exhales in relief when those lips touch mine. I wrap my arms around her, pull her close, take every-thing she has to offer as she tells me between kisses that she loves me. I swallow those words, let them fill me until my body wants more and I'm dizzy.

"Let's get out of here," I say in her ear, our heavy breathing slicing through the still air of the recovery bay.

She pushes back, but I keep my promise this time and don't let her go. She stares right into me and smiles wide, dazzling me like she did the first night we met.

"Alright, Dr. Hotass. Let's go home."

And this time around, we walk out of recovery together.

Acknowledgments

It's been years since I wrote this novel, but I can still remember how special it felt to find Devon in my brain. So many teachers inspired me, both through my own education, and through my career alongside them.

We will start with my husband. Steve, thank you for pushing me to go back to school and step into the classroom. Watching what you do for your students and the way you care will never cease to amaze me. You deserve all the gratitude, all of the accolades, and all of the end-of-year presents you always get more of than me.

Sis, this book started with white wine on your deck as we giggled about a colonoscopy meet-cute. And though the colonoscopy was flushed (I'm the funnier sister), the premise stuck. I love you and all of our laughter.

Mom and Dad, thank you so much for always being there when I needed you. None of this could exist without you.

Barbara, thank you for reading this and believing in it enough to pluck me from the masses. Having you at my back has given me the confidence I could never find before. Cue Bette Midler's *Wind Beneath My Wings*.

Merry, so much of this book is yours. I hope I did it justice because every time I think about you out there sawing through sternums and poking lungs with your spatula, I'm filled with awe and also a little bit of queasiness. Thank you for being my medical insider and my best friend. You are a badass.

Diane, every single lesson that Devon teaches in this book is inspired by you. Some of them come straight out of our classroom together. Thank you for teaching me how to teach. I miss you.

Scott, the difference that Devon makes in Syd's life is the difference you made in mine. I still have a letter just like the one in chapter 48—a letter that has saved me many times. Thank you for always being there for me long after I left your classroom.

Hads and Roarke, you are always cheering for me even when it means that I have to put on my headphones and ignore you. I hope you know how much that means to me. I love you both more than you'll ever know.

Readers and my amazing freshly formed street team, you are the absolute best community that exists. Your excitement and kindness has made me feel safe in a way that I never thought possible. I am lucky to have you and I hope you love this novel as much as I do.

About the author

Christy Schillig is a middle school teacher who lives in a log cabin in suburban South Jersey with her two children, her husband/best-friend since 6th grade, and her dogs, Puppay and Sheep. Christy graduated from Villanova University with a degree in Italian Literature and Language (yes, that's a real degree) and uses that degree to commentate classroom science games in Italian and plan off the grid trips to the Italian Rivieras. On any given day, you can find her reading young adult paranormal romance beneath her desk at school.

www.ingramcontent.com/pod-product-compliance
Lightning Source LLC
Chambersburg PA
CBHW071359300726
48976CB00006B/1936